KANPUR KHOOFIA
PVT. LTD

KANPUR KHOOFIYA PVT. LTD

Richa S. Mukherjee

HarperCollins *Publishers* India

Black Ink

First published in India by
HarperCollins *Publishers* and Black Ink in 2019
A-75, Sector 57, Noida, Uttar Pradesh 201301, India
www.harpercollins.co.in

2 4 6 8 10 9 7 5 3 1

Copyright © Richa S. Mukherjee 2019

P-ISBN: 978-93-5357-151-1
E-ISBN: 978-93-5357-152-8

This is a work of fiction and all characters and incidents described in this book are the product of the author's imagination. Any resemblance to actual persons, living or dead, is entirely coincidental.

Richa S. Mukherjee asserts the moral right
to be identified as the author of this work.

All rights reserved. No part of this publication may be reproduced, stored in a retrieval system, or transmitted, in any form or by any means, electronic, mechanical, photocopying, recording or otherwise, without the prior permission of the publishers.

Typeset in 10.5/14 Utopia Std at
Manipal Digital Systems, Manipal

Printed and bound at
Thomson Press (India) Ltd

MIX
Paper
FSC FSC® C010615

This book is produced from independently certified FSC® paper to ensure
responsible forest management.

*To Ma ... the soul inside, the hand above, and
my angel in the clouds*

CHAPTER 1

'She is dead, isn't she? I just know it.'

Prachand Tripathi was now presented with the onerous task of comforting Nittu Parkash, who had just been informed that her beloved cat Bittu had met her maker. A harmless early morning stroll for the poor cat had led to a high-adrenaline chase involving the neighbourhood terror, Jackie the mongrel (pronounced Jaiki, a.k.a. Jaikishen), which ended with her jumping off a terrace like a confident eagle. Nittu Parkash, fearing the worst, had reached out to the experts, Kanpur Khoofiya Pvt. Ltd, convinced that the cantankerous neighbours had kidnapped her favourite feline. Now, presented with the facts, she sat wailing about why cats did not have leashes.

Prachand stole a glance at his watch. It didn't feel right leaving, but the grieving would have to continue without him. After collecting his payment from the harrowed Mr Parkash, he ran through the day's to-do list. It was a checklist that bore the invisible stamps of unfulfilled desires and the disappointments of a mundane existence that could be better. Of course, one could argue that tailing a voluptuous and adulterous client to her lover's door, or digging into someone's hidden secrets, was infinitely more exciting than pushing papers at a desk, but Prachand Tripathi's ambitions, though stemming from mundanity, were aimed only at the sky. On most days it didn't bother him that his career choice invited ridicule and judgement.

There was a usual slew of questions when he revealed that he was a private investigator:

'Like Karamchand?'

'When were you fired from your real job?'

'Do you eat carrots as well?'

'Are you kidding me?'

'*Pret aatma ka prokop.*' (The symptoms of demonic possession.)

The only object that seemed possessed currently was his favourite scooter, a.k.a. Champa. While the world christened their chariots with names ranging from the absurd to the trendy, the intrepid detective chose a simple one that mirrored his staid, simple self. Of course, sometimes, when he declared in public that he was going to *hose Champa down* or that *Champa needed some oiling*, his comments were met with censure and shock often associated with the decay of societal morals.

'Come on, Champa, don't die on me. I've already handled one dead body today,' he pleaded. No amount of tilting could assuage Champa and like an obstinate teenager, she remained unresponsive.

He looked around and found that he was standing opposite the home of Abdul Kaka, Gwaltoli's most famous and gifted tailor. That was the great thing about small cities. Everyone was anointed a chacha, kaka, mama, phupha, jija or bhaiyya, and was always ready to do you a favour. Champa realized, very soon, that she would have a new home for the night.

With no transportation in sight, he decided to walk, and about half an hour later, he reached Awadh Niwas: the Tripathi ancestral home, where he found his friend Yatish tinkering with a box on the wall. On being noticed, Prachand was waved over.

'What do you want the password to be, Prachand da?'

'Bholenaath.'

'Too easy. The whole neighbourhood will have the same one. Try something else.'

'Okay, try Shivshambhu.'

'Too easy. Let's keep it JSR@2018,' he recommended.

'JSR?'

Yatish shrugged. 'Yes. *Jai Sri Ram.*'

Prachand was a bit wary of technology. What cannot be cured must be endured, but as far as he could manage, he kept himself away from gadgets, Wi-Fi connections, the internet, smartphones, smart homes, and everything that seemed like an assault on the good old ways of life. These duties were usually handed to Yatish, considered an expert as the owner of Sai Nath Computer and Electronics Services. He was called upon more frequently of late – ever since the Tripathi household had opened its doors to the internet.

It had all started when his younger brother Bhushan entered the rickety gates of Dayanand Brajendra Swaroop College. The oily haired, pimply and nervous teenager had, only in a few months, transformed into a gum-chewing vessel of confidence with jeans that barely covered his skinny bottom, t-shirts that proclaimed every colloquial obscenity ever heard, and gelled hair that defied the laws of gravity. After waging a five-month battle, he had been grudgingly handed a second-hand phone and was now usually found singing tunelessly with headphones on. In the tug-of-war between bankruptcy and data, data won. Since they could not get rid of the pimpled nuisance, at least in the near future, they agreed to get something called a Wi-Fi connection, which would help the household stave off financial ruin.

The next person to fall prey to the Wi-Fi gods was mother, Rachna Tripathi, armed with the innocent intention of snooping after her son. Though rare, when the phone had temporarily disengaged from Bhushan (while he was bathing), she would sneak in and poke around the gadget suspiciously, unimpressed with the alien sounding English songs and videos of voluptuous women that made her blush. Gradually, with the help of her neighbour Guddi, she discovered the myriad miracles of the web and learnt to surf the internet when her husband was not home.

Bhushan, meanwhile, was completely unaware that there was a fellow addict residing in the house, but his suspicions grew as fried brinjal recipes, Radhe Ma videos, Baba Ramdev yoga videos and *Yeh Har Ghar ki Kahaani* episodes started popping up as recommended entertainment. Once the secret was out, Rachna Tripathi started running to Bhushan's phone like a heroin addict, tuning out his protests. Her other source of joy was the WhatsApp group Gwaltoli Gilehris, which Guddi had made her a part of. Bhushan was now used to getting videos and weird emoticons from the Gilehris at odd hours of the night.

As Yatish sat down for a cup of tea, Rachna Tripathi laid out some homemade snacks.

'Yo Yo B is most obliged!' Yatish declared, diving for a samosa.

'Yatish, how many times have I told you to stop this nonsense. Such a beautiful name, Yatish Bhatnagar, reduced to a frivolous Yo Yo B,' Rachna Tripathi complained.

'It is cool, Mataji!'

'Cool?' she enquired, puzzled.

'I mean, it's memorable,' he explained. 'I run a competitive binnis. It helps to have a personality that people can remember, to stand out.' He tried to illustrate this point by putting on his sunglasses for effect but it made no impact. 'Look at what your son goes through with his name.'

'What do you mean!' The protective mother bristled. 'Prachand is a great name.'

'Yes. For a cement brand.' Yatish laughed as Rachna Tripathi whacked his hand.

Prachand – a masculine name that meant ample, vast, grand. The Tripathis had no idea what they were innocently doing to their firstborn when they named him. Educational institutions and the streets are often harsh places for people with great, impactful names. In his formative years, whether Prachand tried to blend in or stand out in the neighbourhood gully games, or act as a leader or a lamppost in the school play, his name – juxtaposed against his tiny frame – always entered the room before him, and that was the story of his life. Spending a lot of time in hiding made him introspective and patient, eventually moulding him into a calm and rather unflappable person – a useful trait in the Tripathi household.

CHAPTER 2

It was a sunny Sunday morning. A gentle breeze lifted the papads drying in the sun. Some jars of freshly prepared pickles, a specialty of the lady of the house, lay stewing in the heat. A mound of steaming puris, fried potatoes, mixed vegetables and kheer were kept on a low table in the large aangan. Even the pigeons had decided to take their droppings elsewhere to not vitiate the peaceful and picturesque atmosphere of Awadh Niwas.

The lady in charge of this spread, Rachna Tripathi, was a happy woman. Done with most of her housework, she was looking forward to attending her weekly kirtan. It was hosted in rotation by the members of the Gwaltoli Gilehris. The honour this week was awarded to one of the oldest Gilehris, Ratna Bhatnagar. Rachna Tripathi would be back before her husband and brother-in-law got home from the temple. All was right with the world till a quivering voice rippled through the silence.

'Rachnaaa ... Rachna! Are you deaf? Get me some tea and a few mathris.'

Rachna Tripathi's nostrils flared. And there it was. The voice that usually ruined her carefully laid plans. It belonged to her mother-in-law, Rampyari Tripathi.

The Amma of Awadh Niwas and the doyen of all things gaseous, Rampyari Tripathi could always be found in the courtyard, on the brown charpoy, sunning herself. She was usually silent on account of chewing pan, and her hearing was nothing to write home about either. Her zest for life was now focused around three things – namely, churan, khaana and pakhaana, in her own words and in that order. She was eighty-five years old and, despite her stomach ailments, continued to demand small portions of food every half an hour, something that kept Rachna Tripathi on her toes, 24/7. As a result, one bathroom was dedicated to Ammaji's overactive and unpredictable bowel movements.

'I'll get it!' hollered Rachna Tripathi, barely able to control her anger. She took a deep breath, punched the dough viciously and put the water to boil. Her only hope was wrapping this task up in another fifteen minutes, and still making it in time to belt out a few bhajans, indulge in some gossip, oily snacks and tea with her gang of girls.

Just then, the front door opened noisily and in walked Dinbandhu Tripathi, shattering any remaining hopes that his wife was harbouring towards a getaway. He was followed by his brother, Dinanath Tripathi. After closing the door behind him and letting his younger brother take his bag, the head of the Tripathi household headed to the hand pump installed in a corner of the courtyard. Standing next to it, he trained his eyes towards the sky and exclaimed to no one in particular: 'Do I have to draw water for myself now?'

Prachand, having heard him, recognised his part in this ritual and, without making eye contact, started pumping the lever as water gushed out. After handing his father a towel, he took a seat nearby.

Rachna Tripathi hollered from the kitchen, frustrated at the change of tides. 'Whoever wants tea will tell me right now. I have a headache and don't want to enter the kitchen again. *For* a *long* time!' She hoped the hard-of-hearing Ammaji would get the message. 'Prachand, will you be going to your office today?' she enquired, as Prachand was known to make weekend trips.

'Office!' snorted Dinbandhu Tripathi. 'Circus.'

'Please don't start again,' pleaded his wife, appearing at the kitchen door with a premonition of things to come.

'I'm not scared of anyone,' he thundered, staring directly at Prachand.

'Our little one is doing well,' interjected Dinanath Tripathi, in his favourite nephew's defence, trying to placate his brother, who often seemed agitated in Prachand's presence.

'Little one?' Dinbandhu Tripathi laughed. 'He is a twenty-nine-year-old ghoda who won't listen to sense. Why have I worked so hard to keep Tripathi & Sons up and running? So that Tripathi can work all his life and go to his funeral while the sons can run away from their responsibilities?'

Prachand finally spoke up, but respectfully, his voice always low and his eyes lower. 'I am not running away from anything, Pitaji. I am earning my livelihood. And as for the shop, Chachu helps you...'

'*Ek kantaap dehiyun*?!' (Should I smack you on the head?!) he hollered. 'As it is, business is dying and customers thinning out. We are old and slowing down as well. But we must soldier on because of our cursed progeny. The wayward younger son behaves like he is possessed by some spirit and dresses like a beggar while the older *intelligent* son wants to become a detective and end up on the streets!'

Since he first laid eyes on his elder son, Dinbandhu Tripathi had imagined him, even as a toddler in a cloth nappy, walking into the beautiful, hallowed campus of IIT Kanpur in Kalyanpur. His own childhood had been cooked in the acrid smell of leather, watching his father and uncles slave away at the factory and then the shop, but he knew his son was born to do something special. Hence the choice of his mighty name. They had spent many evenings sitting on the ghats of the Ganga at Bithoor, pouring over forms and guide books, helping his son prepare for the IIT entrance exam. The first time Prachand did not appear on the list, Dinbandhu Tripathi did not panic. The second time he did not clear, he thought someone might have misspelt his son's name.

While often hiding from his father's grand ambitions – career-related and the other one, of getting his family members to use gau mutra, which he considered a nostrum for all ailments in life – sneaking around under the radar to avoid attention had given him enough time to develop his intuitive and observational skills well. Then came the reading obsession, featuring Byomkesh Bakshi, Kiriti Roy, Feluda, Sherlock Holmes and Surendra Mohan Pathak: detectives and magicians of mystery and intelligence. Lost in this fantastical and thrilling world, he suddenly found an ambition of his own. The only hurdle was a large one called: engineering. His father wanted him at IIT Kanpur. Clearly, IIT Kanpur didn't want him, which was evident after two failed attempts. But he didn't have the heart to deny his father's dream and managed to enter the not-as-hallowed gates of University Institute of Engineering and Technology instead. This didn't seem to appease his father, but he completed the course anyway.

The only thing that made those four gruelling years bearable were his non-engineering pursuits as a problem solver. When it came to finding missing dentures, underwear, fans or chairs, to exposing dishonest help or cheating local shopkeepers, everyone had just one name on their lips. This gave him immense pleasure. Then came the day when he announced to his father that he had topped his college and that he wanted to become a private investigator. At first, Dinbandhu Tripathi had gone ominously quiet, hinting at acceptance. Then he chased his son around all of Gwaltoli, without stopping for a water break.

The smart of that betrayal still sent Dinbandhu Tripathi into fits of bitterness, just like it had this evening.

'We have spent years skinning ourselves day and night to run this shop for our family. And what does my son want to do? Look for the neighbour's missing blouse and reunite a lost dog with its owner!'

'Well, it wasn't one blouse, there were multiple that were stolen along with other valuables. Only Prachand was able to help nab the cook, who was the culprit.' This factual intervention was made by Rachna Tripathi in her son's defence.

'Silence!' thundered Dinbandhu Tripathi.

'Pitaji, why are you screaming at Ma because of me? You find my work trivial, but I feel great helping people, solving problems, whatever you might call it. Why don't you at least try to understand what I do?'

'That's all I expect you to do now anyway. Argue and preach to your father. *Par updes kusal bahutere* (Preaching to others comes very naturally to some),' he quoted eloquently, as he often did, and then grunted and walked away in his sweaty vest while Prachand watched helplessly.

Dinanath Tripathi walked up to his nephew, who was now wearing a forlorn expression. Prachand sat with his head slightly lowered, staring at a disciplined line of ants marching across the stone-lined floor. That gave him solace. At-least least the ants were perceptive and gave Prachand something he obsessed about often. Order and structure. Something that always made him feel better and in greater control, in sharp contrast to so much else in his life.

'Son, don't worry about him. You know he is short tempered.' Dinanath Tripathi stroked his nephew's head affectionately. 'I bought some malpuas for you.' He smiled and nudged Prachand.

Prachand smiled at his uncle's feeble attempt at making him feel better after yet another showdown. 'Vidya would love some as well. I'll wait for her.'

Prachand Tripathi looked longingly at the door. Eagerly waiting for the return of a person who could always, instantly make him feel better...

CHAPTER 3

Vidya knew the moment she laid eyes on Prachand Tripathi that she would not marry him. No one could blame her. The photographs that had made their way from Lucky Photo Art Studio to the Sahai residence did not help matters in any way. An awkward-looking Prachand could be seen striking a 007 pose against the backdrop of the Taj Mahal. Next came Superman in front of the Eiffel Tower followed by the pièce de résistance: in the rose garden peppered with hearts, he posed, with oiled hair, in a checked shirt buttoned up to the chin, and tight white pants.

'At least meet him. His father is very well respected in the community,' her father had pleaded.

'He looks like a simple fool,' was her retort. It was not arrogance. Having made good grades and fared well in her last year at the Indraprastha College for women, in the arts stream, why would she assign herself to any small-city bumpkin in haste?

A fly buzzed into the awkward moment when Vidya stood facing Prachand at her Dwarka home, still highly unimpressed. The meeting was set up through common family friends. The ladkawalas sat like birds on a fence in a neat, long row, trying to look important. The ladkiwalas, smiles plastered across their faces, were on the opposite end. A few extremely old women were sprinkled around the courtyard, origins and relations unclear.

The conversation was sporadic and everyone ate amidst long awkward pauses. The father looked a bit stern to her, the mother was a chatterbox, the brother looked bored and sported a torn t-shirt which announced 'I hate youuuuuu!' to no one in particular while the uncle smiled amiably. The grandmother, in a white-and-green starched sari, head covered over dark sunglasses, was perched on the sofa with her feet up, chewing pan constantly.

A rishta usually meant that the whole locality had an appointment on their calendar. A ready audience would be available on neighbouring roofs and homes, and word would spread about the proceedings as the day wore on. Serious betting followed.

After her father had announced the list of her accomplishments and her qualifications, which took about ten minutes, Dinbandhu Tripathi casually suggested: 'Prachand, why don't you sing for them.' It was difficult to gauge from the ripple of titters and polite coughs around the room at the time whether they were laughing at the groom's name or the request made, which would usually have been directed at the blushing potential bride-to-be.

'Next, he will ask you to serve everyone tea.' The brother had nudged Prachand and guffawed while Vidya pretended to not have heard the exchange.

Senior Tripathi continued talking about his son, unfazed by the dagger-like looks from his wife. 'Prachand had multiple talents. Such an intelligent boy I tell you. He always had such potential but ... he decided to...' Cutting into the familiar awkwardness, Prachand smiled, cleared his throat and sang a tuneless Manna Dey song. When the ordeal was over, he requested to speak with Vidya alone. There were audible gasps everywhere, the frying ceased in the kitchen and the neighbourhood news service received its first sensational news of the evening. Then they were grudgingly directed to her room.

Looking at her paintings, he turned around and made eye contact for the first time. She realized then that he had light-brown eyes. Eyes that were warm and kind.

'You feel a bit suffocated in your life right now. You're not much of a reader even though you like people to think you are. Your favourite colour is blue. You have a secret drawer or maybe a compartment in this room where you keep very personal things.'

Her jaw dropped. 'You got all that from my paintings?'

His eyes twinkled as he laughed. 'No. Just the first part. It shows in your paintings. Like you want to break free. The bird in half flight, the broken cage, the woman behind bars, you see the pattern?'

'You seem like you can tell me more about my own paintings,' she challenged him with a raised eyebrow.

He suddenly looked contrite. 'Please, I'm sorry if I've upset you.' His eyes lowered to the ground. 'I'm normally tongue-tied in front of girls. I just felt a strange connection with you so ... I mean ... I'm sorry.'

She smiled. 'Don't be.' She was suddenly intrigued by this shy, oily haired, innocuous looking, yet intelligent, man before her. 'So how can you tell I don't read?'

'Well, when I was looking around, your entire book stack looks like it's in pristine condition. That doesn't usually happen with avid readers. Even the one on the desk right now, which you *are* possibly reading, has dog ears.' He walked up to the desk and picked one up. 'No book lover would ever do that.'

She was impressed and intrigued, but she didn't want to show it. Putting a plate of biscuits next to Prachand, she caught a waft of some putrid smell and wrinkled her nose. She looked at him questioningly and he looked embarrassed. 'It's not my perfume. It's ... it's ... well, it's gau mutra,' he announced shyly. She leapt backwards.

Prachand shrugged. 'My father uses it for almost everything. He made me sprinkle it to rid me of my nerves and as a blessing before an auspicious meeting.'

Vidya started laughing uncontrollably. 'He won't keep it on the menu as a cold drink if we get married, right?'

Blushing furiously, Prachand changed the topic. 'Has my family entertained you enough?' He laughed.

'Not as much as your song!' She giggled.

'My father is well aware of all my other faults, but somehow he is blind to the fact that my singing talent could wake the dead.'

An hour and many shy reminders from various family members later, they finally decided to descend. But before stepping down, he told her something in all earnestness.

'My father will have you think that I work at our shop but, in reality, my passion lies somewhere else.'

'I'm very intrigued now,' she whispered.

He looked at her and said softly. 'I am a detective.'

'*Huh*?' was all she could manage.

'I am a detective, Vidya. A private investigator. And that's how I make my living. Will you be okay with that should we marry?'

After thinking for some time, she asked him, 'You being a detective I don't mind, but will you please stop using gau mutra?'

Prachand laughed, shrugging.

Just before leaving the room, Vidya turned to him again. 'How did you know I had a secret...'

He shrugged. 'Well, that was easy. Girls are usually neater and more organised than boys. Your room seems to validate that theory. So then, there is no reason for a stack of dupattas, old magazines and a big box to suddenly appear in that corner next to your cupboard unless you're trying to hide that space just to make sure I didn't go there by mistake. Makes sense?'

That night, Vidya went to sleep dreaming of fantastical mysteries, crimes and adventures that she would embark on with an unassuming man from Kanpur, with the worst name in the world but the warmest brown eyes.

As she now looked at the same man sitting next to her, furiously punching away at numbers on an old, rusty calculator, she smiled. It had been two years but she still felt warm and tingly looking at her husband. The habit change had taken some time but he no longer depleted Gwaltoli's entire stock of almond oil and he was now aware of the clothing universe beyond baggy collared t-shirts and white chappals.

Rachna Tripathi was not a fan of this new look, but kept her opinion to herself, barring a few sly comments once in a while. The change felt like relinquishing control of her son's reigns to the new woman in his life. But Rachna Tripathi was a smart woman. She always felt a little bit intimidated by her Dilliwali daughter-in-law. So when dealing with her, she often reduced the intensity of drama in her conversations and opinions, which seemed to work well for the peace of the house. Of course, during many kirtan sessions with her friends, she had lamented the absolute lack of help from her 'otherwise lovely daughter-in-law'.

'This month, a lot of the cash went into repairs. We need more cases.' Prachand frowned.

Vidya sat up. 'The bathroom needs repairs as well! Do you know that hole in the wall has become so big that I try to bathe with clothes on? What if someone sees me naked? I accidentally saw Ammaji yesterday, and I've not been able to sleep,' she complained.

'Poor Ammaji,' Prachand replied. 'I hope she never finds out.'

Their conversation was interrupted by a big commotion outside. Vidya quickly threw on a dupatta as they ran out.

Rachna Tripathi was sitting on the ground in her favourite position, holding her head. Dinanath Tripathi was running behind his brother, who was giving chase to someone that resembled Bhushan Tripathi.

Ammaji had broken her silence temporarily and kept bleating '*Hai Dayya!*' (Oh my!)

'*Ullu ka pattha! Bewakoof!*' thundered Dinbandhu Tripathi.

'What happened, ma? What is going on?' asked Prachand, utterly confused.

'Your brother has gone mad,' she said pointing at the darting figure of her younger son. 'That's Bhushan?' Vidya enquired quizzically. All she could see was some bald boy who vaguely looked like her brother-in-law.

'Of course!' she responded. 'He shaved off his hair and apparently something is written on the back of his head.'

Prachand joined the chase and intercepted his father.

'Pitaji, stop, stop. Please. I'll talk to him,' he begged his father.

'*Paglait kahin ka*! He has lost his mind. Too busy to become an engineer. Too busy for an IAS exam. But all the time in the world for these gimmicks!'

'Please, Pitaji, calm down. I'll speak to him,' Prachand pleaded again. Then he turned to his uncle, who was gasping for breath. 'Please stop running. Everyone calm down.' Vidya was trying to placate her agitated mother-in-law. 'Black magic. This is black magic,' she muttered.

Prachand caught hold of the man of the moment. His brother had always looked like an indecipherable mix of his mother and father. Shorter and skinnier than most kids, his most striking features were his slightly brown eyes, just like his elder brother. Now with his bald head, he looked like a little brown mongoose.

'What have you done now, Bhushan?'

'Nothing, P.'

'I'm your older brother, not P.'

'Same thing, P.' He smiled cheekily.

Prachand turned him around to inspect his head. Lettered tufts of hair announced boldly: BELIEBER.

In the sea of blank faces, Vidya was the only one in Awadh Niwas who had a very, very vague idea about who Justin Bieber was.

'He is my God,' Bhushan announced passionately. 'I am going to become *the* Justin of Kanpur,' he proclaimed like a fervent patriot.

Before Prachand could manage the situation, Dinbandhu Tripathi picked up his other slipper and resumed the aborted chase while Rachna Tripathi ran to her puja room to pray to Bholenaath for the return of her son's sanity.

CHAPTER 4

Chotu was busy cleaning the big signboard that read: 'Kanpur Khoofiya Pvt. Ltd'. Right next to it was the image of an animal. He had never quite figured out which animal, but once his Prachand Bhaiyya had explained that it was a fox, because they are clever and sharp. This had confused Chotu further. To begin with, it looked more like a cat. Secondly, if someone spent money and started a business, why not just put their own name on it, like the Champakram Anaaj Bhandaar nearby or Purohit Mithaiwala or Mishra Paneer Centre. Why use a fox? Pondering such mysteries of life, little Chotu wanted to dust the entire two-room office clean before bhabhi and bhaiyya arrived at 9.30 a.m. But he knew that bhaiyya would spend another half an hour re-dusting and rearranging everything in a particular order.

He also never understood why they had to come to office so early when, on most days, they did not get many clients. When they did, no one walked in before lunchtime. Their friends visited often and that was when Chotu had the most errands to run. Like picking up piping hot tea from the shack nearby, or running to the market for hot snacks. He had heard bhabhi muttering that most of their income was wasted on feeding their greedy friends.

After sweeping and dusting, he filled two bottles of water, cleaned three used glasses from the previous day, filled the jar on the table with biscuits, which were special treats saved for clients, and uncovered the desktop computer gingerly. The office was declared open for business as two flowers were placed in a vase on the table. As if on cue, the owners arrived and brought their scooter to a halt right outside the shop.

After lighting the incense stick in the small puja behind the desk, Prachand stared at his favourite Bholenaath picture for an entire minute, praying hard for new business and world peace in the same breath. Then he went about rearranging everything, exactly as prescient Chotu had predicted. The books needed to be in descending order and the mat with WELCOME written on it had to be a few centimetres from the door.

When he returned to the table, Vidya was already seated, turning on the computer. Receiving no response, she had to employ the most time-tested technique for booting electronics. She whacked it many times till the screen reluctantly blinked to life.

Vidya frowned. 'Nothing works properly. Stupid computer.' Prachand smiled. 'Poor thing. You're too hard on it. You are the sole user and friend of this contraption, so you must treat it a bit better.' Vidya rolled her eyes in response. Not finding anything of value in her inbox, she sat back in contemplation.

'How will things ever improve if we don't get more work? Maybe it's time to start marketing ourselves, Prachand. In the last few months two more detective agencies have opened up. One on Meston road and one in Gwaltoli itself. They have all these fancy ads coming out in the paper.'

Prachand docked the incense stick in the holder and then started sharpening pencils. 'I really don't think all that works, Vidya. Their ads are senseless.'

'Prachand, this *is* what works today. If you are not visible, you are finished.'

'I agree!' chimed in another voice. They both turned to see Yatish a.k.a. Yo Yo B walking in. He gestured towards Chotu who immediately stood up to embark on his snack collection duty.

'Chotu, finish sweeping the foyer.' Vidya said sternly. 'It's very dirty.'

Yatish sighed at the missed opportunity of a free breakfast. Being half Bengali, thanks to his mother's hometown in Midnapore, West Bengal, his foodie blood ran thick and though housed in a small container, his stomach was always magnanimous and accommodating to all kinds of food at any point of the day.

'Getting back to bhabhi's point,' he continued, 'You must advertise. My posters have definitely brought more binnis. You should also take an impressive picture and run a promotion. Oh, I have the perfect line!' he snapped his fingers, 'Let the Chacha Chowdhary of Kanpur solve all your problems!'

'Are we selling comic books here?' Vidya asked, unimpressed.

'Bhabhi, imagination is important,' he snapped his fingers. 'And add an irresistible offer.'

'Like what,' asked Prachand, laughing at this display of enthusiasm. 'Sniff out the betrayal of a loved one and get one surveillance free free free?!'

Yatish laughed. Vidya sighed. Prachand looked at his wife scrunching her nose in concentration at the screen and smiled.

When Vidya entered his life, Prachand knew he had truly met the woman of his dreams. Instead of setting theatrical conditions (namely, *it's either me or your career*), she had been excited by what he did, singlehandedly convincing all her family members who were having palpitations about the son-in-law's farcical career choice and economic prospects post marriage.

He still remembered the day she suggested that he open up a detective agency. 'How long will you run around chasing petty cases? It is now your time to shine,' she had insisted. He couldn't have possibly guessed at the time that her additional motive was having an opportunity to do something exciting and away from home. Having never fit into the homebody mould, she balked at the thought of having to roam around like a 'good little daughter-in-law' at home all day long.

It was an exciting time. Two newlyweds were embarking on a new life and enterprise. There was so much to discuss, so much to plan, but nowhere to do it in peace. Every time Prachand was spotted at home, his father would invariably launch into a tirade or try to get him to join the family business. So they made movie plans every time a discussion was due. But instead they would go sit at a restaurant, the most scandalous event in any locality of a small city. When a newly married couple couldn't get enough of each other.

They were out of the house so often that Dinbandhu Tripathi was forced to share his opinion on the matter with his wife. 'This young generation is shameless. *Varn dharm nahi aashram chari, Shruti virodh rat sat nar nari.*' (No one has any shame or desire to behave in accordance with the Vedas, religion or dharma as enshrined in our holy books.) Little did the family know that instead of holding hands and staring into each other's eyes, Vidya and Prachand Tripathi were busy designing their new life.

'I have savings worth around 50,000 rupees. Happy to pool that in as well. Let's make a rent reserve for six months at one go.' Vidya had chewed off half her pencil in deep thought as her new husband watched this beautiful woman in awe. Someone who was everything he could have ever asked for. He held her hand. She smiled.

After much planning, their decision had been announced to both families over a Diwali dinner. The announcement was followed by pin drop silence in contrast to the blast of firecrackers just outside the door. The painful silence had thankfully been broken by Ammaji who passed a great torrent of noisy wind. She looked unabashed and continued chewing paan while her son hissed 'My reaction won't be very different from hers.' Dinbandhu Tripathi walked out after announcing, '*Vinaash kaale vipreet buddhi.*' (Self destruction is often preceded by your own mind turning against you.)

Now, a year into the business, they were wiser but still hopeful. Though they still had no regrets, they realized time and patience would need to be constant companions. Large dollops of patience, especially given the kind of clients that usually came to them.

While some at least needed them to investigate something, such as exposing a kleptomaniac domestic help, or a cheating business partner, most others had bizarre requests. Someone wanted an old parent with memory loss followed, some wanted their children to be dropped to school, while some even wanted them to hire a maid for them. Prachand had to physically restrain Vidya once when someone came in asking for security at a wedding function. 'Haven't they ever watched a detective movie?' she had asked him, exasperated. What frustrated her more was that her husband even indulged some of the inane requests because he didn't have the heart to say no.

Yatish suddenly jumped in his seat. 'I have an idea that will guarantee more business!' Prachand looked sceptical. 'Let's hear it then.'

'Why don't you announce a free holiday with every big case brought to you?'

'Yatish, we are not selling toothpaste or furniture here. I can barely keep us afloat and you want me to advertise free holidays for the cheap cases we get?'

'You just don't value my suggestions.'

Before Prachand could respond, there was a knock on the door. A timid-looking man walked in and sat down.

'Namaste.' Prachand smiled. 'How can I help you?'

'Son, my rent agreement has lapsed. Can you renew it for me?'

CHAPTER 5

The entire Tripathi clan was bundled in a silver Innova as they sped away to Nirmal phupha's second cousin's daughter's wedding. A very *close* relative, at least by Kanpur standards. The window seat occupants stuck their heads out, enjoying the breeze, while the rest fanned themselves furiously.

As the car had pulled up outside Awadh Niwas that morning, each family member made an Usain Bolt-like dash with their belongings, in their haste to occupy the window seats. Ammaji stood her ground knowing that she could get a window seat with zero effort. No one wanted to venture between her gas and the window. Dinbandhu Tripathi had been outrun by Bhushan, but after growling and pulling rank, acquired a spot up front. Bhushan backed up, keeping a safe distance from the gau mutra bottle his father carried with him like a little pet. Coming in next was Rachna Tripathi who had tucked in her sari and tripped over her mother-in-law in an effort to get to the last window seat across from Ammaji. Chachu Tripathi and Bhushan had to make their peace with sandwich-meat positions in the middle seat while Vidya and Prachand were relegated to the hottest, window-less back end of the car.

As was tradition, enough food had been packed for a one-and-a-half hour drive, an approximately eighty kilometre distance, that could feed an entire locality caught in the throes of a famine. Puri, khasta kachauri, aalu ki sabzi, achaar, papad, mathri, besan laddoo, imarti, the car smelt like a busy bhojnalaya. The other frequent stop was for Ammaji's bathroom needs. The time allocation per stop was approximately eight minutes for disembarking, another ten to reach the bathroom, five to ten minutes for the business, and then the return journey to the car. By the way things were going, it was estimated that they would reach just before the bride and groom were leaving for their honeymoon.

Road trips tend to have a transformational effect and the Tripathi clan was feeling the magic as well. Conversation was flowing, jokes were being cracked, the wind was blowing away any shreds of resentments wafting in the air and life seemed good. Even Dinbandhu Tripathi's characteristically furrowed eyebrows had been given a day off. The only unhappy occupant of the car was Bhushan Tripathi, who literally had to be dragged to the wedding. He had recently been chosen as the lead singer of a band called 'KPB Rocks' (Kanpuriya Beliebers Rocks), a dream come true for him. Unfortunately, their first performance was due at a teenager's birthday party, also on this weekend. He ranted about missing a golden opportunity, but threatened with dire consequences, had to relent. However, he was firm in his refusal to wear the wig that Rachna Tripathi had picked out from Maganlal Dresswala. After a lot of pleading, when

Bhushan remained adamant, she had secretly stuffed the wig in her luggage, determined to throw it on his head at some point over the next two days. She would not let her bald son become the highlight of the wedding.

After many pit stops, the Tripathi's dusty Innova pulled into Aman Residential Society in Gomti Nagar, a modest enclosure of a handful of two-storied buildings. Most of the exterior walls looked like they were in need of immediate repairs but all was forgotten in the glowing curtain of fairy lights that were installed for the wedding. Even in broad daylight, they sparkled away, in preparation. Both Nirmal phupha and his own second cousin whose daughter's marriage it was, lived in the same building.

The small community hall nearby was to host the ladies' sangeet, marriage ceremony and other small rituals. The guest accommodations were sprinkled across various neighbours' homes, which was the usual practice. Amidst the accommodation announcements, Bhushan was dispatched to share a room with some fellow pimply teens, two buildings away, which did nothing to improve his mood.

The day was well spent over multiple cups of tea, gossiping and making arrangements for the functions. It was only a few hours to the sangeet function when the bride's mother came running down the stairs, tears streaking her face. She ran straight to her husband and whispered in his ear as all the guests stood up in concern. Dinanath Tripathi and Prachand walked up to him and enquired if everything was alright. With resigned eyes, he took off his proudly perched pagdi and sat down. 'This wedding will not take place.'

'What? Why?' Prachand prodded.

'A necklace, the groom's family heirloom that was given to the bride to wear during the wedding, has been stolen!'

A Spanish wave of 'what' 'what' 'what' and other appropriate reactions broke out. 'We might as well call off the wedding. They will blame us for sure,' he continued moaning.

Prachand quickly enquired. 'Where was the necklace stolen from?'

'From Ritika's room, where she was getting ready.' She pointed upstairs to the first floor. Prachand ran up the stairs, surveyed the area that held a teary-eyed bride and ran back down. Vidya walked up to him. 'What are you doing, Prachand?' Her husband looked like he was struggling with something. 'I ... I ... I'm helping.' Before she could investigate further, he had already started walking to the spot where all the relatives were gathered. 'Let's call the police,' someone suggested.

'Wait,' Prachand shouted. He turned to the bride's father. 'Chacha, do you trust me?' The distant relative, now under pressure could, only offer a feeble, 'yes, sure, son.'

'Then I'll find your thief in the next ten minutes.' Another wave of murmurs and exclamations swept through the gathering. 'The theft has taken place minutes ago. So I am positive we can locate the thief as per my plan,' Prachand announced confidently.

Dinbandhu Tripathi switched to a deep red as he addressed his elder son. 'Prachand, this is no place for your games.' The ever polite Prachand Tripathi looked respectfully at his father with lowered eyes and replied: 'Pitaji, I know what I'm doing.' Then he turned to the crowd in front of him that included guests and help. 'Please follow my instructions,' he announced loudly. 'All people on the first and ground floor who had someone with them at all times please move to the right.' Around twenty people moved away. 'All those people who are here from the kitchen, please show me your hands.' About eight to ten helpers came forward and displayed their still greasy or stained hands. They were asked to move away as well. 'Anyone who needs any support to move, sit or stand, please move to the right.' With a high geriatric component amongst the guests, a large number of elderly people shuffled away looking irritated for the effort. Even Ammaji gave Prachand a scathing look.

'What is this nonsense. Tripathi bhaisaheb, your son thinks we are all thieves!' An incensed relative shouted. The Tripathi bhaisaheb in question was looking like he would pop a vein. Prachand tried to placate the frazzled nerves around by folding his hands. 'Two more minutes please. Bear with me.' He looked at the six people that now stood in-front of him. The line-up made him gulp. Rachna Tripathi, Esha Devi an old friend of the bride's family, the house help Golu, an electrician and the bride herself. 'Please tell me exactly where each one of you were.'

'I was in the bathroom.' The bride sniffed, trying her best to not smudge her mehendi despite the possibility of not having a wedding to go to.

'Prachand, are you insane?' Then, since her son pleaded with his eyes for her to cooperate, Rachna Tripathi relented. 'Errm ... I was ... taking some ... selfies on the balcony,' muttered his embarrassed mother. Even at that distance, she could clearly hear her husband's sharp intake of breath.

'I was fixing the light in the adjoining room,' said the electrician, shivering with fright.

'Sir, sir, I had just delivered tea in the room and left,' Golu informed.

Last in line was the bejewelled and dignified-looking Esha Devi: 'I was resting in the room as it was unoccupied. I felt a little faint.' She flapped her fingers in front of her face. 'I'm sure this servant took the necklace. Check his pockets.' The boy started howling in protest. 'I'm innocent. I didn't take anything!'

Prachand suddenly sprang up, ran back to the brides' room and came down panting. He smiled. 'I found the necklace.' There were shocked expressions all around. He turned to Esha Devi and folded his hands. 'I'm sorry, aunty, but you took the necklace.'

Esha Devi stood up. 'How dare you, you chit of a boy! The bride is like my daughter. Besides, I can buy this entire city with my own money. I don't need a stupid necklace.'

'Sometimes need is not the only motive, aunty,' Prachand explained. Vidya ran up to her husband. 'Prachi, what *are* you doing?' He looked at her in a very composed manner and said, 'When I announced that the jewellery had been found, there was relief on everyone's face except Esha aunty's. She looked worried. I went back upstairs on a suspicion and sure enough, a small silver Ganesh idol was missing, something I had seen earlier while visiting the room. It was right by the sofa where she said she was resting. I am almost sure it is in her bag right now. She can't help herself.' Esha Devi clutched her bag possessively. 'And if I'm not mistaken, in haste, she has stowed the necklace temporarily in a place where no one in a busy house would care to look, deciding to pick it up later when things cooled down. A place where her eyes have been darting nervously to ever since I started talking.' He walked to a flower pot right by the staircase that was covered in decorations. His hand disappeared for a few seconds and reappeared with a shimmering necklace, as thunderous applause broke out.

Some tears and accusations later, it was discovered that the very affluent Esha Devi was a habitual kleptomaniac. As the news spread, everyone instantly recalled how they had witnessed many objects disappearing over the years around this elderly lady. No one would ever know if this were true or a mere confirmation bias but Esha Devi was asked to stay away from the wedding celebrations, which was punishment enough for her.

Eventually, someone remembered that there was a wedding on hand and the preparations for the ladies sangeet swung back into action. Prachand, feeling hot under the spotlight, was standing under a tree, some distance away when Vidya found him. His hand was shaking.

'Hey, genius husband. What happened? Are you okay?'

'I have no idea how on earth I worked up the courage to do that! Is Pitaji looking for me?'

CHAPTER 6

Even though sangeet functions were usually meant for the ladies, an exception had been made, possibly due to the lack of space, to include the men as well. The most significant problem of the evening was that alcohol could not be consumed openly. As a result, the man of the hour was Ashfaque Bhai, a man Friday and the sole supplier of alcohol to the male members in attendance. A well-hidden fact of the evening was that forty per cent of Ashfaque bhai's stock had been secretly depleted by the womenfolk in attendance.

Prachand, after his recent display of stellar detective work, was being pulled aside by various relatives. Such as the inebriated Sheila Bua from Mugalsarai.

'Son, your Kailash phupha is cheating on me. Please help me catch him red-handed with that bitch.'

'I only take cases in Kanpur, Bua. Besides, I'm sure he is very much in love with you.'

She wasn't even listening. 'I know why,' she wailed. 'Look at my stomach. It jiggles. And I have a moustache. Look.'

She offered him a better view while he desperately looked around for his wife, in the hope of being rescued.

'He had told me many times that mine is longer than his. But what can I do! This problem runs in my family. My mother, my grandmother – both hairy. He thinks I look like a man. That's why he is chasing after that young bitch Shobha from the sweet shop nearby. I just know it.'

Fortunately, his mother came looking for him and he smiled at her gratefully.

'Come on, Prachand. The dancing has begun.'

'Ma, I do *not* want to dance!' he begged his mother. She shrugged and pulled him towards the area where scores of women were sitting in a circle around the blushing bride. An additional factor making the bride blush was pride. She was marrying an IAS boy; that in Uttar Pradesh is akin to having found God. Two women sat by the dholak, one playing, and one tapping it rhythmically with a spoon. A manjira chimed away in another pair of hands. After a few moves, the women dancing would rush away giggling and embarrassed. Some heavyweights, who were convinced about their dancing prowess, refused to leave the circle and had taken permanent positions.

As Prachand stood clapping, he saw the next victim being dragged in. His beautiful wife. Dressed in an emerald green sari, gold earrings and shiny green bangles, she reluctantly started moving to the song.

'*Banna banni se pooche milogi kahan? Usi mandap ke neeche aadhi raat ko!*' (The groom asks the bride, where will you meet me? Where we got married, at the stroke of midnight!) announced the scandalous lyrics as the women laughed and sang enthusiastically. It became very evident that Vidya was no dancer but to her credit, she held the pretence for a good five minutes before rushing to her husband. Her position was soon taken up by Chachu Tripathi who danced with joyful abandon. Ammaji sat watching, having found a charpoy to her liking and was blowing smoke in varied shapes from her bubbling hookah, a scandalous indulgence for a woman that she was allowed only due to her age.

The afternoon show had garnered a lot of interest and curiosity about their line of work and Vidya was dealing with a barrage of strange questions through the evening.

'Have you met any celebrity because of your detective work?'

'How much money do you make?'

'Do you have to wear pants to work?'

'Do you snoop on your mother-in-law?'

'Why do you have to do a man's job? Why can't you just sit at home?'

Vidya shook her head. 'You know, sometimes it really makes me wonder. No matter how qualified or capable you are, the kitchen, the cooking and child-bearing hips are the forever yardsticks for how *good* women are. I think the first woman must have been born with a ladle in her hand and a chapati for a face! Who says a woman can't be a detective? And, I do realize that I'm technically in the admin and finance department, but what if I chose to be one? Would you object?'

'Never,' Prachand smiled.

'So why can't these women just accept that I willingly work for my husband?'

'*With*, not *for*. And they are just curious, Viddu. It is an unusual choice you'll agree,' ruffling his wife's hair. She swatted his arm away.

'Well, for better or worse, we are famous here, Prachand,' she said, shrugging. He laughed and slipped his hand into hers, under her sari fold. She looked around shyly.

'If ma sees us like this she will beat her chest and tell everyone that I have made her son shameless.'

'My poor ma,' Prachand said in his mother's defense as Vidya laughed.

'By the way, a lot of people have taken our business cards. Going by some of the conversations I've had, I'm expecting decent business,' predicted Vidya.

'That's the alcohol talking' Prachand countered.

'I don't care what is talking as long as we get more clients. By the way, did you know that Prema chachi is waiting for her *father-in-law* to die?'

'What!' Prachand asked incredulously.

'Yes, she bribed me with a plate of dessert and asked if we could help find her father-in-law's will.

'Really, you end up ...' Mid-sentence he felt a hand on his shoulder, turned around and froze.

His father stood before him with an odd expression on his face. An investigation of the glass in his hands revealed the mystery behind the cryptic expression. Dinbandhu Tripathi was drunk.

'Prachand,' he said, then cleared his throat, looking confused about what to say next.

'Yes, Pitaji.' Prachand said softly.

'Umm. How are you?'

'I'm good. Shall I get you some food?'
'Is there good food?'
'Yes. I think so.'
'And tolerable dessert?'

Prachand laughed. 'Maybe. I'll have to check. Let me get you a plate.' He looked at Vidya who smiled and turned to speak with another relative.

'Prachi?' his father called out to him again.
'Yes?'
'You know ... if you need money for your business ... I can ... you know ... I mean ... I can...'

He smiled at his father as his heart melted. The poor man was financially in dire straits himself and was still offering to help.

'I know. Thank you very much. You sit here. I will bring your food.'

Prachand's heart was dancing with joy as he picked up a plate for his father. He however guessing that the alcohol induced window of affection might close up soon, he wanted to maximise it to the hilt. As he filled the plate with his father's favourite food, Prachand heard a familiar sound.

Ooh whoa, ooh whoa, ooh whoa
You know you louuuue me, I know you keeyar
Just shout whenevaar and I'll be theeyar
You are mai louuuee, you are mai heart
And we veel never, ever, ever be epaaaart
And I was like baby, baby, baby oooooooooh
Like baby, baby, baby nooooooooo

Bhushan had clearly met Ashfaque bhai and had also managed to wrest the mike from the aunties.

Prachand balked as he realized that the suspicious Sheila had caught up with him once again. She asked quizzically. 'Son, is something the matter? With Bhushan?'

Prachand smiled and energised himself for all the queries that would come his way, now that the lead singer of KPB Rocks had just made his debut.

CHAPTER 7

'Sir, this is a fixed rate' said Prachand, looking uncomfortable. 'If you can hold on for a second, I will hand over the phone to my finance manager.'

Before she could protest, Vidya was handed the phone and found herself in conversation with Motilal Narottam Bhai who wanted Kanpur Khoofiya Pvt. Ltd to keep an eye on his business partner, suspected of working with their competition now and causing him major losses. Being a businessman though, he was bargaining about the fee like he would at a vegetable market.

'Sir, we charge 2,000 rupees per hour for this kind of job, which is a very good rate. We execute each job personally, we don't hand it over to amateurs like most other detective agencies.'

'You do good price for me. You tell me how many days you take. I reduce days. You reduce cost.'

'Sir, that depends on his movements and how detailed you want the surveillance to be.'

'You give me two days free. You give me good price. I'll give you more business. Many people to follow in my house as well. All useless.'

'I'm sorry,' whispered Prachand and gestured for her to continue talking. Before she could express her anger, he quickly turned away, pretending to read something.

After a thirty-five-minute negotiation, Vidya looked like she had been in a wrestling bout.

'That was not fair!' she complained.

'I can't handle bargaining, Viddu, whereas you excel in this area.' He explained with the intention of placating her. Her haggling skills had been honed shopping on the streets and shops from Sarojini Nagar to Chandni Chowk. And Prachand was well aware of this.

Not looking pleased at the compliments, she went back to the computer.

'I don't even know why I check emails. No one mails us anyway.'

'Even I was expecting at least a few calls after the wedding. So many people seemed to be interested.' Prachand wondered aloud.

Vidya shrugged. The emails that usually came to her inbox were spam. Some emails had links to Indian porn sites. She had a vague suspicion that Yatish had been through the trash folder where these emails were junked.

A knock on the door interrupted their banter.

A man with a medium build walked in. He was wearing an incongruous attire comprising a long jacket and a hat that covered most of his face. He stood looking at Prachand for a few seconds and then started walking towards him.

Just a few inches away, he stumbled over a low stool and sent papers flying everywhere. Prachand made to help him up but he refused the hand offered, brushed himself and spoke with as much dignity he could muster after that fall.

'Srikhand?'

'No.'

'Srikhand Tripathi?'

'No. Prachand.'

'Oh. Prachand Tripathi from Awadh Niwas, Gwalto...'

'A big yes!' Prachand said, losing his patience. 'It really is me. Believe it.'

'A message for you.' Then he started reading it out like a robot: 'Please be warned that under no circumstances will I reveal my identity to you. In a few days, the details of the person I want followed will be shared with you. Your fee will be dropped to you after the completion of the job. I will pay you two lakhs for this job. Half will be paid midway and the remaining, on completion of the job. Remember, do not tell *anyone*.' He looked like he was trying to remember something else. 'Oh. PS: Please fix your email server. Emails are bouncing back.'

Vidya smacked her head in frustration. 'I was wondering why we didn't have a single email. Why can't Yatish fix it once and for all? How embarrassing!'

Prachand looked at the curious fellow. 'Who sent you to us?' Prachand enquired.

'You must tell no one,' he shouted, a bit repetitively and darted out the door. But not before falling again. In his haste, he left his hat as a souvenir.

Prachand ran after him. 'Mister, your hat!' he shouted as the man disappeared around the corner.

'Now what was that all about?' asked Vidya, sounding perplexed as they walked back into the office. Prachand's eyes were twinkling. 'Anonymous. Hmm ... you know, that man is a cook.'

'But then why hire us?'

'No, no.' Prachand corrected Vidya. 'The man who delivered the message. Fingernails stained yellow with turmeric, small cuts and burns all over his hands and he smelt a bit of onions.'

'How does it matter who is chosen to deliver a message? And whether he smells of onions or eggs?'

'Because it tells us a bit about who is sending the message.'

'You sometimes over analyse things, Prachi.' Vidya shrugged and then pinched her husband hard.

'Ouuuch!' he howled. 'What!?'

'Two lakhs!' Vidya was dancing. 'Two lakhs, Prachand! We can put ads in the paper, lots of them. I'll get a new laptop, new clothes.'

Her enthusiasm was infectious. 'We can buy that new spy camera and a better pair of binoculars!' Prachand chimed in. 'And we will take the family for a holiday and I'll give money to Pitaji for his business...'

'And our honeymoon ... finally!'

'Wait,' Prachand said furrowing his brows. 'What sounds too good to be true, usually is. I smell a rat.'

'Stop overthinking everything, Prachand!' But he was too deep in thought to listen.

'Why would someone pay me two lakhs to follow a person. Something that could easily be done by any other agency, even smaller and cheaper than ours. I'm telling you...'

'Alright,' Vidya said, throwing her hands in the air. 'Your instinct is usually correct. But honestly, maybe it is someone who is new to these matters, and just happened to pick us.'

'There are usually no coincidences in life,' said Prachand, not convinced. 'Look at the man who delivered the letter. That was strange you will agree.'

'Yes. But we now know, thanks to you, that he is clearly no hardcore criminal. The worst crime he may have committed is chopping garlic in the kitchen with unwashed hands- after- kitchen!'

'But why this anonymity? Getting someone else to deliver a message?'

'Maybe he is some famous celebrity' suggested Vidya, unable to hide another tremor of excitement in her voice.

'Or a famous gangster,' countered Prachand.

'Well, we will find out soon enough. For now, just let me dance while dreaming of that money!'

CHAPTER 8

Two men were squatting on the ground surrounded by cans of paint and brushes. One only had to sweep their gaze down the street to witness the handiwork of these modern-day Picassos. Every empty wall they could find had been painted on with an impossibly happy-looking man holding a bottle in his hands. The text read – '*Yeh humaara nara hai, bawaasir se chhutkaara dilana hai!*' (This is our mission/slogan, to rid people of piles!) This was not an unusual sight in Kanpur. All across the city these ads could be found plastered in all shapes, sizes and colours, rivalling the number of chaat and sweet shops.

'Hey! What are you doing? Get away from that wall,' an angry voice shouted at the men who dropped their paint brushes in fright. They had clearly chosen the wrong canvas this morning. Bhushan's wiry frame stood over them menacingly. Although usually averse to any emotion or physical activity, he wasn't about to let Awadh Niwas look anything but its best today.

Kanpur Khoofiya Pvt. Ltd

After all it was a special day, and every inch of the house had been scrubbed and cleaned like it was Diwali. The single-storied house was compact but generous in the matter of open areas. A beautiful little courtyard with a customary Tulsi plant, a terrace on the first floor, a small backyard where all the washing took place gave a sense of openness. The original Tulsi plant unfortunately didn't survive and after a few tries at replacing it, they had now resorted to a lush green artificial substitute from Naveen Market. But it was still watered dutifully.

The main wooden door of the house opened on to a narrow street but it was green and distinctive. Right next to the door was tied another distinctive personality, Hirwa, the family cow. She was more an object of reverence and devotion than a source of dairy for the family and was bathed, pampered and worshipped by the whole neighbourhood. She was fed hay all day long by passers-by who touched her frisky hooves. Whatever came out of her other end was also collected and taken home by them, for making *kanda* (dung cakes), so for Hirwa, life was good. And today she was going to be a star.

A week ago, a strange-looking gent with curly hair, torn shorts (just like Bhushan) and large tattoos on his arms had come calling while Rachna Tripathi was peeling peas. He represented a company that wanted to shoot an advertisement in her house. The setting of this house was perfect for them. For a local flavour, they said. Her initial apprehensions had melted as soon as 30,000 rupees for the one-day shoot was mentioned. The cow would feature in the ad as well. Glasses of buttermilk had suddenly appeared and the deal was sealed.

'Ma, won't Pitaji object?' Vidya had asked, questioning her mother-in-law's sudden bravado.

'I will convince him, saying they want to capture our culture and roots. He can't say no to that appeal. And the delicious food I make for him will take care of the rest. Don't you worry about him.'

The day of the shoot had arrived. It was a Friday but it looked like the weekend had arrived early at Awadh Niwas. Every surrounding terrace was overflowing with onlookers. There was a big crowd of people blocking the narrow street, one half of which was taken up by a van and a few cars. The crew, the lights and the cameras had attracted a lot of attention. Of course, the Gwaltoli Gilehris had also done their bit by ensuring that everyone, from the shopkeepers to the priests, knew that a member of their group was hosting a shoot at her home.

Despite the heat, Rachna Tripathi had worn her best Banarasi sari with purple and orange borders. Her bun was adorned with flowers and she had even worn the nose ring from her wedding. 'You look like an actress, Rachna!' her neighbour Guddi had gushed, decked in her brightest sari, not to be left behind. In order to help with the management of the day, no one except her husband was allowed to go to work. Of course Chachu Tripathi had begged his brother to let him be home. Bhushan pretended to be nonchalant but was equally eager to be around.

'Lights, camera, action!' shouted the director, a British gentleman called Harry.

Hirwa gave a great shot, mooing to the crowds and chewing the hay with great starry abandon. While the set up moved inside the house, the crew came to meet the family. The crew tried to speak in broken Hindi, as if they hailed from another country, and the Britisher was trying very hard to make friends with the language. Prachand acted as the translator.

'Ma, meet Harry.'

'Hello Hairy ji.'

'*Naamaaste*!' replied Harry with an elaborate folding of the hands. 'Did she just call me hairy?' joked the director. Prachand smiled.

'Hey hey, I learnt something in *Hinday*. Can I tell your mother?'

'Sure!'

'*Tuumra ghar boot kachcha haai!*' (Your home is very underwear!) He announced proudly with a thumbs up.

'Kachcha?' Rachna Tripathi looked confused.

'Kachcha means underwear, Harry. It's achcha,' corrected Prachand. Harry guffawed, thrilled to bits. Soon he was being introduced to the others. Bhushan sniffed an opportunity and jumped in, pumping the director's hand. 'Myself Bhushan. I am Kanpur Justin,' he announced proudly, pointing at the back of his head.

'Like Justin Bieber?'

'Yes. But I'm better Bieber! Let me show you.' Before Bhushan could unleash his deadly song, Prachand made an excuse and herded Harry to his next shot as per the crew's instructions.

'Hey Prashaand,' Harry called out to him again.

'Yes, Harry?'

'Hey man, I love India, you know. I love the cows and the honking, the noise. Where can I go to see more of the *real* India. You know, the crowds and the poverty. Is there like a special tour I can take?'

'Just hop onto any mode of transportation, Harry. You'll see it all around you,' smiled Prachand. 'But there's so much more to this country. I hope you get to see how beautiful it is before you leave.'

'Sir, I show you poor,' offered Chachu Tripathi. 'You come on my phatphati.'

'*Phatati?*'

'No, no, my phatphati. My scooter. *Vroom vroom!*'

'Shot ready!' screamed someone and Chachu Tripathi's rendezvous with the stars ended abruptly.

By five in the evening, most of the shots were taken, snacks had been served and a gigantic pot of tea brewed for the guests. Rachna Tripathi looked nervously at the clock.

'Son, just ask them how much longer. I want them to leave before your Pitaji arrives or he will make a fuss.'

'I'll just check.'

Prachand was returning from a chat with the production manager when he saw his Chachu standing next to the first-floor balcony, otherwise his father's usual perch.

'All okay?' he enquired. Chachu Tripathi smiled wanly.

'Yes, beta. All good,' he sighed.

Unbeknownst to many, and something only his brother and Prachand were privy to, was Dinanath Tripathi's unrealized dream of becoming an actor. Between home, the shop, and studies, he had spent every other available moment reading movie magazines, listening to Bollywood songs and creeping into cinema halls without paying for tickets. Once in his twenties he had even tried running away to Mumbai to try his hand at becoming an actor with the classic prescription of fifty rupees in his wallet, the popular and sure-shot mantra for success in Bollywood.

Unfortunately, his tattletale brother had informed his father of his whereabouts and he had been dragged back to Kanpur by his Dev Anand-like hair puff, looking black and blue. Now, in his late forties, the passion was still alive but buried under the stacks of leather that he dealt with at the shop each day. Every Friday when the entire family thought that he was making devout circles around the famous JK Temple, he was in reality munching popcorn while enjoying the morning show of the latest blockbuster.

'I wonder sometimes what life would've been like if I hadn't been dragged back to Kanpur. I could have been the next Sanjay Dutt!'

Prachand hugged his Chachu, smiling at his dated fantasies. 'Then how would you have been in our lives? Who would I have stolen money from? Who would Bhushan run to when Pitaji ran to hit him? This house would fall apart!'

He looked seriously at Prachand. 'Son, *you* live your dream, okay? If it's this detective thing, then be a detective. You should not have any regrets. I will fight with my brother if I have to.'

'Chachu! So brave! Are you sure you'll fight with him?'

His uncle's expression conveyed that he was re-evaluating the offer. 'Well, maybe I'll stand behind you while you're doing it!'

'Pack up!' a loud voice announced and the show at Awadh Niwas came to an end. Hirwa swished her tail and made a big deposit as the equipment was dragged past her, signalling her need for restoration of some peace and quiet. In this melee of men and machines, Prachand's eyes fell on one of the crew members. He was wearing a cap but his eyes were piercing and distinctive, even at that distance. Nothing seemed out of the ordinary except that this particular man seemed to be doing nothing amidst the flurry of activity. He seemed to be looking for something. Prachand couldn't put a finger on it but something in his manner was odd. The production manager passed by just then.

'Excuse me, who is that?' he asked, pointing at the man he had been watching.

The production manager turned and shrugged. 'I'm not sure, Mr Tripathi. I thought he was one of your friends. He is not with the crew.'

Just then, the stranger's eyes locked with Prachand's. He seemed startled but kept staring. Prachand quickly made his way down the stairs. When he arrived, the mysterious stranger was gone.

His instinct prodded him to give chase and he obliged. Reaching the main door just seconds later, Prachand turned his head both ways to ascertain which way the intruder had turned. In the crowd of adverting folks, cows, rickshaws and inquisitive neighbours, picking up any speed was out of the question, so Prachand gathered the man couldn't have gone very far. That's when he spotted the cap as he turned a corner.

'Hey you, wait. I just want to talk to you,' he called out.

Without as much as turning around, the man broke into a run. Unfortunately for Prachand, he turned out to be the reincarnation of Milkha Singh.

'Wait, wait! This is not track and field practice. I just want to talk.'

While the man kept sprinting ahead effortlessly as if he were gliding on butter, it became painfully obvious to Prachand that his legs and lungs would desert him very soon. Also, now obvious to him was why stamina and a fit body were such essentials for runaways and criminals.

They were now in a more deserted by-lane, some distance from Awadh Niwas and the gap between the man and his pursuer had opened up considerably. Sensing an opportunity, the stranger picked up a rock and without turning much, hurled it backwards in Prachand's direction. The only way to avoid it was to duck. Not only did Prachand duck, he sprawled out on the road. Brushing himself, Prachand stood up, only to find that the Olympian runner, who also turned out to be a shot-put expert, had disappeared into thin air. Dismissing the incident and labelling the man as some disgruntled person he might have helped put in prison, Prachand started walking back home.

CHAPTER 9

'So you didn't get a good look at his face?' Vidya enquired. Prachand was filling her in on the chase from after the shoot.

'Good look? Not at all. I just saw him for a short time when I was standing upstairs. His eyes were quite distinctive though, even from that distance. Piercing, like an eagle's.'

'It could be a coincidence you know. In case you are trying to connect him to the new case we have.'

'Viddu,' Prachand said while lighting some incense sticks, 'you know what I think about coincidences. It is a convenient term coined by lazy people for when there is no explanation at hand.' He smiled as Vidya hit him on the arm.

'Get serious, Prachand. That man tried to hit you with a rock. What if he is someone who has a bone to pick with you? Maybe from a previous case. He can come after you again.' She looked worried.

'Umm. The nature of the cases I take on are ... let's just say, too mild to leave arch enemies in my wake. But point taken, whether it is a lone offender or connected to the case, we need to be careful.'

'I have one more important concern,' Vidya said with a furrowed brow.

'Yes, Viddu?' Prachand enquired.

'You must improve your stamina. I don't want to be embarrassed next time a criminal comes calling!' She laughed as Prachand made a sad face.

'Prachand babu, where are you hiding?' someone called out.

'I'm coming!' Prachand responded.

'This Ashok uncle has no other work. Why must he come by so often? I know the reason for this frequency. His wife is visiting her parents again. So who better to fleece than the gullible Mr Prachand!' Vidya muttered in frustration.

'Viddu, relax. He is old and lonely. How will a few cups of tea and snacks affect us?'

'Oh, you will be surprised. Come, take a look at the expenses sheet one day. And buckets, not cups, when it comes to him,' Vidya countered. 'And Yatish is no less, mind you.'

'Now come on.' Prachand caught hold of her hand. 'Let's go sit with them.'

Yatish apparated soon enough. After exchanging pleasantries and ordering tea and snacks, they started chatting about the competitive nature of the private investigation business.

'What kind of name is Kanpur Cats Detective Agency?!' laughed Yatish. 'It sounds like they specialize in locating lost cats.'

'It doesn't matter if they have a funny name. I've heard that a rich industrialist's son has set it up. It will be the largest detective agency in Kanpur,' Prachand countered.

'Apparently they didn't even have to apply for a license. They have so many political connections that an officer delivered the license to their office.'

'This is what is wrong with this country,' chimed in Ashok Srivastava, reaching for his fourth samosa as Vidya, who was watching from the other side of the room, frowned. 'Hardworking people like you get left behind and these new thugs get everything easily.'

'Ashok uncle, I never said they're thugs. Just well connected.'

'You don't need to. Go to their fancy office on Birahna Road once and you will know for yourself.'

'Anyway, you tell us, how is your business faring?' Prachand enquired politely, wanting to change the topic.

A long thirty-second sigh was supported by a visible slackening of the shoulders. The head drooped theatrically as well. 'What do I tell you, son. Before I begin, can I get another cup of tea?'

Vidya could only fume internally as Chotu was sent off on yet another tea mission. Not one to miss an opportunity, Yatish had also ordered some snacks and another tea for himself.

Ashok Srivastava continued woefully. 'Aah. What amazing things I've seen as a child. Those glory days of being the grandson of a wealthy landlord in Farukkabad. Eating berries and mangos of our own trees. Living a life of luxury.'

'Berries and mangos don't sound that luxurious to me,' pontificated Yatish as Prachand gestured for him to be silent.

Ashok uncle continued, as if in a trance. 'Then there was so much internal fighting over property that my poor father took a small share and came away to Kanpur with us, starting his leather goods business.'

Prachand nodded sympathetically despite having heard this story a million times before.

'Things were fine back then. But see what is happening now. The raw hide godowns are as good as gone from Pech Bazaar. All because of the big machine slaughterhouses. They charge us much more for raw material. Then you have the worker problem. Most of them have run away because of the cow crusaders and then even the demand has slumped. Things are looking very, very bad. Sometimes I feel I'll have to sell the clothes off my back to survive. But why am I boring you! Being part of the trade, your father must've already told you about this state of affairs.'

Prachand suddenly felt very guilty at being so clueless about his father's plight.

Not very interested in this exchange, Vidya decided to run some errands while their meagre budget for the month was being exhausted over snacks.

The last one on her list was a secret one. Picking up a silk nighty, a raunchy little number, to wear for her husband. The opportunity to add some spice to their marital life presented itself very rarely. Living in a joint family was detrimental to their sex life. She often thought of telling her mother-in-law that if she really wanted grandchildren, the family would have to stay out of the house longer. On the other hand, somebody or the other was always visiting, whether it was the children of an aunt's mother's cousin sister, or a mauseri bua, or a long-lost cousin from the States who wanted to discover his roots. As a token of respect to the guests, their room was the first one to be donated along with Bhushan's sleeping cot, which was parked right outside. They never had the privacy a married couple craved. Very seldom, on nights when the others were out, by virtue of some miracle, they attacked each other like inmates serving a life term, who had just been allowed a conjugal visit.

Most of the 'nighty shops', as they were called, were always found in small corners of the market, as if the women wanted them to be a well-kept secret and wished away their existence. But in larger markets like Naveen Market, they were hung out in the open with men peddling bras and panties with all the wisdom of experienced grandmas. She walked into Lovely Nighty Shop, one of the few still helmed by a woman, and was greeted by the owner, Bimla aunty.

'Namaste aunty, I need bra hooks.' While Bimla aunty was digging in a box of hooks, Vidya's eyes strayed to one poster displayed to her left, featuring a model sporting a blue lace nighty that left little to the imagination.

'Should I take that one out for Prachand ... I mean you?' Bimla aunty winked. Vidya's cheeks turned crimson.

'It's on discount anyway. Let it be a gift from me.'

Vidya brushed her away again. But while her bill was being made, as casually as she could, she asked for the product to be added to her shopping bag. A delighted Bimla aunty made the bill, sent off her embarrassed customer and made a quick call that would take care of her entertainment for the day.

CHAPTER 10

'How dare he question gau mutra! The nerve!' Dinbandhu Tripathi looked visibly upset.

His brother, as always, tried to reason with him. 'We can't expect everyone to take to *gau mutra* the way you have ... maybe he thought there was a better solution for his diabetes and eczema than rubbing urine all over himself and drinking half a glass of it every morning.'

'As if I would suggest something unscientific to that stupid shopkeeper. Bloody village bumpkin. Ask any foreign doctor. They all recommend it. I am approached by so many people every day asking for Hirwa's ... well ... you know, product.'

A large dekchi of dal was placed noisily on the low table by Rachna Tripathi.

'Can we please talk about something else while having dinner?'

Everyone made their way to the table. 'Auntyji, is there any special food made today?' asked Yatish, who had joined in for dinner, a frequent practice for him.

'Again this boy is here?' Dinbandhu Tripathi scowled. 'Don't you ever eat at home?'

Rachna Tripathi jumped in to help the poor lad who doubled up as another son and man Friday, by trying to change the subject. 'Vidya, is there any *good news* you have for us?'

Vidya's smile faded and was replaced by a hacking cough. Prachand looked at her wide eyed as well. 'You mean, the discounts that Narottam Bhai is offering on pulses this whole month?' Vidya asked innocently.

Rachna Tripathi placed a large serving of vegetable curry on her daughter-in-law's plate and smirked. 'I mean, the *other* good news. I've heard from Bimla, you know.'

Vidya imagined Bimla aunty's severed head in the curry that she was eating. 'That gossipy old woman,' she muttered under her breath. Prachand started coughing. Ammaji farted and asked for water. Yatish felt bad and decided to break the awkward silence.

'Prachand, did you find the intruder who had entered the house during the shoot?' Success was instant. All awkwardness was forgotten and every head turned towards Prachand.

He shot Yatish an angry look while the latter just shrugged.

'If someone entered the house, we should call the police.'

'This is what happens when you let so many unknown people into the house.'

'What was he wearing? A kurta-pyjama? I saw a strange man standing next to Hirwa yesterday. No, wait a minute, he was wearing a dhoti.'

'Everyone relax,' Prachand said firmly. 'He might just have been here by mistake. Anyway, even if there is something more to this, I'll find out. I'll take care of it.'

'Of course. Just like you take care of everything else,' snorted Dinbandhu Tripathi.

It was around 1 a.m. Rachna Tripathi couldn't sleep. She kept dreaming of a faceless person following her around the market and stealing her vegetables. He had just about taken the last brinjal from her basket when he came close to her face and she woke up sweating.

'No one takes my brinjals!' she shouted defiantly in her sleep and reached out to the jug of water that turned out to be empty. Now awake and muttering curses, she made her way to the stairs with the jug where she heard a noise. Her sleep entirely gone, she was now frightened. There was another noise. Of breaking glass.

'Who is it?' she managed to squeak.

No response.

She then saw a shadow run across the stream of light being thrown in from the street.

A shriek emerged from her mouth and she ran to the bottom of the steps, wanting to hide in the shadows.

A light came on in the downstairs room and Prachand walked out bravely with a big lathi, Vidya on his heels with her Rampuri knife drawn. Another loud crash brought Dinbandhu Tripathi and Chachu Tripathi running down the stairs. Their arrival was met with a hailstorm of vegetables from the kitchen behind them. Rachna Tripathi, possibly still half dreaming was convinced the vegetable thief from her dream was in the house and launched her best nutritive defence.

'Stop it! What's going on?'

'Someone switch on the veranda lights!' someone screamed.

'They aren't working. Where is the intruder?'

'It was you the other day. Wasn't it, you scoundrel?!'

'I caught him!' screamed Prachand, yanking a cloth on which red chillies were drying.

Finally everyone seemed to have their wits about them and collected around Prachand and the moving white figure, now sneezing uncontrollably because of the sharp smell of chillies.

'Who are you!'

'*Acchchho*!!' came the response.

Vidya finally yanked the cloth away.

'Bhushan!' everyone shouted together.

'What are you doing sneaking around?!' shouted Prachand. 'Why is the front door open? Were you out?'

'But I saw him sleeping a while ago,' said Vidya sounding puzzled.

'I sneaked out after everyone went to sleep,' admitted Bhushan sheepishly. 'The KPJ Rocks had a performance tonight. I knew I wouldn't be allowed.'

Before Dinbandhu Tripathi could contribute with abuses and a befitting punishment, Rachna Tripathi rose like a tigress and held Bhushan's ears.

'Tonight I will make a chutney out of you, you stupid boy. Always lurking around at night, troubling everyone. Once I'm done boxing your ears, the ghost of that American boy will be exorcised from your body!'

Long after the commotion died down and everyone was back in bed, Prachand lay awake for a long time hugging

Vidya, his mind working overtime. He tossed and turned, wondering about the strange message, the stranger who had delivered it and the other uninvited stranger in their home, responsible for everyone being on edge. Were all these events connected in some way?

CHAPTER 11

Prachand used to treat the computer in his office warily. They would stare at each other on warm summer afternoons like suspicious enemies, keeping their distance. But Vidya considered this attitude archaic and detrimental to their growth.

'The world isn't just moving but running forward, Prachand. And here you treat the computer like a flea-infested street dog.' No tech wizard herself, she was however smart enough to know that being computer literate wasn't an option anymore. In the hopes of new business, she would even send emails and emailers. While checking the inbox diligently every day, she prayed for a case to arrive. And one day, her wish was granted.

Sitting atop the pile of rubbish spam and unsolicited emails was one marked 'urgent business'. She stared at it suspiciously. The last time she had fallen for the subject, her computer was attacked by a virus and opened up vile and pornographic animal sex videos for a week. Of course, this had taken place in front of a weary client who

Kanpur Khoofiya Pvt. Ltd

was briefing the agency on his adulterous wife. He had left with alacrity.

She stared at the subject for a few seconds before clicking on the message. But once she did, she knew exactly what it was. 'Prachand, it's here!'

'What's here?' Prachand asked, putting down the files he was organizing for the umpteenth time.

'The case details!'

Much like the verbal brief, it contained a paragraph of instructions:

> This is the woman you must follow. She is Shailaja Kapoor from Mumbai and is coming to stay at Lily Bungalow, Ratan Lal Nagar, after three days. She will be there for two weeks. I want details on all her movements. Where she will be going, who she will be meeting, what she will be doing. I'll send half the money at the end of the first week, after you submit a report. If I am happy with your work, I will continue with your services otherwise the remaining deal stands cancelled. This information is confidential and must be kept that way. NO ONE SHOULD KNOW.

Vidya clicked on the attachments. There were pictures of a woman and a few more of a house. She then checked the sender details out of curiosity. The email id looked like it was from an encrypted server, that you cannot trace, something she had learnt about in college during student election time in Delhi, when malicious campaigns were the flavour of every election season.

'Wait a minute. Shailaja Kapoor. That's who this woman in the picture is. I remember her face. She has acted in a few movies,' announced Vidya excitedly, not immune to the Bollywood bug.

'Now that you mention it, her face does look familiar,' agreed Prachand.

Vidya stood up and started pacing around. 'I can't believe it! *We* have a Bollywood client.'

Prachand smiled. Her enthusiasm was infectious. 'This is the first time I've seen you so excited about a case and I have Bollywood to thank for it.'

While he was watching, amused, Vidya opened up a browser window to search for something. The screen suddenly flickered and switched off.

'You stupid old computer!' shouted Vidya irritably. Then she banged her fist all over it. With a shudder and a hiss, the screen reluctantly came back to life.

'This stupid box will be the first thing to go once we get that payment.'

'Sure! Now, can we focus?' Prachand requested.

Vidya clicked and skimmed through a few articles.

'So it says here that Shailaja Kapoor is the daughter of a wealthy industrialist, Dhirendar Raj Kapoor and Pamela Kapoor. Doesn't he sound like a military-grade weapon' laughed Vidya. Prachand nudged her to continue.

She scrolled over a bunch of pictures of Shailaja Kapoor. 'Look how pretty she is.' She read a bit more. 'Wow!' she smirked. 'The mummy sounds like a colourful personality I must say. She was an actress as well. Featured in a few movies that apparently her husband financed. Then got married and that's when her acting career came to an end.

Says here that apparently when Shailaja was five years old, her mother ran away with another man.'

'We are talking about someone's mother here, Viddu.'

'Prachand, I'm just reading what's written!'

'Anyway, did they get a divorce?'

'Ummm ... I don't think so. I'm not sure what happened. She went back to her husband after a few months, but soon after he died of a heart attack. Oh. And she had an accident and landed up in a wheelchair. One tragedy after another. Poor thing.'

'That's horrible.' Prachand's heart went out to the poor lady. 'Did Shailaja ever get married?'

'Umm,' Vidya continued scrolling. 'She is married ... but I don't think it's a happy one. At least that's what it says here.'

'Oh.' Prachand was pensive, ticking off all his instinctive questions. 'And who is the husband and what does he do?'

'Doesn't say. Oh wait, Sujit Oberoi. Some big builder. A few reports claim that he had suffered business losses but then managed to recover. According to me, some people can live a rich man's life without being rich. Look at the Tiwari Mithai Bhandaar brothers. Three shops shut down, all the cows and poultry sold off and they still live the good life,' she said incredulously.

Prachand's eyes bore into the screen. 'She is sad about something, you know. Someone with a troubled life.'

'How can you tell?'

'Look at this picture. The close up. She's beaming away, but her smile doesn't reach her eyes. Also, if someone smiles a lot, it shows up as curves and wrinkles around their eyes and mouth. She has none.'

'Or it could be great skin,' Vidya offered. Prachand shrugged his dissent.

'And there is some friction between the mother and daughter, according to me.'

Vidya smiled, accepting the familiar routine. She had now learnt to absorb instead of constantly marvelling at her husband's intuitive eye on life and people.

'There was definitely some hidden tension running in this family. Look at this picture of her as a little girl standing in between her parents. The father's eyes are hard and his jaw is set, lips in a thin line, usually suggestive of underlying anger. The mother's fists are clenched and Shailaja looks scared. The tension is obvious.'

Vidya laughed. 'Only to you, Prachi! Trust me.' Then she trained her eyes back to the email. 'So who do you think wants her followed? And why?' pondered Vidya aloud.

'I don't know yet. The usual motives are money or love.'

'This is just too exciting!' Vidya chuckled.

'We must be very careful and not tell anyone. That is what the client has demanded and I would like to honour that.'

'You have my word.'

'Vidya, I mean it. Not a word to anyone. She is a known face.'

'My lips are sealed.'

'You know...'

'With Fevicol...'

CHAPTER 12

Prachand had always liked being part of a large family. It gave him a sense of belonging and comfort. But today was not one of those days. Vidya Tripathi, who was like a sieve when it came to keeping secrets, in Narad Muni fashion, had accidentally slipped the information about Shailaja Kapoor to the closet starlet, Chachu Tripathi. In his excitement, he had passed the information to Bhushan. Bhushan had in turn told his mother, swearing her to silence and begging her to be non-reactive. Clearly this strategy failed as she was found bounding around like an ebullient goat when Prachand returned. It didn't take a detective to connect the dots.

'Ma, you must not say a word to anyone. Swear on me,' he warned his mother as sternly as he could. Soon, with the exception of Dinbandhu Tripathi, who was missing in action, everyone had collected in the courtyard where there was palpable excitement.

Watching his excited mother dance to some tuneless song in the kitchen, Prachand was convinced he needed to take further action to rein her tongue in.

'If I am not enough, then you have to swear on this Tulsi.'

'It's artificial. She will break her promise,' muttered Bhushan into his ear.

Prachand looked at him testily, 'Aren't you getting late for college?' He then shifted his gaze to Vidya who was looking apologetic, having being the official broadcaster of the news. 'I am warning everyone here. No one, and I mean no one, can know about her whereabouts or the fact that we have anything to do with Shailaja Kapoor,' he reiterated.

Ammaji, who was relaxing on the charpoy, sat up.

'Chacha Gafoor? Where is he?' and looked around confused.

Rachna Tripathi corrected her. 'Not Chacha Gafoor, Ammaji. Shailaja Kapoor, the actress.'

'Aah' she lay back down with a loud belch, convinced that nothing of interest to her was being discussed.

Prachand returned to the task at hand, only to be interrupted by Chachu Tripathi.

'Son, what have I ever done to you?'

'What do you mean, Chachu?'

'After years I see a ray of sunshine and you want to eclipse it?'

'Chachu, I have no idea what you're talking about.'

'Son, this could be the break I'm looking for. My father isn't around anymore and I'm too old for your father to fight with me. I know my destiny lies in Bollywood. She is an older actress with connections. This might be the stepping stone to my dreams!' Chachu Tripathi announced with a theatrical flair, his arms stretched on either side. Prachand discretely gave his poor Chachu a once over.

The just-about peppering hair swept back in a tidal wave of pungent oil, the gaunt cheeks that looked like life had been sucked out of them, the grey kurta and a soggy white dhoti made him wonder if his Chachu had looked any different even when he was twenty years younger or that his own mind had etched a permanent picture of his uncle that would never change. His heart went out to the poor guy.

'Chachu, I know you've always only encouraged me to follow my heart. But I really don't think Shailaja Kapoor is your key to stardom. We might not even get to speak to her. The job is to follow her.'

'Then let me come along!' he pleaded.

'Can you take a few pictures for me?!' Rachna Tripathi sensed an opportunity and dived right in. This was also her only chance to shoot to stardom in her Gwaltoli Gilehri group, becoming the one with insider access to a real Bollywood celebrity.

Prachand, mild mannered in the harshest of situations, was finding it difficult to keep his composure. 'I am saying this for the last time. This is my work. I will not have anybody taking it lightly.'

'Hey there, Tripathis!?' a jovial Yatish entered, carrying a packet full of samosas.

'Prachand, so when is that Bollywood star of yours coming to Kanpur?? Look, I've got snacks for us to celebrate!'

Prachand looked at Vidya. She held her ears as an extended apology.

The next morning was a busy one at Kanpur Khoofiya Pvt. Ltd. A client that had approached them for investigating a property dispute was packed off hastily without the usual tea session. Prachand had singular focus. To get things started.

He had lit two extra incense sticks this morning. His intuition told him that after this case, things would change around here. For the better. So he had to do everything in his power to get this one right.

Realizing that Yatish could be useful in this investigation with his network of contacts, for the first time, he had officially been inducted into the case after being re-sworn to secrecy.

Sitting around the table, Prachand shared the groundwork that he had done. 'So, Lily Bungalow is a little more isolated compared to the other houses around. I went and scouted the area. It will become a bit difficult for me to remain hidden but I think I've found a spot that gives me a good view of the house. It's an empty shop very close to the bungalow.'

'And what will you do if she leaves the house?' enquired Vidya.

'I will use your cycle. The scooter will make too much noise.'

'That's a good idea but my cycle is purple. Will you ride a ladies' cycle?'

'I don't want to waste money on a new bicycle just for a case. I don't mind. Can I use it?'

'Sure.' Vidya shrugged but made a mental note to remove the silver tassels from the handles. 'But don't complain later. You won't find it comfortable.'

'I won't. Don't worry. Yatish, I want you to find me a good pair of binoculars. Mine are really old and cracked at one end.'

'Okay.'

'I need a new audio recorder as well. Just in case.'

'Okay.'

Kanpur Khoofiya Pvt. Ltd

'Vidya, can you please dig out some more information about the family. Every bit of information is important.'

'There isn't very much online really, but I'll get whatever I can. Don't worry. It'll be done before we start the surveillance,' she assured him.

Prachand paused and turned around to look at Vidya. '*We*?'

'Of course,' she said innocently.

'Vidya, you are not coming with me.'

'I am.'

'This has always been our division of work, Vidya. I do the ground work and investigations. You help me in office with the paperwork, clients, finances, etc.'

'Well, I don't accept the division of work for this particular case.'

'What makes you think I will allow you to put yourself in danger and come with me?'

'I'll be in as much danger as you will be, eating peanuts and training your binoculars on a woman as she moves about her house.'

Yatish kept his silence, his neck twisting to either argument like a chair umpire at a tennis match.

'I have taken this case, but am clueless about who wants this information and for what reason. There is always an element of danger with the unknown.'

'There is always that other danger of my leaving you for being so bossy and finding myself a more pliable IAS boy.'

Prachand started laughing. 'Please don't be like this. You know, this is for your safety.'

'So you won't take me along even for a few days?'

'Absolutely not, Viddu!'

CHAPTER 13

'Would you like a laddoo?'
Prachand frowned.

'I would like one!' chirped Yatish, before Prachand trained an eye on him.

Prachand Tripathi was a harrowed man. He looked at his companions. Yatish was casually squatting on the ground like he had been invited for a village panchayat meeting. Vidya was sitting next to him on a low foldable stool. Between them sat a large cloth bag. It contained sweet treats, roasted peanuts, biscuits and an Eagle thermos flask filled with tea. There was easily enough food at this stakeout to feed a few families.

'Vidya, firstly you accompany me against my will, and then you pack a picnic basket that looks like a *mata ka bhandara*. This is not how stakeouts are done!'

'You will thank me once you feel hungry.' She shrugged. 'This will be the first stakeout that you'll thoroughly enjoy.' Looking around in the food stash, she found a chocolate that she unwrapped and started eating. 'You know, I've noticed that you get rather grumpy during ground work. Relax!'

'I agree with her. Relax,' chimed in Yatish.

'You were not supposed to come either. Don't you have some other work, Yatish?' asked Prachand, uncharacteristically irritated at this gang up.

'Prachand da...'

'Shhhhhhh ...' Prachand had his binoculars trained on the entrance of the house where a car had just pulled up. In true Bollywood fashion, a long black car blew up a curtain of dust and haze. Through this cloud emerged a woman. With a porcelain complexion and long black hair, she looked radiant in a navy-blue dress.

'Please give me the binoculars for just a second' requested Vidya with her mouth still stuffed with chocolate. 'Her pictures don't do justice.' She gaped, looking a bit awestruck. Once Yatish had taken a look as well, Prachand took back the binoculars.

'There is a male caretaker in the house. Otherwise, she seems to have arrived alone.'

Vidya snatched the binoculars once again. 'I just counted six suitcases and two bags! Has she come to stay here for the rest of her life?'

'Maybe that's just how actresses travel.' Prachand shrugged and took a few notes in his small diary.

'Ex-actresses,' Vidya corrected him.

A few hours later, the excitement had fizzled out and the three investigators sat in silence, waiting for some action. Vidya nudged Prachand.

'I need to go to the toilet.'

'Huh?'

'Toilet.' She stuck her little finger up for visual confirmation.

He looked around. There was a big clump of trees a little distance from them.

'Would you be able to go there?'

Vidya surveyed the area. 'I need more cover. Can't have my behind hanging out for the world to see.'

Some more twisting of the neck. 'How about that big bush over there?' offered Prachand.

'It's just one bush. And there is a house right behind it. How can I go there!?'

'I did not scout the area for bathroom arrangements?' he said plaintively.

Yatish coughed discretely.

'Lower your voice,' hissed Vidya. 'Do you want Yatish to hear about my bathroom needs?'

Prachand sighed and turned to Yatish. 'I need to take her somewhere. You'll keep an eye on the house?' He thrust the binoculars into Yatish's hands. 'Do not move from this spot, at all. Not at all.'

Yatish felt very important. He now had the reins and he was the boss. He trained the binoculars onto Lily Bungalow. Everything looked peaceful, normal. The gardener was pottering around ... sometimes digging, sometimes watering plants. Shailaja Kapoor appeared on her ground floor balcony very often, each time with a mug in her hand. The only irritant was that he was finding it increasingly difficult to keep his eyes open. The alcohol session with his neighbour from the previous night followed by the fatigue from the early morning surveillance had caught up and he was now yawning steadily.

In the middle of one such yawn, he noticed that a white car drove into the gate and a man in a black jacket alighted from the rear seat. *Could this be a friend*? Yatish wondered. The man walked up to the front door and rang the bell. To Yatish's surprise, Shailaja Kapoor stormed out. Her body language and hand movements clearly showcasing her anger. He was happy that finally something interesting had occurred on his watch.

Half an hour later, Prachand and Vidya returned to see Yatish curled up on the ground. He had a slight satisfied smile on his face and was snoring peacefully. Prachand shook him awake.

'Yatish! You're sleeping?' asked Prachand incredulously. Yatish woke up and the smile disappeared. He wiped the drool off his mouth and looked embarrassed.

'Oh, don't worry. I barely slept for a few minutes' he lied.

'You really couldn't hold on till I returned?'

'Anyway, forget all that.' He was desperate to change the topic. 'There is something important I must tell you. A man drove up to the house to meet Shailaja.'

'What? Who?'

'I don't know. And it looked like they were arguing.'

'This could be important. Show me the picture.'

'Picture?' Yatish's eyes darted nervously. 'You see ... picture ... yes ... so...'

Prachand controlled his temper with great effort. 'Yatish, one thing. The first substantial thing to happen and we have no pictures!' Then he took a deep breath. 'Please go back home and take Vidya with you. Before you go, I want you to give me that man's description.'

'How will you manage on your own, Prachand? You need our help.' Vidya tried to reason.

Prachand didn't know whether to laugh or cry.

'A picnic party, then washroom problems, then naps. I appreciate the intention but you both have done enough for one day. Really, I'll manage.'

After Vidya and Yatish left, grumbling, Prachand sat down in his spot. He spent the rest of the day waiting for a glimpse of the man who Yatish had seen and hoping he would turn up again. Neither did anyone leave the house, nor enter. Yatish was to take the night shift but Prachand decided to not let anything else get botched up on day one of the investigation and volunteered to continue the surveillance himself.

As he nibbled on the food that Vidya had left for him, an owl came and sat on the window sill and started hooting. He looked at his watch and then the owl.

'Please keep me awake!'

CHAPTER 14

'Ammaji! Should I give you hot turmeric milk?' bellowed Rachna Tripathi from the kitchen.

'Why don't you just give me some poison, Rachna? That'll do wonders.'

It was a busy morning and Ammaji had been unusually vocal. To make matters worse, she had a cough that in her hypochondriac world meant she was going to die of pneumonia. Adding to the list of demands, Dinbandhu Tripathi had an urge to have kheer for breakfast and there was not a drop of milk. Rachna Tripathi had Prachand to thank for it. As was the case every morning, she had woken up to the clatter of the milk cans on the milkman's cycle. Two empty vessels were kept outside the door next to Hirwa who had long stopped demeaning herself with minor mediocrities like milk production.

To Rachna's utter surprise, Prachand had walked in just when the milk was delivered. Before Rachna could warn him, his foot collided with the full vessels, leaving the threshold of Awadh Niwas bathed in milk.

'Satyanash!' was all Rachna could manage, looking at the mess. She turned to look at the culprit and then sniffed around his mouth.

'Prachand, are you drunk?'

'What! No.'

'Why are your eyes red?'

'Because I've been awake all night, working.'

'Where?'

'The new case.'

'I told you, let us help.'

'No, thank you. Don't worry. I just need a few hours of sleep.'

Rachna Tripathi ended the exchange with a frown, made him a cup of black tea to drive in the point and went to the bathroom.

'This tastes different.' Dinbandhu Tripathi looked suspiciously at the bowl in front of him.

'Then don't eat it,' Rachna Tripathi muttered.

'I never said I won't eat it. Just that it tastes different.' He noticed his wife's glum mood, while she quickly tucked the packet of milk powder under the gas stove. 'Why are you frowning?' he probed.

'I am worried about Prachand.'

'What happened?'

'He came back this morning. Poor thing was up all night keeping an eye on that Bollywood woman.'

'He has dug this pit for himself. Let him do his work.'

The shape of the amorphous roti mirrored the irritation she felt. The work was never-ending and her daughter-in-law never seemed to have the time. Adding to her list of woes, she was tired of this father-son friction. It was like a stale Bollywood formula that the makers wouldn't let go of.

'It was tasty,' Dinbandhu Tripathi concluded, sensing the adverse atmosphere. 'Where is my langot, Rachna?'

'Vidyaaa,' she hollered. 'Can you please bring down the langots drying upstairs?'

'Are you mad?' whispered Dinbandhu Tripathi. 'You'll ask Vidya bahu to get my underwear!'

Rachna Tripathi turned around. 'All day long it flutters in our faces from the clothesline, like a royal flag. Everyone in Gwaltoli knows that you are possibly the last person in Kanpur to still wear a langot, so why hide it?'

All he could do in response was look annoyed. On difficult mornings like these, Rachna Tripathi, the ideal, obedient wife would transform into a belligerent battle axe and let even her husband have it.

'Why don't you try the new-age underwear? The ones that Prachand wears. It holds everything properly,' she said, cupping something imaginary. 'Small and easy to wear. Should I get you one?' she offered.

'Get your brain checked. I'm going to finish my prayers.' He grunted and trudged towards his room while Rachna Tripathi grunted back at her husband's obstinacy.

'Are you growing the turmeric in the backyard?' hollered Ammaji and Rachna Tripathi smacked her forehead in exasperation. With the demand for milk growing steadily, she decided to ask the one responsible for the crisis to replenish her stocks but in his sleepy state, he had returned with a litre of cooking oil instead of milk.

After hearing an earful from his irate mother, when Prachand finally made it to his office, Vidya was already there, filing some papers. She smiled and gestured for him to sit down.

'Still sleepy?' she enquired.

'Little bit,' lied Prachand. 'I asked Yatish to fill in but I have to head back soon.' Then his eyes sparkled. 'That was the first time I had to stay up all night you know. It was exciting!'

'I'm glad. I just wish it wasn't so tiring for you.'

'Don't worry,' Prachand said stretching out his body. 'By the way, who was that on the phone?'

'Motilal Narottam bhai. I analysed the accounts and the records you shared with me. He was right. His partner has been dipping into a lot of the company money. But there is no threat of him joining a competitive business.'

'Then? What's happening?'

'I got Chotu to follow his partner. For two days. And there is a woman involved. He is having an affair with her and stashing away cash into an account they are joint owners of. I traced it from a copy of the financials that Narottam bhai gave me. He is either naive or arrogant to not hide the trail.'

'Chotu? You got Chotu to follow him?'

'You'll be surprised. He is quite the nosy one. Just needs strict instructions. Besides, you need all the help you can get right now.'

He came and sat next to Vidya.

'You take care of everything, don't you?'

'That's my job, Mr Tripathi.' She blushed as he kissed her lightly on the cheek. 'Now tell me about last night.'

'Aah, yes. I waited for quite some time. Not much activity. I was almost calling it a night when someone drove in at around 12.30 a.m. From Yatish's description, it seemed like the man he had seen earlier but I can't be a hundred per cent sure.'

'Did he look anything like this?' Vidya pulled out a printout. It showed a handsome middle-aged man, dressed impeccably, holding a glass of wine in one hand while the other was tucked in a trouser pocket.

'Who is this?'

'Sujit Oberoi. The husband.'

'Like I said, it could be him.'

'So if it is him, he comes in earlier, she has an argument and chases him away. Then he returns in the dead of the night. What happened after that?' asked Vidya.

'Nothing.'

'Nothing?'

'Absolutely nothing. There was no noise, no commotion. Lights went off soon enough. He hadn't left till the time I started for home this morning.'

'How long have they been married?'

'About seven years. You know, they're a very well-known family, but I am not finding much online. Possibly because she gave up acting a long time ago. We need to dig.'

'I think we might have to dig very deep,' added Prachand with a faraway look.

CHAPTER 15

It had been three days. Of watching and waiting. The only respite came at night when he went home to get a bit of shut-eye. Prachand was tired but still focused on the job. This part of the neighbourhood, full of second homes for the rich and creamy, looked like a sleepy old hamlet. Devoid of crowds, traffic and the din of regular city life. While on the one hand this backdrop and lack of intrusive passers-by made it easier to snoop, it made a stranger lurking around become equally conspicuous. So Prachand had to be alert at all times. Most of the houses had one man multitasking as a security guard, gardener and man Friday. Which was the case with Lily Bungalow as well.

Vidya called at some point.

'How is it going?' Vidya enquired.

'Fine. But it's a little frustrating. I have no idea what she is doing in there but it must be really interesting. Either that or she hasn't slept for a year and is catching up.'

'Why?'

'Why? Because she hasn't left the house at all. Not for a walk, not to run an errand.'

'She doesn't need to. She is used to people running around her, doing everything she needs. Imagine. What if we had a few, running around our house?' Vidya had a mental flash of a battalion of servants in Awadh Niwas. One was washing a mountain of her father-in-law's langots, one was pressing Ammaji's constantly aching legs, another was cooking up a storm while her mother-in-law sat and chatted with her friends. Of course, she herself featured in it as well: getting a long luxurious massage as delicious food miraculously presented itself on the table. The truth was that she managed to skilfully evade most tasks at home. But in a joint family, it was hard to dodge them consistently.

'Vidya, stop daydreaming.'

'Huh. Oh. No, no, I was just...'

'Daydreaming!'

'Anyway, what else?'

'Well, there is a Govind in the house who does all the work. I had found out earlier from the neighbour's gardener.'

'Why don't you come back home?'

'I'll have nothing to report at the end of this week, Vidya. I'm getting a bit desperate here.'

'But manufacturing news is not our job, we just report what's happening. How is it your fault that she has no friends here and does nothing? If the person who wants her followed found out, he would probably get bored and call off the investigation.'

'I'm not leaving till I find out more. I can feel it in my bones. There's more to this.'

Prachand's bones felt a host of other things. The hard ground. The bed of pebbles, the heat beating down on his head despite the tree cover and the sticky bird droppings that were constantly falling on him like mini pellets.

'Can't you find some other place to do your potty? How much do you birds eat, anyway? You and Ammaji must both seek consultation.' Prachand tried to rationalize with the pigeons hopping around on the branch above his head and then felt alarmed that he was finally losing his sanity and talking to birds. That's when he decided to take matters in his hands and get closer to the house. It was the only way in which he thought he would truly earn his fee.

A solution lay at the bottom of his faithful black bag, a collection of small handy items, disguises, binoculars, etc. The contents had not been employed very often, barring the use of an occasional moustache or a pair of thick glasses for some undercover action. But today, it had to be something that could help him get close to the house without raising suspicions and after some rummaging and some thought, he made his decision. The neatly combed hair was ruffled. He changed into a tattered vest and pyjamas. Out went the Bata sandals and out came tattered ones. He rubbed some dirt on his face for good measure and added a fat stick as a befitting prop. His transformation into the friendly neighbourhood beggar was complete.

It was showtime. He emerged onto the main road that led to Lily Bungalow. The pace was slow and unhurried and he kept looking around every now and then to ensure no one was watching. Crossing the gate a few times, he looked for some sign of activity, but there was none.

A few hours passed and the pretence of being miserable became real. The mosquitoes were feasting on his legs and ants had joined in too. Just before he was about to turn away, he heard someone approaching the gate. It seemed to be

Kanpur Khoofiya Pvt. Ltd

the caretaker, Govind. He had a bag in his hand, possibly embarking on an errand. Halfway to the gate, he saw the shabby-looking man standing outside. Prachand averted his eyes and focused on looking wretched.

'Hello! Who is there?' Govind asked suspiciously.

'A poor beggar,' he answered in a weak voice.

'Go away!' said Govind, shooing him off while shutting the gate behind. Prachand's mind raced and he decided to employ an oft-used trick. He called it the 'loosening of the heart with the purse string' that began with throwing a 100-rupee note near the gate.

'Mister, I think you dropped some money,' he said innocently.

The arrow met its mark. Where the money came from and who it belonged to notwithstanding, Govind's heart melted looking at the beggar who had his moral fibers intact, despite the poverty. He took the money and buried it in his shirt pocket.

'What is your name?'

'Banwari Lal.'

'Named after a God and resorting to begging? Why?'

'Why does anyone beg, mister?'

'You weren't always a beggar, were you?'

'No.'

'I guessed as much. You don't really look like a beggar.'

Prachand made a mental note to work on his beggar look for the future.

Govind was in deep thought for a minute. 'Hey, why don't you come in? I was going to get some cigarettes and eggs but I can do that in the morning. Don't mind some company either. Do you want something to eat?'

'Absolutely!' Prachand genuinely perked up at the sound of food.

'Come with me. But don't make any noise. Madam likes it quiet.'

The gate opened and Prachand tiptoed in behind Govind. He was led towards the back of the house.

'Madam is resting. She eats late. So I can get you something to eat now.' He ushered Prachand into a room which was attached to the kitchen. It was spacious but quite sparsely furnished. A bed sat at one end with a table and chair next to it. There was a set of blue sofas, possibly discarded from the main house that filled in another corner of the room. This is where Prachand was given a seat.

'Banwari Lal.'

Prachand looked around, taking in his surroundings.

'You there! I'm calling you,' hollered Govind.

Prachand turned around immediately. 'Sorry. I'm a little hard of hearing.'

'Banwari Lal, please dust your clothes before sitting down on the sofa. You can wash your hands in that sink outside.'

Govind bustled into the kitchen and returned with a plate full of food. Prachand graciously took the plate and ate silently.

'Thank you.'

'*Mensan naat*.' (Mention not.)

'It must be very hard for you to manage such a big house alone.'

'It is, but I've been here for years now. I'm used to it.'

'Your madam is good to you?'

'She doesn't talk much,' he said pensively. 'Seems a little unwell, if you ask me.'

'Something troubling her?'

Govind was about to respond, then stopped and frowned. 'You should focus on the food.' Prachand nodded and continued eating, reminding himself to be careful and not put the old man on his guard.

CHAPTER 16

After dinner, Govind offered Prachand a drink that he politely refused, claiming his stomach was full. With each successive sip, Govind loosened up further. It turned out that his magnanimity was proportional to the amount he drank. By the time he was ten sips down, he asked the poor beggar to stay and rest for a while before heading out. A sofa would be a welcome change from the hard, dusty ground. Prachand readily agreed.

'Govind!' hollered someone from inside.

'Yes, madam!' Govind was suddenly alert and seemed to have lost any trace of inebriation as he put on his slippers.

'I'll give madam dinner and come. You rest. Don't make a noise.' He sprayed some perfume, popped some mouth fresher and ran in.

It took about an hour to wind up dinner. The clanking of the used dishes in the kitchen announced the end of the day's proceedings. Govind returned and sat on the sofa.

'Sriram, sriram,' he groaned, holding his knees. 'My bones hurt all the time. I'm getting old.'

Kanpur Khoofiya Pvt. Ltd

Then he glugged whatever remained in the small bottle.

'Careful. Don't drink so much.'

'This is my medicine, Banwari Lal. It is my friend. My family,' he hiccupped.

For Prachand this was an ideal opportunity to dig a bit further while Govind's *family* was in charge of his senses.

'So, does your madam come down very often? You must feel quite lonely here.'

'No, no. Just once a year. You know she was very famous at one time, a teenage star, almost as famous as her father was in his business. Everyone used to line up just to get a glimpse of her,' he announced almost with parental pride.

'But why does she come alone? Doesn't she have any family?' Prachand enquired innocently.

'Kapoor Sahib is in heaven. Madam's mummy is in a wheelchair in Mumbai. And that husband ...' He looked disgusted.

'They don't get along?'

'No one would get along with him. He doesn't care about her. They just fight all the time.'

'He is also in Kanpur right now?'

Govind Chacha, still sitting up and leaning against the side of the sofa, was silent.

Loud snores announced that sleep had finally claimed the old man.

Prachand was torn. He could go back home with the information he had gleaned and continue his investigation the next day or he could stay. After all the effort, it made sense to look around a bit more.

He exited the kitchen and started walking around the bungalow that was surrounded by greenery and trees on all sides. The fact that maintaining this property was a gargantuan task for one old person was evident in the state of the gardens. Overgrown bushes and grass made certain sections of the property look ominous at night time. There were windows running through the entire circumference of the bungalow. He passed by the hall which was dark. Two spiral staircases protruded from either end, connecting to the upper floor. He passed by a few rooms and then to the largest room that had an attached balcony. He had seen this very balcony from his hidden perch. This had to be Shailaja's room.

Kneeling just below the last window granted him a discreet view of the balcony as well. The room seemed to be empty but loud music was audible. At the farthest end of the room, there were two big wooden trunks. One of them was open, with some clothes falling out of it. Prachand waited patiently. Maybe she is in some other part of the house, he thought. And then his eye caught a movement.

From the other end of the room, a woman emerged. Striking features bathed in a milky complexion, a svelte body clasped in a silk robe, all painted a picture of a life of affluence and privilege but that's where the fairy-tale-like references ended. Upon taking a closer look, there was a peculiar expression on her face and her eyes looked haunted. She walked around the room as if unsure about where to sit and then almost fell onto the bed with a loud maniacal laugh. Prachand watched her in astonishment as she lined up boxes of what seemed like medicines and started popping one pill from each. She would eat one, then rock back and forth for a few seconds, followed by another one, like some crazy assembly-line operation. The next time she laughed,

Kanpur Khoofiya Pvt. Ltd

she sounded positively deranged and Prachand decided that before she indulged in any further behaviour worthy of a spot in a mental asylum, he should leave.

He got down on all fours and started crawling back towards the gate when a phone started ringing. The music suddenly stopped and he could hear a pair of heels clattering away. Prachand paused as well, got back on his knees and peeped into the room.

'Hi, mamma,' said the strange-looking lady. She was now sitting at the edge of the bed and looking at her nails casually as if she had just emerged from a deep meditative yoga session instead of acting like a mad woman.

'I'm fine. Yes. Hmmm. Hmmm.'

She nodded while listening. 'So why don't you do it yourself? Am I your personal secretary?' She sounded miffed. 'Yes. The house is in good condition. Yes, he keeps it clean.'

Suddenly, Prachand's phone started ringing. With his heart pounding inside his ribcage, he desperately tried to locate his phone inside the bag. To his horror, Shailaja Kapoor had hung up and was walking towards the source of the sound, directly to him. He finally managed to find the phone, switched it off, sighed with relief and looked up to find Shailaja Kapoor's face peering at him through the window.

Her large, round eyes were now fixed on him without any other expression on her face. Prachand smiled disarmingly, not sure what else he could do in the odd situation.

'Who are you?' the lady asked Prachand. 'Are you a ghost?' she whispered.

'No, no. I am Banwari Lal,' he murmured. 'Please don't be angry, madam. I thought I saw some intruder near your room so I came to check. To see if you were safe.' He lied through his teeth, desperate to salvage the situation.

'Don't lie!' she shouted. 'What are doing in my house?'

Prachand's mind was racing but he managed to steady his nerves. 'I am a beggar, madam, passing by when I was offered a meal by your generous watchman. God bless him. I was on my way out when I heard noises and came here.'

'Oh.' It looked like Shailaja was also trying to process what she was being told.

'And where is Govind now?'

'He is sleeping,' he explained.

She rolled her eyes and then looked at him curiously. 'Did someone send you here? My husband, maybe?'

This disguise and the act must really be sub par, Prachand thought to himself.

'Please, trust me, madam. I'm just a poor man trying to help the home that gave him some food.' Prachand tried his best to sound sincere but she didn't seem entirely satisfied with the explanation. He had no idea what she was thinking.

'Banwari Lal, I'd like to sleep now,' she said abruptly and then yawned. 'And now, before I change my mind and call the police, I think you should leave.'

Taking this slim window of opportunity, he bid adieu and rushed towards the gate.

As he left the property, beads of sweat broke out all over his face. He folded his hands sending thanks to his Bholenaath and walked away at lightning speed.

CHAPTER 17

'It's twenty kilometres away, Prachi. We don't have money growing on trees,' complained Vidya.

'I have a setting with an autorickshaw driver, Viddu. He gives me a discount both ways.'

'But it's all coming out of our pocket right now. A week is over. Where is the money?' Vidya insisted.

'It will come when the report is ready. Someone should be contacting us today or tomorrow as promised.' Prachand had decided to take the day off with his wife, partially because the week had taken a toll on him, and also because he needed her help in typing out the report.

While Vidya lazed, Prachand continued assembling the pages and crosschecking some facts from his diary.

'Do you think Yatish will be able to keep an eye on the house today?'

'So far he has been able to when called in,' Prachand responded.

Vidya rolled closer to Prachand. 'I wish I was there with you last night, Prachi. It must have been amazing! So much action and I miss all of it!'

'Amazing? I almost had a heart attack!'

'I think it's thrilling and such a relief from the usual, humdrum cases. Mysterious messages, an eccentric actress of yesteryears, hide-and-seek, a midnight chase. Wow!' she chirped excitedly. 'By the way, Prachi, you must stop scaring Ma with your sudden entries. She said she almost had a heart attack when you came home last night looking like a beggar.'

'How could I know that she would be awake so late? Thanks to the earphones she had on, even after I said it's me she kept screaming thinking I'm a thief.'

'You can't blame her. First that intruder in the house, then this recent scare of the Lota-Balti Gang. The whole neighbourhood has been terrorised.'

'That's true.' Prachand shook his head in dismay. 'They've attacked again?'

'Oh, yes. Just last night, when you were on your vigil. The Nigam's home, a few streets away. This once they were so quiet and light on their feet that they made away with much more than lotas and baltis. The family had a lot of giveaway boxes stacked in the balcony for a puja today. All gone, while they slept peacefully.'

Prachand made a quick mental note to take Ammaji's charpoy indoors.

'Vidyaaa!' Their conversation was interrupted by Rachna Tripathi, hollering from downstairs.

'Ma should be an announcer for All India Radio, Prachi. Without a mike, all of India would be able to hear her.' She rolled off the bed as Prachand protested. 'Hey, let my poor mother be.' Vidya laughed and kissed him on the cheek. 'Ready for lunch?'

Prachand scrunched up his nose. 'I feel like eating something different today.' His face lit up. 'Should we eat out? Something chatpata?'

Vidya smacked her lips. 'Great idea! Where do you want to go?'

'We can go to Naveen Market. And how about Moti Jheel for some boating after that?'

'Perfect!' Vidya clapped her hands.

'And I'm done with this report as well.'

'Great. Now it's your job to convince Ma and Pitaji.'

'That I will do. But what about Yatish?' Prachand felt guilty.

'Yatish won't mind, Prachi. You've been working too hard on this case. Moreover, we will reward him handsomely once the money comes in.'

The suggested plan was met with scepticism and joy in equal measures.

Dinbandhu Tripathi: 'Why do we have to waste good money? We can eat *home* food.'

Bhushan: 'Can we watch a movie after eating? Boating is for kids.'

Chachu Tripathi: 'Which movie should we watch, Bhushan?'

Dinbandhu Tripathi: 'What a dumb idea. I don't want to waste my time watching silly people dance to senseless songs.'

For all the reservations floating around, Rachna Tripathi was sold on the plan. The prospect of a cooking-free day combined with an outing made her heart dance. Besides, she would have pictures to proudly post on her WhatsApp group. Stamping her approval on the plan, she turned to her husband. 'Oh, come on!' she insisted. 'For the kids.' Looking at Bhushan just then with his torn clothes and black eyeliner, she decided that a more compelling reason would need to be furnished. 'And tomorrow is Holi,' she added. 'I'll be able to pick up whatever I need for the puja.' This religious missile found its pious target and the plan was actioned.

It took about an hour and a half for everyone to get ready. Ammaji had decided to stay behind. Everyone guessed why, but it was one of those family secrets that no one spoke about. Once a month, Ammaji would refuse an outing. Because it was time for the solid steel trunk to surface. As legend had it, the trunk had come with Ammaji when she was married, originally titled *saans ka baksa*, which traditionally is the suitcase filled with goodies and gifts that the bride brings with her post marriage. It undergoes inspection by the mother-in-law and the other elderly women of the house. Once the original objective was met, Ammaji had continued to stash away all her goodies and valuables in it (who needed banks anyway?) and it was forever under lock and key. No one was allowed a peek. No one had ever seen it open. There were many urban legends and rumours around the contents. Gold, cash, emeralds and pearls, a year's stock of food, medicinal herbs with magical cures? But even the family members didn't know for sure. Now with the entire lot off for an outing, she would be able to open, inspect and clean her beloved trunk. There were however strict instructions to pack two kilos of jalebi for her from the market.

Meanwhile, two rickshaw pullers were summoned and the passenger load of five Tripathis was evenly distributed. 'First, Naveen Market, beta. How much will you charge?' Dinbandhu Tripathi enquired, taking the reins of negotiation. The delicate art of bargaining was something that everyone was born with in this city. It was a necessary skill. But Dinbandhu Tripathi had a strangely persuasive tactic.

'Eighty rupees,' the rickshaw puller announced.

'Thieves! Twenty and not a paisa more. Otherwise we walk.'

'Okay, sir. Please walk.'

'Thirty and not a penny more. Otherwise we walk.'

'Please do, sir. You will enjoy great health.'

'Forty-five and not a paisa more.'

'Papa, at least use a different threat,' suggested Bhushan from the adjoining rickshaw.

'Shut up!' Dinbandhu Tripathi hissed and then turned to the obstinate man.

'Seventy and not a paisa more. That's it!'

They finally relented, possibly to put an end to this tedious negotiation.

As they pulled away, the houses and shops dotting the side of the roads started flowing past with the rhythmic striking of the pedal created by the rickshaw puller's bare feet. Every part of their rickety rides rattled as they weaved through narrow crowded streets, small cars jostling for space, footpaths milling with people. In the distance, smoke billowed from factory tops, lining the suburbs of the city. As they entered Naveen Market, their nostrils were hit with the familiar smells of desi ghee and frying jalebis.

Rachna Tripathi turned in her seat and hollered to the rickshaw behind them, occupied by her sons and daughter-in-law. A surprised cyclist consequently banged into a scooter.

'Prachannnnnd,' she hollered, 'Please don't forget to stop at Chowdhary Jewellers on the way back. Your moonstone ring is ready. You must start wearing it today! Auspicious day!'

'Okay!' Prachand shouted back. 'Please don't lean out. You'll fall.'

Her head popped out moments later. 'And we need to stop at the Sahakari Bhandar. I need to buy a few things.'

'I can't hear you!' hollered Prachand as Bhushan covered his ears and another cyclist banged into a scooter.

At Tiwari Mishti Bhandar, table number twenty-two was overflowing with mouth-watering chole bhature, jalebi, tokri chaat, raj kachauri, dahi bhalle and aalu puri.

'This is my treat,' Prachand announced. Everyone smiled but Prachand looked at his father from the corner of his eye.

He knew that his father must be itching to say one of the following:

Option 1: I am not dead yet. I can take my family for a meal!

Option 2: If you had cleared the IIT exam, you would have been treating us at a five-star hotel.

But Dinbandhu Tripathi kept his silence. Unbeknownst to Prachand and the rest, he had been trying to keep a check on his sharp tongue off late. His friend Santosh Kumar Tyagi had told him that due to constant taunts and bickering, his son Bittu had left home. Inserting himself into a hypothetical situation, Dinbandhu Tripathi admitted that the departure of either of his sons would sadden him, but what made him most apprehensive was Rachna Tripathi. She would blame and mentally torture him for the rest of his life if this were

Kanpur Khoofiya Pvt. Ltd 99

to happen. So all he did was grunt in response, surprising everyone with this rare display of restraint.

As they were hailing down autorickshaws to take them to Moti Jheel for the boat riding plan, another auto came and stopped before them. A woman stepped out and Prachand's eyes opened wide. He nudged Vidya.

'That's Shailaja Kapoor,' he whispered.

'Oh yes, that is.'

To avoid any discussion, they sent off Bhushan and the senior Tripathis ahead, promising that they would follow soon.

'What is she doing here?' Prachand wondered aloud.

As if inadvertently responding to his query, they saw her entering a small deserted lane and followed her, finally ducking behind a few stacked boxes to remain hidden. A short man was waiting for her. She seemed nervous, reaching for something in her purse. Out came a fat envelope that was handed to the short man. Vidya squeaked in surprise as she saw what had been exchanged between the two. It was a small black revolver.

CHAPTER 18

Vidya, Prachand and Bhushan were on one boat. After the initial shock of being so close to a revolver, they hadn't had much time during the short auto ride to discuss what had happened. Thankfully for them, Bhushan was not keen on conversation. Large headphones were stuck on his ears and a larger pair of sunglasses, possibly four times the size of his face, severed any remaining connect with the outside world. 'Prachand, that was a gun. A real gun,' hissed Vidya, sounding nonplussed.

'I know that. Calm down. The other boat is nearby.' He said this looking sideways, while waving at the three occupants who were tightly squeezed into the limited space on the other paddle boat. His father and uncle were working the paddles on either end of the boat, while his mother was wedged in the middle, with hardly any space for her feet, so they were suspended in the air.

'What did Yatish say? He didn't inform us that she had left the house. So how did she get here?' Vidya enquired.

'I am sauuu uuu rryyyyyy ... baby ... saauuuuury!' Prachand elbowed Bhushan and gestured for him to sing softly.

'He says he has no idea when she slipped out. He never saw anyone leave. In fact the husband drove in about two hours ago and is still there.'

'I'm sure Yatish was sleeping,' complained Vidya. 'This is all too confusing. Do you think she wants to shoot her husband?'

'Or maybe she wants one for self-protection. She did sound suspicious of her husband when I spoke with her briefly.'

'Suspicious enough for her to buy a gun?'

'I know I lait you dowwwwn ... uh uh uh. Down down ...' sang Bhushan. Prachand whacked him softly behind his head.

'Sorry, P.' Another whack behind his head helped him reform his apology. 'Sorry, big brother!'

Prachand squeezed Vidya's hand, returning to their conversation. 'Don't worry. I'll be careful.'

As the evening wore on, the preparations for Holi began. Rachna Tripathi and Vidya had taken up their positions in the kitchen. Ammaji had tactically placed herself on her charpoy and was keeping an eye on the preparations as a vanguard of the Tripathi traditions. The proceedings were peppered with her keen instructions, some useful, some disparaging, and some unintelligible.

In a few hours, mountains and rivers of sweetmeats, beverages, snacks and the potent thandai (alcoholic local beverage made with milk) had been lined up. While the women, including Vidya for once, were proving their prowess in the kitchen, three Tripathi men had been dispatched to procure logs and sticks that would star in the soon to be commenced Holika Dehen. Chachu Tripathi had chosen to stay behind and help with the washing down of the courtyard and general arrangements in preparation for the scores of guests that would descend the following day.

Prachand was walking back home from an errand when he spotted a familiar jacket and hat. A man was standing across Hirwa and they were staring at each other like adversaries. Every time the man came too close to the house; she would either moo or swish her tail frantically. Prachand walked up to the stranger and tapped him on the shoulder. Startled, he turned around. It was the same man who had delivered the case to them.

'You are Srikhand?'

'Srikhand? Are we really doing this again? We've met.'

'Are you Srikhand Tripathi?' The man was undeterred.

'It's Prachand. Not Srikhand.'

'Whatever,' the man shrugged.

'You have a report for me?'

'I might.'

'I am to take a report from you and then give you this.' He pointed at the plastic bag he was carrying which had Hina Ladeej Tailor written across the front.

'Wait here,' Prachand advised him. 'Hirwa, don't let him in.' Hirwa mooed in response.

Prachand handed him the file and the man gave him the packet. Then he turned on his heel and walked away speedily. Prachand went to his room and shut the door behind him where Vidya had just returned from a bath and was drying her hair.

'Prachand, we must install a commode in the bathroom. My legs have now started hurting with all the squatting,' she complained.

'Maybe we can do that this week.'

Vidya flipped around, shocked at the ease with which her demand had been considered.

Prachand was smiling and gestured at the packet on the bed.

'What's this?' she smiled. 'You bought me a salwar kameez for Holi!'

He shook his head. 'Open it.'

She turned the packet upside down and emptied it on the bed. Crisp bundles of money started cascading down as Vidya's cheeks turned crimson with delight.

'We are rich! We are rich!' she started jumping.

'Shhhh,' Prachand laughed, looking at his wife's childish glee.

'You must put it in the bank.'

'I will, but the banks will be shut tomorrow because of Holi. I'll deposit it day after tomorrow.'

'I thought after all your hard work, we might not even get paid. But this is amazing! So Yatish is still there?'

'No, I called him back. Even private detectives deserve a Holi break!'

CHAPTER 19

The courtyard of Awadh Niwas had transformed into an MTV Grind-like scenario. It was the 'it' destination during Holi celebrations. Thankfully Rachna Tripathi had insisted that Lord Shiva be invoked first thing in the morning for purification, as she knew fully well that the rest of the day would be spent under a bhaang-induced stupor for most of the people involved.

The small winding streets across Gwaltoli were filled with merry makers throwing colours on each other. Every street was playing the latest Bollywood Holi tracks, competing with each other for the title of playing the most ear-drum-splitting music. Portable water tanks had emerged overnight and were dotting the streets. Big pots of thandai along with little *kulhad*s (small earthen cups) had been placed inside building compounds and individual homes.

Aawdh Niwas looked like it had undergone a makeover. The walls were lined with long strings of colourful flowers. Big pots of water had been placed on either side of the courtyard filled with rose petals, to facililate the *pichkari* (water gun) wars. Two platefuls of colours sat on the ground and the food was placed in a buffet style alongside the kitchen to prevent them from becoming a multicoloured offering.

Ammaji, atop her usual throne, looked like the uncontested and reigning queen. Multicoloured sari shining in the glittering sun, dark glasses, slick against the backdrop of her purple-coloured face, she was enjoying the hookah that her beloved son had personally filled for her. Her foot tapped to the songs being sung by a bunch of giggly, inebriated womenfolk.

'Ma, Ammaji has been through a lot of dessert. Isn't that harmful for her at this age??' Prachand enquired.

'That woman has the constitution of an ox, son. Don't be fooled by the lack of teeth and hearing. She is as sharp as a needle and nothing, I mean nothing, escapes her!' Rachna Tripathi whispered to her son conspiratorially.

'Oh, come on!' laughed Prachand, hugging his mother.

'Bhaiyya!' Bhushan had unceremoniously cut into the conversation. This gave Rachna Tripathi a chance to scold her errant son.

'At least today you could have tried not looking like a monkey. What is this underwear you are wearing she enquired, staring at his extremely short shorts?'

'Oh come on, mom!' Bhushan protested.

'Mom!? When a stick lands on your head, you'll forget all your English!' Rachna Tripathi announced ominously.

'Okay, enough' Prachand intervened, breaking up the altercation. 'What is it Bhushan?'

'You promised me something, remember?' He looked at his elder brother beseechingly.

'Yes, I remember. Come with me.' Bhushan had pleaded for Prachand's help with the consent form for an intercollegiate competition. Something his father had pointedly refused to sign until now. Prachand had no idea how his intervention would benefit the cause but he had promised Bhushan that he would try. Taking Bhushan's arm, he led him upstairs where his father was perched high above the madding crowds with some of the menfolk.

They were expecting the men to be having a heated political or religious discussion with the intoxicating beverages playing a key role, but what they found instead was a bunch of revelers, singing, clapping and trying to shake their hips as hard as their generous girths would allow, to the tune of a local song.

Goria jhoom jhoom gawe ho gajariya na
Ho gajariya le gajariya na
Kaili solaho singaar tikuli chamke laal lal
Goriya lachak jaat tohri kamariya na

Leading the pack was Dinbandhu Tripathi who had let down his hair and all characteristic restraint. Both sons looked on in mute admiration as his whole body shook. They hadn't in their wildest dreams imagined that their father was capable of such movement. During one particular swivel, his eyes fell on Prachand and Bhushan who were standing rooted to the ground. Far from looking embarrassed at being caught with his festive pants on, he pulled his sons into the circle.

'I've seen him do odd things when high, but this is a first!' whispered Bhushan, desperately trying to match his father's steps. Prachand just shook, which was his usual response when requested to dance. When their father finally came close to them, Prachand pulled him aside gently.

'Pitaji, Bhushan wants to request something. There is an intercollegiate festival on Friday. Can he please participate with his band?'

Dinbandhu Tripathi went through a range of emotions. As his sons watched, he first looked upset, then irritated and a second later, he burst out laughing, guffawing and slapping them on their backs as they reeled in pain.

'What did Amrish Puri say in that new movie I saw?' he tapped his head, trying to remember. '*Ja jee le apni zindagi, Simran.*' (Go live your life, Simran.) And he burst out laughing again, tickled with his own sense of humour.

'Pitaji, that movie released even before I was born,' murmured Bhushan, being factual. Prachand squeezed his arm to silence him.

'Thank you, Pitaji,' Bhushan shouted and turned to run.

'Wait!!'

Bhushan turned around slowly.

It was Murari Bhatnagar who lived nearby.

'Why don't you sing a song for us?'

Bhushan looked like a helpless deer caught in headlights as Prachand laughed and made his way downstairs.

As the day wore on, Prachand started feeling unsettled. The hair on the back of his neck stood on instinct. A premonition of something bad about to happen. He played Holi, ate, drank, laughed along, but his mind kept straying to that ambiguous feeling.

Vidya pulled him into the kitchen and planted a big kiss on his cheek. He looked around furtively and then hugged her tight. She pulled back to stare into his eyes.

'What's the matter, Prachi? I know something is on your mind.'

He smiled. 'How do you know me so well?'

'It's my job. Now tell me.'

'Will you be upset if I pay Lily Bungalow a quick visit?'

She pulled back. 'Prachi, why are you doing this? You've done half the job, we got paid for it. A few more days and we are done. It's not your job to become the police and get involved.'

'I can't explain it, Vidya. I just have an intuition. No one has been there all day. Let me go for a short while. Then I'll keep a watch at a strict distance for the last few days. I promise.' He turned around as someone laughed raucously. 'Now the only problem is how on earth do I get out of here unnoticed? If anyone, especially Ma, finds out that I'm planning to go somewhere, even for a few minutes, she will scream her head off.'

Vidya still looked like she wasn't entirely in agreement with his plan but decided to help. 'I'll create a distraction. Just wait for my cue' she said.

'You're the best, Viddu!' He hugged her as she laughed.

'Now let me get to it.' She wriggled out of his grasp and ran to the kitchen.

After a few minutes, she returned, covering one hand with her dupatta and pulled Prachand to a corner. Under the dupatta, she revealed a slightly swollen finger with a ring stuck on it.

'What is this!?' Prachand asked, bewildered.

'A distraction,' she smiled.

'But doesn't it hurt? How did you do it?'

She shook her head. 'No. And it's very simple. I pushed a smaller ring onto a fatter finger, placed it on ice repeatedly while flexing it and magic! It swells up like a pakoda!' She smiled proudly.

'Viddu, what if it doesn't come off?' Prachand asked, questioning this seemingly inane plan.

'Bah!' she waved her hand dismissively. 'All it needs is hot water to reduce the inflammation and heat to expand the metal. Then a dash of oil to help it slip out. It's a childhood trick.' She winked.

'Someone was a bright Science student I can see,' Prachand smiled.

She smiled back proudly, changed her expression to that of pain and walked out the door, putting her acting skills to test.

'Ouccccchhhhhhh! My ring is stuck. Help! Prachand, go find a doctor, I don't care how long it takes.'

A grateful Prachand followed her to the courtyard, nodded vigorously and darted out of the house. The music was stopped as the guests started gathered around the stupid woman who had a ring stuck on her fat finger and had brought the festivities to a halt.

CHAPTER 20

Rachna Tripathi was holding her head. 'A ring getting stuck is a bad omen I tell you.'

'I've never heard that before,' her husband countered. 'And you've emptied a whole bottle of oil already. How will the ring slip out if the swelling doesn't go? Let me get you some gau mutra. It'll work wonders.' He ran in to get his go-to solution for all problems while Vidya gulped.

'Just give it some time,' Chachu Tripathi suggested.

'Absolutely!' Vidya chimed in, finding some support. But the enthusiastic guests were not to be deterred from this now public mission.

Rajni Pandey from the house down the road had a suggestion. 'Move away! All of you. I know exactly what to do. Keep wrapping thread around the finger to thin it down and then just slip the ring off. Rachna, give me thread.'

'You women are clueless,' scoffed another lady, dialling up the existing political tensions between the different groups of women from the neighbourhood. 'A heated knife is the best way. A flick of the wrist and you're done.'

'No knife, heated or otherwise is coming near me! I'm waiting for a doctor. Prachand will be here soon,' Vidya lied, now leaning towards forgetting all about the plan and just rescuing her poor finger which really looked like it needed help. The pretence was turning into reality.

Ammaji banged her stick on the floor, bringing the arguments to an end. She beckoned Rachna Tripathi as her mouth was full of paan. Her daughter-in-law leaned over for a few seconds, nodded and straightened up to make an announcement.

'Ammaji knows what to do. The answer lies in her trunk and she will go get it now.' Horrified at what could emerge from the trunk from twilight zone, Vidya pretended to talk to Prachand on her phone, snatched her dupatta and swollen finger and ran out the door towards a friend's place, saying that she was going to meet the doctor Prachand had found.

Meanwhile, a multicoloured Prachand found himself standing in his usual hiding place near Lily Bungalow. The husband's car that he had seen earlier was in the driveway. There was no other sign of activity outside. It didn't even look like anyone had played Holi in or around the house. Remembering his promise to Vidya, he kept his distance but after some time, he couldn't help but walk a little bit closer. Even if Govind or anyone else were to see him, he would look like a wandering Holi reveller.

He slowly started towards the house, when a loud horn sounded right behind him and he was forced to jump out of the way. A Maruti van sped past him. The van turned towards Lily Bungalow and forced open the half ajar gate as the tyres screeched to a halt. To his shock, two masked men jumped out holding guns. They banged on the door and once it was answered, barged into the bungalow.

Prachand's limbs froze, battling his fight-or-flight instinct. Realising that he had to do something, he ran towards the gate. But before he could reach, the same men rushed out, one holding a blindfolded Shailaja Kapoor while the other rushed to open the door. They shoved her into the backseat, and drove away while she continued screaming.

As the car sped past him again, he hid himself behind a nearby tree and sat down to make a phone call.

'Vidya ...' he said in a calm voice, far from what he felt inside.

'What happened, Prachi?' Vidya asked.

'Shailaja Kapoor has been kidnapped.'

CHAPTER 21

An urgent round table meeting was called the following morning at Kanpur Khoofiya Pvt. Ltd. Since some guests were still scattered around Awadh Niwas, Prachand did not want to cause any unnecessary upheaval, given his wife's penchant for sharing news.

He paced the length of the room. Vidya was staring at a spider suspended from the ceiling fan, her tapping feet betraying the anxiety she felt.

'Where is Yatish?'

'I told him to come quickly.' Vidya said looking at her watch. 'Why do you need to meet him so urgently?'

'We need Yatish's informant network to help us.'

'Prachi, we are not the police. What will it achieve trying to get any information? Let the police do their job.'

'So what do you suggest? We go to the police?'

'I'm not sure myself. But what I do know is that we are way in over our heads.' She picked up the landline. 'Let me call Yatish again.'

There was no dial tone. 'The phone bill wasn't paid, Prachi?' Her husband looked at her apologetically.

'This stupid case has taken over our lives,' grumbled Vidya.

At this point, they both noticed that something had darted across their door.

'Did you see that?' Prachand looked at Vidya for confirmation.

'I think so.' Vidya looked equally confused as they walked to the door to investigate further.

They just about made it in time to see the disappearing figure of a man followed by what looked like Yatish's figure chasing him down the road.

'You there, stop!' he hollered and they both disappeared around the corner.

Prachand and Vidya exchanged a puzzled look wondering what in the world was happening.

After about five minutes, a profusely sweating Yatish entered the office panting.

'What is going on, Yatish? Who was that?' asked Prachand, walking towards him.

Yatish sat down and Vidya gave him a glass of water.

'I saw a man peeping into the office window just as I arrived. With that intruder in your home and with all that's happened yesterday, I had to check. But I shouted out too early and he ran away.'

'You startled him. Otherwise he might have come in, Yatish!'

'If he wanted to come in, he wouldn't be lurking,' shot back Yatish.

'Now we won't know, will we?' frowned Prachand.

'There's one more thing. Just before jumping into a rickshaw, he screamed, 'Warn them to stay away from the police.'

Prachand became silent. He spoke after a few minutes.

'I know we can walk away from this situation. But I will not be able to live with myself knowing a crime was committed and we kept quiet. That we didn't even report it. What if the same happened to us?'

Everyone fell silent.

'So we are going to the police?' asked Vidya.

'Yes,' said Prachand firmly. 'I thought the husband wasn't guilty, but a whole night has passed and he still hasn't gone to the police. Yatish, did you check again with your contact at the Ratan Lal Nagar Chowki?'

'Yes,' confirmed Yatish. 'I know a constable. He checked and told me, nothing reported yet.'

'That is fishy. Maybe she did buy the gun to protect herself,' surmised Prachand. Then he got up. 'There is no choice. We can't wait for him. The police must know.'

Senior Inspector Navin Srivastava of the Ratan Lal Nagar Police Station was a simple man with simple needs. If a Bollywood stereotype had to be created of a dishonest, loud, garrulous, rotund cop from Uttar Pradesh, the creators would have to look no further than this khaki-clad idol. But he hadn't always been this way. His career started as a starry-eyed recruit. As he climbed the ranks, slower than at snail's pace, his integrity and righteousness had shrunk like his meagre earnings and by the time he had reached the position of subinspector, his honesty had been wiped clean off his slate. By then he had created a self-serving ecosystem that comprised of corrupt seniors whom he served, and scared or ambitious juniors who served him. Round with prosperity, pliable bosses and a happy wife and two kids, life was good and nothing else mattered in the world. But today as he sat before Private Detective Prachand Tripathi and his wife Vidya Tripathi, he was a confused man.

'Dubey, get me some tea!' he shouted, trying to adjust his voluminous girth in the meagre chair.

A small cup of steaming and sickeningly sweet tea was placed in front of him. He took his first sip noisily, dipped a Parle-G biscuit which partially melted into the cup, and the rest disappeared in his mouth. Prachand watched him go through these motions, waiting for his turn to speak.

'So you want to report a kidnapping?'

Prachand nodded. 'Yes, sir.'

Navin Srivastava signalled to someone to come and start writing. A bored-looking bald man in a faded uniform took his position next to them with a pen and a register.

'Which family member of yours was kidnapped?'

'Not a family member, sir.'

'Huh? Okay. So a friend then?' he prodded.

'Umm. No sir. I don't know her. Well, I've met her but I don't know her well.'

Navin Srivastava's gaze shifted from him, to the bald officer and came back to rest on Prachand. 'Does she have any family that you know of?'

'Yes, sir. Her husband and an old mother in Mumbai. She was also from Mumbai. The lady who was kidnapped. Shailaja Kapoor.'

'Was from Mumbai?'

'Is.'

Navin Srivastava's eyes brightened up with some recollection. 'Shailaja Kapoor from the movie *Angrezi Mem*?'

'Yes, Sir.'

'Hmm.' He sat up, looking a bit more interested now.

'How are you involved in all of this?'

'Let me tell you from the beginning, sir.' Prachand then went on to tell Navin everything. As per Vidya and Yatish's advice though, he left out the part when he had entered Lily Bungalow. It was information that could unnecessarily get him into trouble.

After Prachand was done with his narration, Navin Srivastava sat back in his chair, processing what he had been told. He kept scratching his stomach instead of his head, almost as if his grey matter was stored in there.

'Your case is very confusing, Mr Tripathi. Also because it is not your case, you know?'

'I understand how this looks, sir, but trust me, our only reason to come to you was so that an innocent woman can be saved.'

'Hmmm, what a noble soul you are.' He muttered under his breath. 'So you have no idea about who wanted you to do this job, who has been delivering these messages to you, why this woman was kidnapped and who is behind it,' he summarised. 'What work have you done, Mr Byomkesh Bakshi?' he guffawed.

'I can surely tell you that the person behind all of this is not a seasoned criminal. The choice of messengers, the entire plan, even the kidnappers were amateurs. They looked unsure of themselves. That shows their nervousness and lack of experience. In fact, one of them...'

Navin Srivastava started clapping. 'Aye, Ranganathan,' he hollered to a subinspector standing nearby. 'Meet my guru, Pichand Tripathi.'

Prachand felt his irritation rise. 'Prachand. Sir if you don't mind my asking, what will you do now?'

Navin Srivastava's lip curled. 'You don't have to play detective with the police, Mr Tripathi. Not that it's any of your business, but we will talk to the husband and check up on all the information you have given us. You know something else, Mr Detective?' He leaned back languorously in his chair. 'I have often seen that people who commit crimes try to insert themselves into an investigation. Gives them a high. Interesting, eh?'

Vidya pinched her husband's leg and they both got up hurriedly.

'You will also have to hand over the money you received. We can check on the trail that...'

'But sir, that is our hard-earned money and ...' Vidya objected.

'Madam ji,' Navin Srivastava announced with his hands on the table. 'This is kidnapping of a famous person. We have to investigate everything or we will get into trouble. You understand?' Then he looked at Prachand. 'Now if you don't mind my asking, how much do you make in a month with this detective business, Mr Tripathi? Must be hard to make ends meet, huh? You ever feel like doing something desperate to make money?' He asked suspiciously.

Before Prachand could respond, the inspector's phone rang, his ringtone 'Baby doll mein sone di' (famous Bollywood dance song) went off, declaring his delicate taste in music.

'Yes, darling.' He answered, not bothered that everyone around was listening. 'Now stop eating my head about a television repair ...' He waved Prachand and Vidya away.

When they were finally able to leave the police station, Vidya looked at Prachand. 'Is it just me or did you also feel like we were the ones under investigation?'

'You are right, Vidya. You see why I didn't want you to accompany me? But you just won't listen. I'm very sure we are under suspicion now,' sighed Prachand, thinking about the new label that had been pasted on him. That of a suspect.

CHAPTER 22

The atmosphere was charged. Dinbandhu Tripathi sat scowling on his mother's throne that she had tactfully vacated sensing his mood. She wasn't able to gather the exact details, but she did know that her beloved older grandson was in trouble. Moreover, this was potentially looking like a long discussion. Sensing a narrow window of opportunity, she shot out a demand at her usual victim.

'Rachnaaaaaa, get me a bite to eat will you? My stomach's rumbling.'

Rachna wanted to turn around and tell mother-in-law right then that the root cause for her rumbling stomach was that she never kept her mouth shut long enough to let her food get digested. Now in the midst of this tense situation Rachna would have to run to the kitchen.

'You have heaped shame upon our family!' shouted Dinbandhu Tripathi, kicking off the proceedings for the afternoon. Hearing this, Prachand knew that the miniscule stock of goodwill generated during the wedding had been completely exhausted.

Kanpur Khoofiya Pvt. Ltd

'Please don't raise your blood pressure. Just listen to him,' said Chachu Tripathi, rubbing his arm.

'Why don't you ask your dear boy not to do things that will raise my pressure!'

Prachand was waiting for his father's angry tirade to pass.

'Pitaji, there is nothing I could have done to prevent what happened,' he shrugged.

'Who asked you to take such a case? These big people and their big problems belong in the big cities. We should stay far away from them. I've led a simple respectable life and I like it that way. Now my son wants me to get involved with the police at this age. This is the final embarrassment I've remained alive for.'

'How is talking to the police an embarrassment? They are officers of the law.' Prachand tried to reason.

'Yes, my lord! But self-respecting families stay far, far away from them. We don't want to be involved in anyone else's mess. The last time a Tripathi went to a police station was in 1956 when my father's cycle chain was stolen from outside our house, and now my family is involved in a kidnapping!'

'But, Pitaji, we did not kidnap anyone. Someone else did. We are only trying to help,' said Prachand.

'And what was the need to drag your wife into this mess? Our women don't go to police stations.'

Vidya, who had kept her silence, decided it was time to come to her husband's rescue. She kept her eyes lowered but said in a calm voice. 'Pitaji, that was my decision and I insisted. He requested me not to come with him.'

Her father-in-law shook his head and looked away. '*Nari bibas nar sakat gosai, nachai nat markat ke nai* (Beyond a point, men just dance to the tune of women). Everyone has a mind and will of their own these days. Our values and wishes don't mean anything. Not for career, not for advice, not for anything.'

He got up and walked away in a huff.

Rachna Tripathi settled the goodies in front of Ammaji and turned to sit with Prachand.

'Rachna, some juice. My throat is feeling parched,' Ammaji chimed in.

Before her mother-in-law could implode and throttle an eighty-five year-old woman, Vidya prudently intervened and took the new beverage order.

Rachna Tripathi stroked her son's head. 'Son, you know how he is. Give him some time. That over chatty Guptaji told him about seeing you at the police station. He was caught off guard and hates anyone gossiping about the family.'

'But he never listens to the whole story. Ever since the IIT fiasco, I can do no right in his books.'

'Please don't say that. He will come around. I'm just worried about these complicated Bollywood people. I hope you don't get into any more trouble trying to help.'

'I hope so too,' sighed Prachand.

CHAPTER 23

A weathered, wooden board advertised the sweet shop 'Thaggu ke Laddoo' in bright red letters. There were people milling around looking like they were in various states of nirvana. The reason? The special laddoos, kulfis, *peda*s and kachoris on offer. People from all over Kanpur, tourists and even celebrities thronged this humble outlet tucked in a corner of Govind Nagar. It was one of the treat pilgrimages the Tripathis and most of the locals trekked to, especially during the week-long celebration of Holi that started with Holika Dehen and culminated a week later on the ghats of the Ganga in the form of the Ganga Mela. This was a tradition in the city since pre-Independence days and this week-long period of festivities was a great excuse to work less, highly appreciated by the masses, barring two people who were lined up outside Thaggu Ke Laddoo.

'Viddu, ever since the police started their investigations, not even a single client has walked into the office. No phone enquiries. Not even wrong numbers. Nothing.'

'Prachi, honestly, it wasn't as if people were falling over each other to avail of our services to begin with.'

'But I meant, not even our usual visitors.'

'Well, it's also Rangpanchami. A lot of the shops and offices are shut, people are on holiday.'

'But this is usually the period when we receive maximum requests from suspicious clients to follow their spouses. Don't you remember from last year?'

'Aaah yes,' said Vidya, trying to remember the odd requests that had come pouring in. 'I think there were six or seven calls that week.'

Prachand fell silent so Vidya turned to look at him. She took his hand. 'I wish I could do something to make it all go away, Prachi. You are smart, honest, one of the nicest people I know. You volunteered information and the cops are still interrogating you as if you're Gabbar Singh. You're the last person who deserves to be treated this way. But I just wish you weren't so nervous around them. It makes them think we did something wrong.'

Prachand smiled at his personal cheerleader. 'Viddu, I don't need to prove anything to anyone. We did nothing wrong, except maybe give them all the facts. Everything will work out.'

They had almost reached the end of the line and a unanimously selected order was placed. 'Seven badaam kulfis, please!'

As they walked back to their table, Prachand stole a glance at his father's scowling face. It had taken a lot of convincing to persuade him to step out. The entire family was feeling the stress of the week full of interrogations and surveillance.

The police had arrived early in the morning, the day after their visit to the police station. Hirwa's loud mooing led

Bhushan to the door. Navin Srivastava barged in with two constables.

'This cow of yours is more dog than cow.' He laughed and then paused to give Bhushan a once over, from his sparse prickly hair (or lack of it) to the eyeliner to the black baggy clothes.

'Where's Pichand?'

'It's Prachand, uncle,' Bhushan corrected him.

'It's sir to you, not uncle,' Navin Srivastava had said coldly.

'Yes, sir,' muttered a duly chastised Bhushan.

'Is Udd ... what is his name again?'

'Prachand, sir,' filled in Bhushan.

'Is your brother home?'

'Yes, sir. I'll go get him.'

As Bhushan ran in to get Prachand, the inspector came face to face with Ammaji who had just returned from her morning ablutions and was eating her breakfast. She looked at them blankly.

'Namaste,' Navin Srivastava greeted her.

She looked at them with narrowed eyes. 'If you want to shit, then go to your own house.'

Navin Srivastava wasn't entirely sure how he could respond to this strange advice but his officer found enough to snigger about. Before he could chastise his subordinate, the courtyard was filled with a song. From the quality of the voice it was clear that whoever was singing was forever destined to sing in bathrooms.

Mere issq mein laakhon latakeeeee
Balam zaraa hatke, balam zaraa hat ke, un unhu ununhu
Haay haay haay haay

Maarungi aankh toh neel pad jaayega
Main maarungi aankh toh neel pad jaayega. Un unhu unuhu...

A semi-naked man with only a towel wrapped around his scrawny waist, came stumbling out of the bathroom. From thumkas to pirouettes, he performed several dance moves and screeched to a halt right in front of two policemen, dripping wet in his meagre towel. Chachu Tripathi was mortified and dashed to his room mumbling an apology.

'This house is full of namoonas!' Navin Srivastava muttered to Subinspector Ranganathan.

When Prachand finally sat down to have a chat, he knew that his father was watching from above.

'We are here to collect a copy of your report on the investigation. And the money.'

'Do we have to do this here?' Prachand asked nervously as he could feel the back of his neck burn under his father's gaze.

'Are you nervous about something, mister?' enquired Navin Srivastava. 'Seems like when you're nervous you forget to tell people things.'

'I don't know what you mean,' Prachand responded.

'You came and gave us a long story about what happened, and who hired you etc., etc. But you forgot to mention the small detail that you went into Shailaja Kapoor's house. Govind recognised your face.'

Prachand's face felt hot, the white heat of a lie consuming his composure. He berated himself for agreeing to hide this fact in the first place.

'Sorry sir, it skipped my mind completely.'

'That you went in dressed as a beggar? I wonder what else has skipped your mind while giving your statement. Maybe you staged the kidnapping; maybe you're not being honest with me.'

'I was just doing my job sir. I had to keep an eye on her.'

'And on the husband as well?' he asked with a steady gaze.

'Sir, I've never even met the husband.'

'He recognised you from a picture. Says he saw you following him around in the market.'

'Sir, he is lying. I promise you. You know, we noticed that they fought often. Maybe he was involved! Have you asked him why he didn't report her abduction immediately? I can really help if you let me work with you.'

'Why don't you leave the investigations and theories to us, Mr Byomkesh Bakshi! And by the way, he did come to the police station. Just after you. He was apparently knocked around by the abductors and was lying unconscious when the caretaker came home the next morning after a day off. The caretaker verified this. Sujit Oberoi must not have known that some other man was more worried about his wife and would beat him at getting to the police station!'

After some more conversations with the neighbours they had left, but with a promise to be back.

And they did come back, thrice. Neighbours were rounded up again, office records and embarrassing finances were checked. Awadh Niwas became an entertainment and gossip centre for the entire locality, much to the despair and anger of the head of the household.

Thaggu Ke Laddoo was Prachand's obvious way to create a distraction for the harrowed family, which was of course followed by some shopping.

While Rachna Tripathi bargained for a silk sari like her life depended on it, Prachand's mind wandered back to their predicament. Vidya came and sat next to him.

'Hey, husband.' She smiled, nudging his arm. 'You are the best husband ever. Do you know that? Prachand smiled shyly but looked preoccupied. Vidya noticed this and added jovially. 'Hey, Prachi, did you know what the famous tagline of this shop is? *Aisa koi saga nahi jisko hamne thaga nahi!*' She laughed.

Instead of laughing in response, Prachand's eyes widened. 'Husband ... saga ... thagaa ...' He muttered unintelligently.

'Prachand, what are you mumbling? Are you okay?' Vidya shook his arm.

'Viddu, you're brilliant!'

'I am?' she asked, looking confused.

'You have helped me figure out what to do next.'

'I have?'

'Yes! Instead of waiting around, why don't I go confront Shailaja Kapoor's lying husband!'

CHAPTER 24

It was futile convincing his wife to stay back, so Prachand finally gave in. The ruse was that they were going for a late-night movie to divert their minds. Poor Chachu Tripathi was shrugged off the plan with a lot of effort.

'First he invites the problem home and then he wants to run away from it,' Dinbandhu Tripathi muttered to his wife before retiring for the night.

Barring Bhushan's practice session that sounded like a cat was being strangled to death, the house was now silent and Prachand was ready, waiting for Vidya to change and join him. She was briefed to wear something comfortable, which for her usually meant a loose salwar kameez.

'Vidya, hurry up, it's almost 9.30, it will take us half an h....'

What went in was his wife, but what emerged was a black ninja warrior. He looked her over in silence. Vidya was wearing a black t-shirt, possibly his, secured at the waist with a black dupatta. She wore a black pathani salwar from one of her suit sets and a small brown rod stuck out of her waistband. Her face was smeared with black camouflage marks and her hair was slicked and tied tightly in a knot. To complete the look, a shiny beige bag hung casually from her shoulder, in complete contrast to the rest of the look.

'Is my wife in there?' was all Prachand could manage.

'Am I not perfectly ready for our night vigil?' she asked proudly.

'Viddu, we are not signing up to be trained as terrorists for Al Qaeda, nor are we dacoits. Please change. Wash your face, wear a comfortable suit and come quickly. Please!'

'What's the harm in looking tough? Men just don't know how to dress up for an occasion,' muttered Vidya as she went back in to change.

An hour later, they stood a few trees away from the gate of Lily Bungalow. Some of the street lights weren't working and with just one dim porch light on, the bungalow looked haunted.

'Are you sure he is in there?' whispered Vidya.

'Yatish confirmed that he is very much in there.'

'So what do you want to ask him? And why will he tell us anything?'

'I'm not entirely sure. But I will confront him about why he lied about me. If he is lying, he is hiding something. If he is hiding something, he won't report us immediately when he knows we are on to him. So it's worth a shot.'

'Not a very sound plan there. It's, at best, guesswork. We might get into further trouble with the police, you know,' cautioned Vidya.

'I know, Viddu. But we can't just sit around doing nothing. The police have an agenda, our lives have turned turtle and there's no going back till this case is solved.'

Kanpur Khoofiya Pvt. Ltd

An opportunity for an entry presented itself when Govind emerged from one side of the bungalow. He opened the gate and walked out.

'Gossip and drink session, I bet,' whispered Prachand. 'Good for us.'

Govind paused just when he was passing by their hiding spot. Vidya, who was busy slathering Odomos and brushing neem leaves on her arms for added protection, froze. As did Prachand.

Thankfully, a passing car distracted him; he shook his head and continued walking. 'These mosquitoes bite more than the ones in Gwaltoli!' hissed Vidya as she slapped Prachand's arm and her knee in a combination attack move.

'Let's go. This is our window,' said Prachand pulling her arm.

'Do you want a snack? she asked, having returned the Odomos to the bag.

'I told you to pack very light,' Prachand sighed.

'A few bites won't kill anyone. Besides, it's Holi!' she smiled, trying to lighten the mood. 'So do we just ring the bell?'

'No. Let's just see what he is doing first.'

Crouching as low as possible, the duo made it around the house, peeping into windows in an attempt to locate Sujit Oberoi. After checking through a few rooms, he was finally found in the living room, stretched out on the sofa, watching television, with a drink in his hand.

'He doesn't look too anxious if you ask me,' whispered Vidya. 'We can't poke our heads in and just start chatting. What do you want to do?'

'I know,' Prachand said, keenly watching Sujit Oberoi. 'Let's just ensure no one else is with him and then we go in.'

'What if he calls the police without listening to us?'

'We'll just have to pray very hard that he doesn't.'

They went ahead to look around the house when a loud noise from the living room made them jump with fright. Returning to where they had last seen Sujit Oberoi, it now seemed like someone was with him.

'Hide!' whispered Prachand and they both ducked.

The dim light didn't offer much of a view but the body language suggested the two men were arguing. After some heated words, the stranger pushed Sujit Oberoi, who went flailing backwards. In Prachand's memory, everything happened in slow motion after this point. Moving haltingly in a thousand frames, Sujit Oberoi slipped on the rug. His arms sliced through the air like rotor blades as he landed on the ground with a big thud, smashing his head on the glass centre table.

CHAPTER 25

For a few seconds nobody moved, even the man standing in front of Sujit Oberoi. It was a surreal moment. The body lay motionless. A pool of blood spread behind his head like a crimson halo. Vidya took an icy grip on her husband's elbow.

'P—Prachi, is he ... is he dead?' Vidya whispered, hardly being able to say the words. 'I've nnn ... never seen anyone die. Well I saw my grandmother die; I mean she died in her sleep so that doesn't count for much. But I did see my small hamster die. The neighbour's cat swallowed him you know ... right.'

Prachand squeezed her arm to silence her. 'Shh ... it's okay.' He said the words but felt as if nothing would be okay for a very long time. Vidya was trembling and he was finding it hard to control his nerves as well. As they stood frozen like ice sculptures, the man in the hall recovered, and made his way straight to the window they were crouching under. The window opened, he jumped out and found himself facing a man and a woman.

For a few seconds no one moved and Prachand was hit with a peculiar blast of some sickeningly sweet fragrance. It was impossible to see the man's face in the dark.

'What are you doing here?' asked the man menacingly, with no trace of worry or remorse.

'What are you doing?' countered Prachand, finding his courage and tongue after some initial stuttering.

'Get lost!' the man threatened, brandishing a knife at them.

'You get lost!' barked Prachand, pulling Vidya behind him.

In the middle of this very bold confrontation, the man started to move closer, when a loud noise from the street interrupted the odd exchange. He looked unsure, with his knife raised for a few seconds, but decided to bolt towards the exit just to avoid being seen by one more person. He disappeared so quickly that Prachand couldn't even contemplate giving chase.

'Let's go, Prachand!' pleaded Vidya.

'Just one second,' Prachand said. Then he took a deep breath as if to clear his head. 'We must remain calm.' Then he turned to Vidya. 'Viddu, I need to take a look at him.'

'Call an ambulance, call a bullock cart! I don't care. You're not going in!' shouted Vidya.

'Shh! Please don't scream. I'll be back in a minute. What if he is alive and needs our help?'

As Prachand climbed into the house through the open window, he found that he was shivering, not because of the AC but due to the sense of foreboding in the pit of his stomach. Sujit Oberoi was sprawled on the ground, staring up at the ceiling. Once he reached the body, at least one thing became abundantly clear: Sujit Oberoi was very dead.

CHAPTER 26

'So is he really dead?' Vidya enquired timidly from the window.

'Very much.' Prachand confirmed as he walked closer to the body. His stomach felt squeamish but out of some morbid fascination, he continued staring at it. And it seemed as if it was staring back accusingly.

'Prachand, why are you still standing there?' Vidya hissed.

'I'm thinking.'

'Well, you can think when we get back home. Come!'

Prachand went to the window where his wife stood. 'Viddu, now hear me out.'

'Oh no, you don't, Prachand Tripathi!' Vidya knew what was coming.

Prachand pulled her closer to face him. 'Just listen. We came here to talk to him. Clearly, we can't do that now. But looking around for a few minutes might help. What if we find...'

'You'll find nothing this once but trouble, Prachand. Call it a woman's intuition,' Vidya warned him.

'I get your concern. But this is our only chance. Please!'

'You go look around. I'll stand guard here and recite the Hanuman Chalisa.' She folded her hands and started praying to the Almighty feverishly.

Prachand knew what he had to do first. He pulled out his handkerchief and bent down closer to Sujit Oberoi's face.

'What are you doing?' Vidya shouted.

Prachand gingerly shut the eyelids. There was no possibility of rigor mortis having set in so soon, so his task was easy, yet creepy. 'It doesn't feel right, you know. Seems disrespectful snooping around the house while he is watching us. Besides, it is a tad bit spooky as well. I feel as if his gaze is following me around the room.'

'Stop freaking me out, Prachand,' Vidya said, shivering. Suddenly something scraped against her leg and she jumped into the air.

'Gh—ghost!'

The ghost revealed its identity by meowing loudly.

While Vidya was dealing with supernatural forces in her head, Prachand had started looking around. He knew he had very little time so his movements were hasty. First, he went over to the table by which Sujit Oberoi had been sitting and watching TV. There was a bowl of peanuts, some cucumber, a bottle of whiskey and a glass full of it.

'The poor man must not have realized that this drink would be his last,' Prachand said to himself. Then he moved towards the two nearest rooms, hoping one of them would be his.

'Where are you going, Prachi? Someone will be along very soon. I can feel it. Come on!' Vidya said impatiently.

'Just a quick look in his room. It won't take long.'

Kanpur Khoofiya Pvt. Ltd

As luck would have it, he did walk into the room Sujit Oberoi was occupying. A quick peak into the other room told him that Shailaja Kapoor's room must be at the other end of the corridor – a clear sign of less than cordial relations between the husband and wife.

Prachand felt a hand on his shoulder and it was his turn to jump in the air.

'Wha—'

'Hey,' Vidya whispered.

'You scared the hell out of me.'

'Sorry, Prachi. I couldn't stand alone outside. I kept thinking his ghost will pay me a visit.'

'Hmmm ...' Prachand acknowledged and walked to a suitcase that was kept in one corner of the room. Feeling a twinge of guilt, his hand hovered around the handle, feeling reluctant to open it. Vidya leaned forward and with one big movement, pulled back the top cover and opened up the red suitcase.

'There you go. By the time you get over your guilt and open it, the police will be sitting around eating celebratory snacks after arresting us.'

'My hero.' Prachand smiled gratefully.

He carefully went through the contents of the suitcase.

'This man doesn't like banks I suppose.'

Prachand turned around inquisitively. 'Why do you say that?' Vidya, while going through the cupboard, had found a large stash of money in one of the drawers.

Prachand whistled. 'From the looks of it, there must be a few lakhs in there.'

'Do you think that man came to rob him?'

'I don't think so. If he had come for money, he would have created some distraction to get to it despite us being there. No thief would leave so easily without the stash.'

'I guess.' Vidya nodded in agreement.

'Viddu, I think Sujit Oberoi was on the run.'

'Really?' Vidya enquired, 'How can you tell? Oh ... wait, I'm sure you already have a host of reasons for this deduction. Lay it on me.'

'Well,' Prachand started holding up items as he spoke. 'Look at the clothes. All casual: t-shirts, shorts, pyjamas, even the shoes over there,' he said, pointing at a space under the cupboard. 'Remember the pictures you showed me online? Even the ones from his vacation and he is dressed impeccably at all times. Almost always in formals. These just look like under the radar, casual clothing thrown together in a hurry.' Then he picked up a stack of files. 'Who carries their passport, cheque books and property papers for a holiday?'

'You do have a point.' Vidya nodded.

'Some more proof? Look, two family pictures, not even an album, framed, like he picked them up from a table on his way out. And pepper spray? Clearly not for adding flavour to food but for protection. Don't forget the stash of money either, so he wouldn't have to get to a bank and withdraw. I am very certain this man was not just on the run, he was hiding from someone. Someone who was scary enough to intimidate someone wealthy and well connected like him.'

There was a faint noise audible in the distance. 'Was that the gate?' Vidya asked, eyes wide open with terror.

'I can't be sure but let's get out of here.'

They retraced their steps to the living room and passed by Sujit Oberoi's body.

'Just give me a second,' requested Prachand and delinking his hand from Vidya's, ran back towards the body.

'Prachand! What is wrong with you!!' Vidya was seething now.

'It's for closure and respect.' He stood next to the body with his hands folded. 'Goodbye, Mr Sujit. It wasn't nice of you to falsely claim having seen me but I forgive you. You didn't deserve to die. I'll find your murderer and he will go to jail. I promise you. Rest in peace.'

Suddenly, he realized that someone else was in the room. Looking up, he was horrified to see an even more horrified Govind standing frozen by the door.

'Khoon! Khoon! Khoon!' He said it repeatedly as if in a trance. Vidya instinctively shouted from the window 'No, no, we didn't murder anyone!'

At first Prachand thought he would go to Govind and try to calm him down, explain what happened, but his instinct said that this would be futile. While Govind continued to scream for the police instead of actually calling them, Prachand caught hold of his wife's hand and shouted, 'Run!'

CHAPTER 27

Vidya rubbed her eyes, scowling against the bright light. This could very well be a dream. For how could they have slept under a banyan tree by a small dusty road? Some houses were visible in the distance, but for now, in the foreground, she realized that they had an audience consisting of animals and human beings. A dog, two pigs, two children and an adult to be precise, staring at them curiously. She shook Prachand awake as the dog came closer and sniffed him.

Used to this kind of scandalous behaviour in the aftermath of Holi celebrations, the adult covered the eyes of his children and walked away shaking his head, muttering about how people no longer felt any shame.

Prachand looked around, trying to take stock of where they were. After running away from Lily Bungalow at full speed, they had walked on for a few hours, trying to get as far away as possible. There was revelry on every street and a music or dance function in every locality and at some point while weaving in and out of localities, they had lost their bearings.

'I'm not very sure where we are,' Prachand confessed looking around as the two pigs still stood watching them intently. 'Do you have some water?' he enquired. Vidya handed him a tiny bottle. 'Here, have a snack. We've eaten nothing since last night.' She was glad she never went anywhere without her snack pack.

Prachand took a bite and then burst out laughing. Vidya looked worried. 'Prachi, are you alright?'

Prachand continued laughing. 'Couldn't be better! We are fugitives of the law ... yes, from running a detective agency that helps nab the bad guys, we have now become the bad guys. I've even managed to make my wife an accomplice! And here we are sitting by the side of a road, having a snack.'

Vidya sat and watched helplessly as her poor husband muttered and laughed like a madman, with his life now disintegrating before his eyes. He finally came to his senses a few minutes later.

'Look, don't use your phone at all. Hoping you haven't switched it back on. I'm assuming Govind has reported us, He recognises me and Navin Srivastava must have run my photo by him. And of course, you screamed and drew attention to yourself so you're an accomplice.'

Vidya looked morose.

He prattled on. 'Since it's too early and the police will take at least a little time to mobilise, given the festivities, I assume that they wouldn't have gone to Awadh Niwas yet. That's our best bet. Let's go get some basic things that we need. And we definitely need cash. I have some at home. Then we will figure what to do next.'

'You think quite clearly as a wanted criminal. Where did you learn this?' Vidya smiled.

'Books and Bollywood?' He allowed himself a smile as well.

'You don't think we should take help from our families?'

'Vidya, it's bad enough that I got you involved in this mess, I will not let the rest of them be drawn in as well.'

'It was my decision to come, Prachand. You didn't "make" me do anything.'

'Regardless, it was me who took on this case. Remember?'

As it turned out, given the people involved, the case had become high profile and top priority overnight, rendering Prachand's prediction incorrect. The officers in charge had visited Awadh Niwas first thing in the morning. Two police officers were stationed at the entrance to the house, sharing space with a sombre-looking Hirwa.

Prachand and Vidya stood at a distance, watching.

'How about we go around the adjoining house and try to scale the back wall? Call out to Bhushan?'

'Bhushan might not be home.'

'I can try and distract the policemen but that won't help for too long. One of us will get caught,' Prachand pondered aloud.

'What about the long pipe behind Pitaji's room?' suggested Vidya.

'Since I don't have any better ideas, let's give it a shot.'

To their horror, they found that a constable was posted behind the house. Fortunately, he was fast asleep when they approached. They had to act fast. Prachand had never been too inclined towards physical fitness and he regretted it even as he found himself hanging on to a pipe behind his own house.

'Faster Prachand, faster!' coaxed Vidya.

'I'm almost there.'

'Remember to keep the pink suit I wore last week, with the shiny beads. And my favourite blue one as well.'

'Vidya, we are not going for a wedding. We are running from the police. Do you understand that?'

'Yes, I do! And if I always listened to you, then we would have been hungry since last night. Now thank me and get me my clothes.'

Prachand muttered something under his breath.

'I heard that!' shouted Vidya.

'No, you didn't. Now please don't scream! They'll hear us.'

His father's room seemed to be unoccupied. They were possibly all downstairs dealing with the police and wondering what was happening. His heart felt heavy with the realization that he had landed his whole family in a gigantic cauldron of hot soup.

In about five minutes, he had everything he needed; collected in a bag, including the secret stash of cash he kept at home for emergencies. A burner phone with a special untraceable SIM that he had used a few months ago for a case and some of his props and disguises went into the bag as well. Before leaving, he crept to the edge of the balcony overlooking the courtyard to see what was happening. Chachu Tripathi and his father were in a heated argument with Navin Srivastava. Rachna Tripathi was standing by them looking lost. He felt a sting of tears and mouthed a silent 'sorry' to all of them. A tap on his shoulder made him twirl around in fright. There stood Ammaji, balancing herself on her stick.

'Ammaji, you came up the whole way? How? Are you feeling okay?'

She put a finger on her lips and gestured for Prachand to follow her. They walked to the small side room that contained some of her odds and ends and the precious trunk. Shutting the door behind her, she pulled off the covering cloth and cranked open her treasure chest.

First, she fished out a wad of notes and planted it in her grandson's hand.

'No, no! I can't. Please!'

'I might be deaf but I'm surely not dumb. *Hamaar pota galat nahi ho sakat*! (My grandson cannot be wrong!)

Prachand's eyes welled up with tears, but dried soon enough when he saw the next item that was placed in his hand. It was what looked like a desi *katta*, a local, hand-crafted gun. Prachand recoiled. Even as a private detective, he had never felt the need for a gun.

'Ammaji! What is this?'

'A banana for you. Of course, it's a gun, you fool. Keep it. You may need it.'

And before he could protest, his loving Ammaji, who he now believed to be part of the underworld, hugged him and shuffled away. He stuffed the money and scary-looking weapon into his already stuffed bag and made his way back to his father's room. The bag was thrown down to Vidya after which he hoisted himself out of the window. He was about to disappear under the window sill when the last person he wanted to see walked into the room.

Dinbandhu Tripathi for once, was genuinely speechless. The shock of his son not getting into IIT was not nearly close to what he felt when he saw him hanging off a pipe, peering at him from his window. He had a million questions milling in his slack jaw but couldn't articulate even one. Before his son could offer a word of explanation to his gobsmacked father, Prachand had already slid back to the ground.

As he scampered away with his wife, Prachand's biggest regret was that the eldest scion of Awadh Niwas had last been spotted by the head of the family, sliding down a water pipe. So much for last impressions.

CHAPTER 28

Sometimes when luck has left the building, the gods indulge to fill the void. If the cheekiest and most notorious criminals had to pick a day to be on the run in Kanpur, the choice would be unanimous. The last day of Holi celebrations – the day of the Ganga Mela. A day when the 'rangon ka thela' was taken through some of the oldest localities of the city and finally arrived at Sarsaiya Ghat, where thousands would gather, play Holi, eat and make merry. All the while dreading the end of merriment and thinking of getting back to work after an entire week of festivities. Through the many versions in public memory, the most popular story of its origins could be traced back to celebrating the bravery of a bunch of tenacious revolutionaries during the Independence struggle. It was basically meant to be a slap in the face of the British regime, celebration as a mark of revolt. Prachand and Vidya Tripathi were inadvertently on a similar mission.

The brilliant suggestion had come from Yatish Bhatnagar. After Prachand and Vidya went missing, the second person the police came calling on was the close friend. Navin

Srivastava seemed very put out by the tech king of Gwaltoli. He was picked up and shaken vigorously by the inspector as he questioned him about his absconding friends' whereabouts. Still quivering from his encounter, he was walking back home, when he was pulled into a side street by a multicoloured person.

'Shoo! *Hat bhikhari*!' Yatish pushed the seemingly drunk beggar away. Then another familiar face appeared in front of him. 'Bhabhi? Prachand da?' He pulled them behind a wall.

'What is going on? The police think you are involved not only in the kidnapping of Shailaja Kapoor but the murder of her husband as well.'

'Long story. But we ... we saw the whole thing,' Prachand confessed.

Yatish's eyes were bulging. Displaying a half smile and half frown, a part of him was terrified at what was happening but the other half was excited by the proximity to such sensational events.

'Yatish!' Prachand shook him. 'Stop smiling. Help us. We need someplace to hide.'

'Hide ... where can you hide ... Santosh's house? You know him. Or Ramdulari chachi?'

'Preferably a place more than a minute away from home that takes the police at least five minutes to figure out,' Prachand said, exasperated.

'Wait!' Yatish snapped his fingers. 'A second cousin of my mother's stays in Banda. Bappaditya Banerjee. Very good guy. I know you can stay with him for a little while. I'll call and inform him discreetly. Stay with him and use that time to figure out how to prove your innocence. That Navin Srivastava will never think of tracing you to Banda. See, haven't I picked up a few things from you?' He beamed at Prachand.

Prachand hugged him. 'I know you are taking a big risk by helping us. Thank you.'

Yatish teared up. 'Don't you dare thank me! You are my family.'

The emotional exchange was interrupted by a call on Yatish's phone. He took the call and his eyes widened as he listened. 'Wait. I'm coming there.'

'What happened,' Vidya enquired.

'That was Chotu. The police are at your office again. I'll go home, get Chacha ji and head over there.'

'Oh no!' exclaimed Vidya.

'What happened!?'

Vidya smiled politely at Yatish and then pulled Prachand's arm. 'When I came back from the market in a hurry, I left a packet of new underwear in the office cupboard last week,' she informed Prachand with crimson cheeks. 'What if they find it?'

'Trust me, we have bigger problems, Vidya.' Prachand looked at her with a deadpan face and then turned to Yatish.

'Please take care of everyone at home, Yatish. And Kanpur Khoofiya Pvt. Ltd. That's my whole life.'

'I know. Don't worry. For now, you both head to the Ghat. There is no way you will be identified there. Then board Bus No. 212 from the bus stop behind the temple. I'll have him prepared by the time you reach.'

Sarsaiya Ghat was a riot of colours and revelry. It looked like the entire population of Kanpur had descended on its shores to bid farewell to the festivities on a high note. As far as the eye could see, there were people of all age, shapes and sizes. While some were indulging in a final bout of colour wars, a large number were near the Ghat, dipping, rising, praying, turning the mighty Ganges into a massive watery painting. In contrast to the general ebullience in the air, two crouched figures were sitting by a small shop along the river front, eating quietly. They had tried their best to look as inconspicuous as possible, using shawls and stoles to cover their heads and faces. Two tickets to Banda sat in Prachand's pocket, but the bus wasn't scheduled to leave for another two hours. Predictably, a lot of their conversation was centered around trying to sort through the events that had landed them in this predicament.

'You know, Viddu, this is a high-profile case with famous people involved. They want a scape goat. That's quicker and easier than finding the culprit.' He looked pensively across the dancing ripples in the water.

'Do you think we should have gone back to the police and told them the truth?'

'Given how they were treating us the first time we approached them, they would crucify us now!'

'Mister, do you know where God went?'

Prachand turned around to look at a middle-aged man, who was swaying to some inaudible beat.

'The last time I checked he was going down these steps,' Prachand indulged him, looking at a bunch of men sitting nearby smoking a locally made bong, possibly the same place where this funny fellow had started his search for the Almighty.

'Thank you,' he said most graciously and walked back to the group.

Vidya gave a half smile and Prachand looked at her sadly.

'Sorry, Viddu. What will your father say? And your mother? Far from protecting you, I've turned you into a wanted criminal.'

Vidya hugged her husband sideways. 'Why are you always so hard on yourself? When this mess is behind us, they will understand. And I don't enjoy being called a murderer or kidnapper but I'd marry you again in a heartbeat, provided we go on our honeymoon before prison!'

In a few hours, Bus No. 212 was packed with tired passengers, ready to take the long journey to Banda. Prachand boarded first, followed by Vidya. She disappeared into the bus and then looked out of the window wistfully, taking a long last look, wondering when they would be home again.

CHAPTER 29

The atmosphere was charged and the devout were lost in their songs, clapping, with eyes shut. They looked happy and peaceful. Vidya felt neither, but sitting in the big courtyard of the Maheswari Devi temple in Banda, listening to the singing brought her a bit of comfort. However, it was not enough to help dissipate the cloud of doom eclipsing her mood. She looked sideways at Prachand. He sat cross legged on the ground, scribbling furiously, something he took to when trying to get his thoughts organised. Without warning, a dam broke inside her and Vidya, very uncharacteristically, started crying loudly.

A startled toddler ducked behind her mother. Prachand looked at his wife perplexed. When crying, the noises she produced took on such an unearthly quality that it sent people running. A lot of alarmed devotees started moving away from them. Since she sounded like she was being tortured, some even gave Prachand a scathing look. A well-meaning priest approached them and squatted next to Vidya.

'Whatever he has done, I am sure he is sorry about it. God has forgiven him. Now you forgive him.'

'But ... I ...' Prachand spluttered.

'Shame on you!' the priest reprimanded him. 'Don't trouble your wife so much that her patience breaks. Fear the wrath of God!' he warned while Vidya continued to wail.

After about fifteen minutes of the show when the audience started getting bored, the crowd dissipated leaving Prachand and Vidya facing each other.

'Viddu ...' he started. She wailed even louder.

'Shh. Calm down. Please. Talk to me ... Viddu, please,' he begged.

After a few minutes, she finally graduated to sniffling and muffled sobs into her dupatta.

'I know I pretend to be brave...'

'You are, it's not a pretence ...' Prachand interrupted her.

'Whatever ...' she sniffled, then continued. 'I am no detective. I'm a small-town girl from Chandni Chowk with...'

'Chandni Chowk is not a town. It's in the very big city of...'

'Stop interrupting me, Prachand!!' shouted Vidya, finally managing to silence her husband.

'We are wandering aimlessly, Prachand. Moving from place to place will not achieve anything.'

'I'm trying to make sense of all this, Viddu. Since we got here, I've been trying to put the dots together, figuring out what we can do. We could not have proved our innocence inside a jail in Kanpur. Just have faith in me. We will work this out. Just give me some time.' He winked and nudged her. 'And once this case is through, and we are rich and famous...'

'I don't want to become rich!' Vidya screamed.

'Alright. We will be poor. We will beg on the streets and never be rich. Don't be angry.'

'And I don't want fame!'

'Never! I'll ensure no one knows us beyond Gwaltoli.'

'I just want my simple life back again. With Ma's constant complaints and Pitaji's grumpiness, Ammaji's weird antics, Bhushan's horrible singing and Chachu's jokes and our useless clients and the new underwear that I bought...'

'We can get you some new ones here ...' offered Prachand.

'Can't you just keep quiet for a few seconds?' she asked, looking exasperated. Prachand put a finger on his lips in response. Then Vidya grew silent and relapsed into her earlier state of brooding. Prachand hugged her and they sat in silence.

'If you've calmed down, I would like to suggest something.' Prachand asked, searching Vidya's face. She wiped her eyes and drew a sharp breath, nodding her head.

'I had a chat with Yatish.'

'What did he say?'

'The police are crawling all around the office, at home.'

'So? We already know that.'

'So, they are spending most of their energies investigating us, rather than the real culprits. And I know why. Yatish mentioned that he had spoken with his police contact. They have no leads yet on the abduction or the murder.'

'That still doesn't change our situation.'

'Help me here. Now with the husband gone, where would the ransom calls go?'

'To the mother. In Mumbai.'

'Exactly!'

'The police must already be in touch with her.'

'Yes, and we must get in touch with her as well if we need more answers. She is the only link left between her daughter and son-in-law.'

'Prachand, why in the world would she entertain the fugitives who are suspects in both cases?'

'Because someone needs to find her daughter and once we share the information we have, she will know we were only trying to help!'

'That's a long shot, Prachi.'

'It's the only one we have, Viddu,' he said, mentally noting that ever since this case had started, invoking his gut feeling was fast becoming a go-to move.

They were both quiet for a few minutes. Then Vidya's eyes grew wide.

'Prachi, are you telling me we are going to Mumbai?'

'Yes, Viddu.' Prachand nodded.

Bappaditya Banerjee was generally an anxious man. A dangling signboard that could sever his head on a morning walk, hot water that could cost him a trip to a hospital's burn unit, a loquacious neighbour who steadily depleted his special tea leaves from Darjeeling, or the fear that his secret stash of porn hidden under the mattress would one day be discovered by his mother on a visit. He stressed about anything and everything. Acid reflux, gas, antacids and anxiety were his constant companions. Some relatives claimed that he came into this world with a deep furrow on his forehead. So when his young nephew Yatish called him with a request to shelter some friends on the run, he could barely breathe, overcome with fear. But Yatish's plea had also stoked his long-buried sense of excitement and adventure that made him throw his Isabgol and caution to the winds. It had been an exciting few days, but his latest cause for concern was that his guests of three days had suddenly decided to pack up and leave.

'But where will you go, Prochondo da? *Vidya ma ke ekhaane chede dao.*' (At least leave Vidya here.)

'I can't tell you, Bappo da, for your own safety. If the police do end up reaching you, you can genuinely tell them you have no idea where we are.'

'This is very exciting!' He clapped his hands like a happy sea lion. The crime levels that primary school teachers usually deal with are limited to pen thefts, mischief and drawing on the bathroom walls. This fugitive business was rather out of syllabus and fascinating.

'Please wipe the place down once we leave. Our fingerprints must be all over.'

Bappo da's eyes grew wider with excitement, cueing the James Bond soundtrack in his head. 'Thank you very much for everything, dada,' Vidya hugged him, followed by Prachand, as the gentle giant melted like a blob of butter.

As they walked out, he called after them.

'I will not tell them anything, even if they torture me!' he screamed heroically.

Prachand smiled after giving him a thumbs up sign and the husband-wife duo disappeared into the night.

CHAPTER 30

There was pin-drop silence in the courtyard of Awadh Niwas. For once even Bhushan had nothing to sing about. He was at a friend's place and was told upon his return that his brother and sister-in-law were on the run.

'I can't believe no one called and told me,' he punched his fist on the floor.

Dinbandhu Tripathi broke his silence. 'And what would you have done??' he shouted. 'Acting as if he is the prime minister of the country.'

'*Hai daiyya*!' (Oh Lord!) groaned Rachna Tripathi, having borrowed the phrase from her mother-in-law. Ever since the appearance of her son and daughter-in-law on the local most-wanted suspects list, she had barely left the floor, which she pounded frequently in frustration. Even Ammaji's food and beverage demands fell on deaf ears. Rachna Tripathi was inconsolable.

'Bhushan, just check from the window. Are those reporters still outside?' instructed Chachu Tripathi.

Bhushan shook his head. 'Ma had threatened to throw boiling moong dal on a reporter's head. Ever since, they've kept their distance.'

Rachna Tripathi ceased her moaning and spoke up. 'What else am I to do? They are accusing my son of being a kidnapper and murderer?? And Vidya's father is so worried. What do I tell them?' She started sobbing, 'That their daughter is now an accessory to a murder plot?'

Chachu Tripathi lowered his voice. 'Prachand sent a message through Yatish that they are fine. They are with one of Yatish's friends.'

Bhushan banged his fist and piped up again. 'Why are they treating them and all of us like criminals!!? My brother has done nothing wrong in his life.'

'That's what you think!' mumbled Dinbandhu Tripathi.

Bhushan heard this comment and turned purple. He opened and shut his mouth several times and then decided to be brave.

'Pitaji, you are always saying mean things about him. Isn't he your son?!'

In response his father picked up his rubber slipper and aimed it at his son's head.

'You useless buffoon!' he roared. 'You will teach your father!?'

Bhushan tactfully ducked behind Ammaji.

'You can hit me or skin me, but I will say what must be said. He loves and respects you and all you can do is humiliate him. Just because he didn't go to IIT? He completed his engineering just for you, didn't he? Why can't you let it go?'

Another slipper came hurtling his way.

'All he wants to do is make you proud,' Bhushan said, almost sobbing.

Chachu Tripathi decided to be brave as well. 'That's true. He really cares for us. He keeps telling me he will make so much money that we can retire and rest.'

Dinbandhu Tripathi suddenly felt very old and weary. He was tired of everything, his own tirade, this impossible situation and the conflicting emotions. Instead of retaliating, he walked away, with his dhoti trailing behind him, thinking of the last time he had seen Prachand hanging outside his bedroom window. In his room, he lit an incense stick in front of Lord Shiva's picture and prayed for his son and daughter-in-law.

Little did Dinbandhu Tripathi know that a local cable news channel camera was trained and zooming in on his face at that very moment. A voluptuous reporter in a tight red dress soothed her hair and looked into the camera.

'As you can see, this family that the police have been paying many visits to in connection with the Shailaja Kapoor case, is praying very hard to the Almighty. While the police are not sharing details, our sources tell us that their investigations are deeply focused on this family from Gwaltoli. Who kidnapped Shailaja Kapoor? Who killed her husband? Who is the police looking for? How is this family connected? This mystery has rocked all of Kanpur!'

Meanwhile, a hundred odd kilometres from this drama, Prachand and Vidya were moving through the streets of Banda on a cycle rickshaw, making their way to the train station. They were still keeping their faces covered as much as possible, suspecting that police control rooms in nearby cities had been asked to keep a lookout for them. Prachand had even added on a moustache and beard for good measure.

'Have you thought of where we are going to stay once we reach Mumbai?' asked Vidya.

'Yes. I've looked up some cheap hotels in a place called Andheri West. You know, all parts of Mumbai have an East and West? Mumbai overall has South, North, West and East.'

'Wow. That's how big the city is. Tell me more,' Vidya dug further.

'I was checking the map. It's peppered with some funny sounding localities. Dadar, Mulund, Malad, Bhayandar, Bhoiwada, Behrampada,' laughed Prachand as Vidya joined in.

'Sir, if you don't mind my asking, are you going to Mumbai for the first time?' The rickshaw puller interrupted their banter.

'Why do you ask?' Vidya enquired suspiciously.

'I wanted to help, in case you want a cheap and safe place to stay. My nephew works at a lodge in Andheri. I'll share his number and maybe he can get you a good rate from the manager.'

'Sure, thank you' Prachand said, taking a card that had a name scribbled on it.

'His name is Gotya?'

'Well, it was Govinda when he left Banda,' the man shrugged.

'We must look for Shailaja Kapoor's home as soon as we reach,' Prachand whispered to Vidya, not wanting to reveal any more details to the rickshaw puller.

'Prachi! I want to see Shah Rukh Khan's house. Oh, and Amitabh ji's house as well. Please!' Vidya squeezed her husband's arm.

Prachand could feel the onset of a headache and started remembering his Bholenaath. Here was his wife, planning celebrity sightings and acting like they were going on their honeymoon, while he had an intense churning sensation in his stomach as he sat wondering what lay ahead for them in the big city.

CHAPTER 31

Prachand yawned and looked up. A sleepy Vidya smiled back at him. She looked like an angel perched on the clouds, namely, the topmost berth in the AC three-tier compartment. Despite their last-minute reservation, a seat had somehow been snagged. Prachand had a waitlisted ticket but he was meaning to persuade the ticket collector for a seat or at least the 'right to linger' when he came by. There were two essentials to the seat game. First, the designation of the TT would be elevated by adding a suffix of familiarity. The options at hand were any relative. Chacha, mama, mamu, bhaijaan, bhaiyya, bhaiyyaji. If he was a bit elderly and one was really desperate, matters could go as far as babuji and dadaji. Second, the bribe could be in kind or cash. Alternatively, if one had a large amount of money to dispense, then no niceties were essential.

Three hours ago, they had boarded the Tulsi Express at Banda. Prachand moved around like a nomad, smiling, chatting and easing himself into whatever seat was available while people were still awake. Now, at this late hour, most of the berths had been opened up and people were stretched out, sleeping, not leaving much space for Prachand to wiggle into. A large-hearted Gujarati gentleman on the berth under Vidya's seat had offered some space near his feet, but the repetitive kicks and constant flatulence, despite the stellar training from being around Ammaji, sent Prachand running down to the narrow passage outside the bathroom.

No sooner had he reached the passage than the stench of urine hit his senses and he flinched physically. A man who was squatting on a hold-all next to the door started laughing. Prachand stared at the hold-all and it brought back memories of trips he had taken with his family. He remembered a green one, stuffed with sheets and blankets, some shoes, boxes of food, seemingly the entire universe. As a child he had sat atop his green throne with pride.

'Beedi?' the man offered Prachand a drag.

Prachand did not smoke, but these were extenuating circumstances. 'The TT will catch us,' Prachand looked around furtively.

'I have my setting,' winked the man as he took a long drag. Prachand took a few long drags as well. Perhaps too long, because he ended up coughing his lungs out. As the train jerked, he had to hold onto a door to steady himself. The light-headedness he felt indicated that he had just inhaled something more potent than tobacco.

'Does this have ...' Prachand looked at the man accusingly.

The man winked. 'Now you will be happy till the end of the train journey. Then he started laughing uproariously. Prachand's head was swimming. He plonked himself down next to the man on the hold-all and started dreaming that he was a child again, ruling his kingdom from atop his green perch. The fatigue and smoke combined to lull him into sweet slumber.

He woke up and checked his watch as the train was pulling out of Lalitpur Junction. It was 3 a.m. Prachand stood up and protectively clutched his bag, grateful that it was still around. He opened the connecting door and walked into his compartment. People were still sleeping, some were sitting up rubbing their eyes, their sleep having been interrupted by a station stop. The after-effect of whatever he had smoked made him feel like he was having an out-of-body experience, and the other developing issue was that he felt like laughing. Never had he experienced such an intense desire to laugh for no reason. Remembering his current predicament and the sorry state of affairs made him want to laugh even more.

When he reached the berth, the train had started moving again and he stood on his toes to check on Vidya. She was asleep. But this peaceful slumber was short-lived. Some commotion seemed to have broken out at the end of the corridor. Vidya sat up rubbing her eyes. She gestured with her hand asking Prachand what the problem was. He shrugged.

'What was that noise?' someone asked.

'Did someone just break the door down?'

'The train has stopped. Someone has pulled the chain.'

'Robbers! Robbers!' a lady shrieked in terror.

There was pandemonium in the compartment as three men barged in with big laathis. They wore turbans and the lower half of their faces was covered with the cloth at the other end of it.

'Everybody, keep sitting where you are!' one of them shouted.

'Help, help!' screamed a woman in the berth opposite Vidya.

'Shut up!' the tallest robber shouted. Then he opened up a gunny sack. 'Put in all your valuables in this bag. Right now. And no one try to act smart.' He banged the laathi on the ground several times, indicating that he meant business. Everyone started complying except Prachand who just stood still.

'Are you deaf?' He poked Prachand with his laathi. To his utter shock, Prachand started giggling.

'You think this is funny?' he shouted with rage. 'I'll pound you to a pulp!'

What he did not know was that at that very moment Prachand Tripathi was not very aware of what he was saying. All Prachand could see were tiny cartoons of Hirwa running around the robber's head. Some of those cartoons were mooing; some dancing. This was dispatching him into fits of laughter.

'Why is that uncle laughing?' A small boy whispered to his older sister.

'When people are very nervous they sometimes laugh, Chintu,' the worldly wise sister explained while looking at the stranger laughing hysterically.

'I'll break your head!' the robber was screaming hysterically now.

Vidya quickly jumped down from her perch in her husband's defence. She had never seen him behave in such an absurd manner. The stupefied passengers watched in silence as well, equally wary of the robbers and the strange man facing off with them.

One of the other robbers came and pulled the hysterical one by the arm.

Kanpur Khoofiya Pvt. Ltd

'We must go! I think someone has pulled the chain. The police will be coming soon. Come on!'

'Not before I teach this mad man a lesson,' he said menacingly. And with that, he made a lunge for Prachand's bag. With his precious bag and only possessions at stake, the fog around Prachand's head suddenly cleared and he was filled with a sudden bolt of righteous fury.

The robber's friend was pulling the angry robbers' arm. The robber was in turn pulling Prachand's bag. Prachand clung on to the bag for dear life. Vidya clung on to her husband and screamed, 'Help! Help!'

In this commotion Prachand tripped and fell. Very close to the robber now, Prachand stuck his hand inside the bag and found a sinister hold on the gun Ammaji had loaned to him. The veiled gun, sticking out of the cloth was pointing straight at the robber's face.

'Leave the bag or I'll shoot you!' Prachand said menacingly as the robber broke into a high-pitched scream of 'Help! Help!' He pushed Prachand and ran out with the remaining gang.

Vidya turned to Prachand and hugged him, her body trembling with anxiety.

'What is wrong with you, Prachi! Why were you laughing? And why did you put your life in danger?'

Prachand continued smiling but there was a twinkle in his eyes as he looked at his wife. 'I love you, Viddu. I'll always come to your rescue. Trust me ...' He then aborted his own speech, stretched out on the only empty seat he could see, pulled up the blanket to his chin and promptly went off to sleep with a smile on his face.

CHAPTER 32

'Tea, tea, tea!'

A young boy was rattling his spoon up and down a row of tiny empty glasses, holding a steaming kettle of tea in the other hand. He paused in front of Prachand, but was waved away with a smile. After his drug induced act of heroism, Prachand had been unanimously hailed as the saviour and king of the compartment. In their haste to leave, the robbers had even dropped the bag of loot they had collected from the passengers. No one had questioned why Prachand had laughed through such a nerve-wracking experience or why he had suddenly gone off to sleep after the episode. For when you come across a real-life hero, one must suspend all judgement or doubt.

Vidya was still furious with her husband's reckless behaviour and refused to speak with him all morning. As the train pulled out of Manmad Junction, Prachand made another attempt to appease her. Of course by now, the TT had been approached by some influential passengers and Vidya and Prachand were awarded premium lower berth seats facing each other. Prachand set down a plate on the steel table wedged into the wall.

'Try this please, Viddu. It's called puran pohli. It's a famous Maharashtrian delicacy,' he explained. Pin-drop silence.

'Viddu, we are in another state now! Isn't that exciting? Maharashtra. You have always wanted to visit Mumbai and now we are so close.' Vidya continued to look out of the window.

Prachand took her hand. She shook it off.

'Come on, Viddu, please,' he pleaded.

'Please?' Vidya thundered. 'Did you listen to me when I was pleading earlier?'

'Vidya, I was not in my senses!'

'Of course, you weren't in your senses. You don't have to convince me!'

'Let me explain. Please.'

Prachand slowly narrated everything to his wife.

'So let me get this straight. You smoked a cigarette, then you took some drugs, then you fought a robber and pointed a gun at him. And none of this is your fault?!'

'It really isn't and the drugs were in the cigarette.'

Vidya's frown silenced him.

She pulled his arm hard as he howled in pain. 'How can you carry a gun, Prachand?'

'Ammaji gave it to me. For protection.'

'So what? She gave it to you and you took it? Knowing how dangerous that is?'

'Viddu, I was in two minds before taking it as well, but now that I think of our current predicament, it's not such a bad idea holding on to one.'

'Stop with your conspiracy theories. The police are the ones chasing us Prachand, we can't shoot them!'

'We don't know anything yet. All I know is that we went to help and they turned the heat on us.'

'You know what they'll do if they find out that you've been smoking drugs and pointing guns in trains?'

'They've already convicted us in their heads.' Prachand shrugged.

'I don't believe that yet. And I'm sure, deep inside, you don't either. This defeatist attitude is so unlike you Prachand. Please don't lose faith.'

Prachand looked away, indicating that he would like the conversation to end.

They travelled in silence for a while and then Vidya glanced at her husband as he stared out the window. Her heart went out to him. A gentle, non-controversial simpleton, who was caught in a confusing web of lies and murder, unable to stop the wheels that were in motion.

'Prachi ... I...'

'Viddu,' Prachand interrupted her. 'I think we must change compartments. It's not safe here.'

'Huh?' she exclaimed, trying to look around. Prachand stopped her.

'There is a man who I have seen at the last few stops. He is watching us but keeps his distance.'

'Do you think he is a policeman in disguise?'

'I'm not sure' he said. 'Hey, I'm going to buy some peanuts from that boy standing at the door. When I come back, just run along with me.'

'Okay,' she whispered.

Prachand adjusted the bag on his back and casually started walking towards the peanut vendor. The man outside also walked in the same direction. He had a cap on, so his face wasn't very visible. As the man reached the door and lost the sight of Prachand for a few seconds, Prachand turned on his heels and dashed back to the seat where Vidya was waiting for him. They both ran and moved into the next compartment. Prachand looked behind but the man had still not caught up.

They weaved through a few coaches till Prachand finally stopped and pulled Vidya into a crowded seat. Vidya, who was panting violently due to the exertion, looked around.

'Couldn't run towards the AC compartments, could you?'

'There's much more of a crowd here. Easier to remain hidden.'

'Talking about hiding, half your moustache is dangling like a pendulum,' Vidya remarked.

Prachand quickly pushed it back into place. Not that it mattered. Amidst the general commotion of people and possessions, it was hard to notice anything in the compartment.

Prachand was in deep thought when Vidya tapped him back to the present. 'You know,' Prachand surmised, 'That man was not from the police. Had they caught wind, there would be checkpoints and a larger number of people deployed and, instead of this cat-and-mouse chase, we would have been arrested right away.'

'That's right,' Vidya frowned.

'Bappo da didn't even know we were headed to Mumbai. That just leaves...'

Prachand looked stricken. 'Yatish?'

CHAPTER 33

Prachand woke up with a start, sweating profusely. As he stirred, Vidya whose head was resting on his shoulder also moved, but she didn't wake up. After a lot of begging, pleading, Prachand and Vidya had been granted a tiny spot for their buttocks. Being in no position to contest, they had decided to try and get a nap, sitting straight up, plastered to each other. Prachand barely slept. For he was on the lookout for the person who was following them. Ever since their coach switch, the man had completely been out of sight. This should have made Prachand happy, but his mind was preoccupied and rejecting the possibility of his childhood friend being somehow involved in this mess. The prudent thing to do would've been to keep no contact even with his untraceable burner phone but he did the exact opposite. He made a call to Yatish, using the method they had agreed upon, knowing fully well that Yatish's movements and calls might be monitored by the police.

The phone rang several times before someone picked up.
'Halloo. Naaz restorunt.'

'Chotu,' Prachand whispered.

'Bhaiyya!' an excited voice piped up at the other end. Chotu worked part-time at the restaurant. Prachand knew he could be reached there and get Yatish, when need be, from his shop next door.

'Chotu, don't shout!' Prachand cautioned him.

'Matar pulao, jeera rice, biryani, boneless biryani.'

'Okay, so is it safe to talk? Any police, any guards nearby?'

'Not spicy at all sir,' Chotu mumbled, hoping his bhaiyya would get the message.

'Everyone okay at home?'

'Yes sir. I have that as well.'

'Yatish there by any chance?'

'Butter chicken, gosht keema, nalli nihari, galauti kebab!' shouted Chotu and then there was no response for a minute.

'Dada!' It was Yatish, but Prachand didn't know what to say.

'Yatish, have you spoken to the police or anyone about us?'

'No, dada. Not at all. Why are you asking?' Yatish sounded puzzled.

'Are you very sure?'

Yatish hesiatated. 'Yes ... yes, I'm very sure. But what happened? Where are you right now? Have you reached Mumbai?'

Prachand's heart skipped a beat. 'How do you know that we are going to Mumbai, Yatish?'

There were a few moments of silence and then Yatish started stammering. 'I ... I guessed. Just the way you do all the time. Ha ha. Where else would you go, right?' He laughed. Nervously. 'Hello ... hello?'

Prachand had hung up.

In another part of the train, sat a very agitated-looking man. Bhima Shankar had lost track of the man he was following. His wife was nowhere to be seen either. The last time he had laid eyes on them was almost four hours ago. They were most probably still on the train but after scouring the length and breadth of it, he still had no idea exactly where they were. This interfering husband-wife duo was responsible for his current plight as he looked at the two irritating kids hanging around his neck and dropping crumbs of food on him. All he really wanted to do was wring their necks but with the mother sitting on the opposite seat and watching indulgently, he had no option but to force himself to smile. Staying put with a family as opposed to arousing suspicion lurking around seemed like a better bet till the train reached Mumbai.

Oh, how normal his life had been just about a month ago, he thought. A life of petty crimes suited his needs. The police had mostly learnt to look the other way, treating him as a harmless nuisance as long as he kept them happy. Bijli, the bar dancer, was the highlight of his day. He would visit her late at night after all her customers had left. He had vowed to whisk her away from that hellhole one day and live happily ever after. But one call had changed everything. The call from 'the Boss'. Just thinking of 'the Boss' made his stomach churn and his palms sweat. He couldn't dare to say no to any job. Besides, the ten-lakh-rupees price tag had been the ultimate incentive. He had taken care of that Sujit Oberoi, but 'the Boss' was angry because the detective had seen him. How was he to know that two critters were sitting around at the time in the front-row seats? Now he had that mess to take care of.

Lady Luck finally shone down on him when he bumped into the gullible Yatish Bhatnagar in Kanpur, round about the same time that he was desperately looking for the detective and his wife. Already having snooped around for Yatish in the past, all he had needed was some alcohol to dilute the inhibitions and the latest news came pouring out. Sitting at Naaz Hotel, Yatish had cried and told Bhima about a peculiar problem with one of his close family friends, something Bhima knew only too well, having been on their trail. Sniffing an opportunity to make money while serving his own interest, Bhima had offered to keep an eye on the 'too proud to ask for help' friend, and Yatish had readily agreed. Once Bhima had Bappo da's address, all he needed to do was lie low and follow them. Since Mumbai was where they were headed, he followed suit.

'Pee-pee.' The podgy boy raised his little finger.

'Uncle, even I want to go' his brother would not be left behind.

The indulgent mother smiled, signalling her approval while the tall stranger led the children to the bathroom, wishing he could chuck them out of the door on the way.

CHAPTER 34

'Sir, tea?' enquired the constable timidly. His boss was not in a good mood. Maybe it had to do with the number of calls he was receiving with regard to the Shailaja Kapoor case.

'Keep it on my head,' shouted Navin Srivastava.

'But sir, it will fall and...'

'Moongalal! Just keep it on my table and go away.'

Moongalal scurried away, reminding himself to keep his distance.

Nothing was going right in Navin Srivastava's world. The wife had locked horns with him over an objection to excessive shopping. Consequently, her room turned into a 'kop bhavan', a sulking chamber like the angry maharanis of yore would turn to. This meant the husband was transferred to the sofa. Moreover, she had relinquished the reins of the kitchen to the maid who was like a misfired missile; cooking whatever she liked, usually things that turned out to be inedible.

To compound his problems a terrible toothache was making his head throb. Sitting on top of this weary pile was the damn new case that had put him in the eye of a storm this past week. And to think that the key person of interest had walked into his police station and sat under his very nose with his wife! He cursed the moment he allowed Prachand to walk away. Now his only suspects were on the run and he had no clue where they were headed. The kidnapping itself had left wafer-thin clues in its wake and the murder was even more confounding. The post-mortem report had concluded death due to head trauma and internal bleeding. Was it just a mix of circumstantial evidence and 'being in the wrong place at the wrong time' against the detective and his wife or could they really be involved? But their recurrent involvement could not just be written off as a bunch of coincidences. All these facts were whirring around his head like a high-voltage blender.

'Saar, Mr MLA has called again.'

'Tell him I am in the bathroom.'

'Saar, that is what I told him last time.'

'Then tell him it's number two this time.'

From MLAs to journalists, to women's' organizations, to civil rights NGOs, no one could keep their noses out of this case. Fame, money, power and media were like mounds of jaggery. A tiny whiff and everyone would come crawling like ants, hungry for the limelight.

He was in deep thought when Subinspector Ranganathan came and sat in front of him with a bunch of files. Navin Srivastava drummed the glass tabletop with his fat fingers.

'Did you get the husband's financial records checked? That Sujit Oberoi?'

'Yes, saar. Despite being a builder, nothing unusual. Some debts in the market. But that's expected. So, either he is squeaky clean or really good at fudging accounts.'

'Hmm, last few calls on his phone?'

'To his office, a friend called Kala Shastri in Switzerland, Shailaja Kapoor and a landline number that appears a few times.'

'Have we traced it yet?'

'They are still trying to, sir.'

'It's been a week already and you can't finish such basic legwork on the case?' Navin Srivastava thundered.

'Saar, because of the Holi festivities, everything slowed down.'

'Maybe salary transfers should slow down as well then?'

Subinspector Ranganathan, without a rejoinder in place, started staring at the wet patch on the wooden table in front of him.

'What about the footage from the hotel cameras near the main road? They might have some footage of the car used for abduction speeding past. The detective had given us a description.'

Subinspector Ranganathan's eyes opened up really wide as his senior sighed loudly and leaned back in his chair.

'Let me guess – that footage hasn't been checked yet.'

'No, no. Saar, we will get it any minute now. In one hotel the camera stopped working a long time ago and in Hotel Suvarna, the tapes have not been touched for so long that it's taking time to retrieve them.'

He then checked the file he was holding.

'Saar, Govind, the servant in Shailaja Kapoor's house has given a list of all the people who visited or who Shailaja Kapoor went and met, at least to his knowledge. It was hardly a list, but we have spoken with all of them. She mostly kept to herself.'

Navin Srivastava started browsing through the stack of menus lying on his table.

'Any news from stations in nearby cities that we've alerted?'

'Saar, Lucknow, Banda, Etawah, Allahabad have all been alerted.'

'I underestimated this bloody detective! He really can hide well.'

'Saar,' piped up Ranganathan in the hopes of picking up atleast a crumb if not a whole brownie point. 'Two people are still stationed at Tripathi's house.'

'Anything else from Oberoi's family or Shailaja Kapoor's mother?'

'Sujit Oberoi does not have many relatives. Just a stepbrother who lives in London and never comes down. They had last spoken five years ago. Pamela Kapoor just keeps crying and asking for her daughter. I feel bad for the poor woman. She has shared a list of all close friends and acquaintances and I'll follow up with the Mumbai Police.'

'Ranga, I think you should keep a close watch on that Yatish. I have a feeling he knows more but is on his guard.'

'Okay, saar.' He nodded in agreement as his phone rang. After listening and nodding for a few seconds, he stood up and shouted. 'What!' and then felt silent again.

Navin Srivastava, who was watching his face, nudged him impatiently.

'Stop building suspense like you're in a soap opera. What is it?'

Subinspector Ranganathan cut the call and looked excited. 'Saar, the footage from the camera verified that the only car that sped past around that time was the

Maruti van the detective had described. We got part of the number plate.'

'Good. That's good. Now we need to look for this damn car.'

'Saar, that's the second news. The car has been found.'

'That's great!' Navin Srivastava stood up with open arms, ready to welcome the first piece of good news. 'Where?'

'Saar, in the compound of a building on Birahna Road. It belongs to the Kanpur Sarvajanik Natak Mandli.'

'Natak Mandli?!'

'Yes, saar. That car has never been loaned. It belongs to them. We checked with the manager.'

Navin Srivastava sat down again.

'Saar, and the landline number on Sujit Oberoi's phone also belongs to the same Mandli office.'

'Ranga, order some food for me from this restaurant.' Navin Srivastava passed on one menu from the pile to his officer.

'What, saar!' Subinspector Ranganathan was desperately trying to connect the dots between food and the missing car.

'I need some spicy food to fire up my brain. This case is becoming even more twisted than a jalebi with every passing day!'

CHAPTER 35

The train was chugging a bit slower, now that it was in the city and passing through the suburbs of Mumbai. Vidya had napped quite a bit but Prachand was sleepy given the constant vigil, barely allowing himself to shut his eyes, lest they were rediscovered by the man following them.

'Legs up,' was the general chant around the train as passengers suspended their legs in the air to allow passage for the luggage stashed beneath the seats. Then came the unlocking of chains. Trust no one, being the general sentiment. While some people had linked their luggage to the legs of the seats, some paranoid passengers had even tied the luggage to themselves while sleeping. Prachand was clearly travelling light, so a gentleman from Kerala, who occupied a seat nearby had requested permission to tie Prachand to his luggage.

'Mister, it will take two minutes. I need to use the toilet.'

'Just leave your luggage on the seat. I'm not going anywhere. I promise I'll keep an eye on it.'

'Mister, that's how I lost a bag on my last journey. I don't doubt you but there are too many people milling around.

Please! Mister, help me. I really need to go!' he started dangerously shuffling from one foot to another. 'Please help me!'

Without waiting for another protest, he hastily clicked the chain around Prachand's wrist, and made a dash for the bathroom. Vidya was laughing.

'Maybe this is Bholenaath's way of mentally preparing me for prison.'

Vidya hit his arm. 'Don't talk like that.'

Prachand looked out the window. Rows and rows of small hut-like houses with blue tarpaulin tops were rushing past, blurring into a hazy sea of blue. His nostrils were hit with a heady mix of spices, sweat and smoke. As they rocked with the rhythmic beat of the train, his heart thudded quietly as well, excited and scared all at once. It had always been his dream to visit the maximum city but what he could have never imagined were the circumstances under which this dream would materialise.

As Tulsi Express rumbled onto Platform Seven, there was a mad rush to the exits. The people leading up to them were glued to each other, their limbs moving in line with public will. The Keralite who had safely repossessed his suitcase was now clucking the loudest.

'Such lack of manners these days.' Of course, he said this as he shoved the man right in front of him with all the force he could muster.

'Move ahead!' someone screamed from behind.

'Do you want me to climb on the person in front of me?' came the quick retort.

Prachand allowed everyone to alight before them, his eye always scanning their surroundings.

Kanpur Khoofiya Pvt. Ltd

They finally landed on the platform in a heap of humanity. Coolies darted all around them, balancing stacks of luggage on their heads while doing the precarious duck walk. Shrouded in the cacophony of people and announcements, Prachand tried to locate the whereabouts of their stalker but he was nowhere to be seen. Vidya had been looking uncomfortable ever since they had alighted.

'I desperately need to go to the toilet,' she pleaded.

It was very easy to find the toilet. All one had to do was follow the stench right up to the large brown door that had 'Mahila' (Ladies' toilet) printed across. With her dupatta wrapped tight around her nose, she gathered her resolve and entered the bathroom looking like the bandit queen.

Prachand decided to use this opportunity to relieve himself as well. Once inside, he found it difficult to breathe. The floor was wet and dirty while the pots looked like they hadn't been cleaned since the British left India. Conforming to the trend of most public toilets across the country, the walls were tattooed with provoking artwork from pan stains, hand prints and odd love declarations like 'John loves Salma'.

He had just finished relieving himself when he was pushed towards the wall. He didn't have to see the attacker's face to fathom who it was. The man tried to choke him from behind but Prachand refused to let go of his arms. He banged Prachand's head on a wall but the dizzy yet tenacious detective held on. In frustration, he strengthened his hold on Prachand's neck. With the air supply dwindling, Prachand started thinking of all that was dear to him and his mind played pictoral flashes of scenes from back home, laughing family members, a simple life, even a happy Hirwa mooing freely, his precious office, much like a beautiful montage that belonged in a dreamy Yash Raj movie sequence.

But before this sequence could be completed, the door swung wide open and a slack-jawed man, possibly the janitor, stood in the doorway. On his arrival, the attacker dropped Prachand's almost limp body and pushed past the man, making a speedy exit.

The cleaner knelt beside Prachand. 'Boss? Are you okay?' he enquired.

Prachand slowly opened his eyes.

'Do you know where you are?'

'Chandigarh, of course' Prachand replied confidently.

'I think you need to rest,' suggested the man. Then he looked at the floor and added. 'And take a bath soon after.'

Vidya almost fell from shock when she saw Prachand being brought out with support.

'Sister, please handle your husband,' the man said when she ran up to Prachand.

'I want food. Get me some toys,' Prachand muttered away.

He was taken to the waiting room and Vidya ordered him to rest on the bench. In about half an hour, he was almost back to normal but did not divulge anything about the attack to spare Vidya further anxiety.

'I slipped and fell, Viddu,' is all he mentioned of the entire incident.

As they stood at the entrance of the station, looking on at the sea of people, Prachand wondered how they were to embark on this journey. With no immediate answers, they walked out, only to run into a herd of enthusiastic taxi drivers.

'*Ae bhau, bhau, eh bhau.*' (Hey bother, brother, hey brother.)

Vidya muttered to Prachand, quite puzzled. 'Why are they barking?'

'*Bhau, bhau*, idhar, discount milega,' another man offered.

'Viddu, I think *bhau* means brother in Marathi.'

'Aah!' Vidya responded, looking visibly satisfied with the explanation.

Instead of braving the two-mile long autorickshaw queue, they decided to settle with one of the taxi drivers who offered them a discount.

'Belcum to Bumbaee.' The jovial man smiled. 'No luggeg? No poblaim!' He walked ahead of them with a triumphant swagger, a colourful scarf fluttering around his neck. The remaining style statement was completed as he flicked on his dark sunglasses in the middle of the night.

'Please come,' he smiled and opened the door of his car. His black-and-yellow taxi looked like it had been driven out of a low-budget Bollywood set. Pictures of every imaginable Bollywood star clung to the insides. There were two shiny silver poles in between the front seat and the back seat, as if ready to host an impromptu pole dancing session. As he started the ignition, disco lights came on and a song blared from the back seat.

'*Hungama ho gaya ... ha ha ha ha hangamaaaaaa...!*'

He screamed over the music as the passengers watched with mouths agape. 'Where will you go, mister?'

Prachand screamed back, 'I'm still deciding, mister!'

CHAPTER 36

Yatish Bhatnagar knew that something was wrong. He had always known, even as a child, when trouble was around the corner. Like the time when his teacher was about to hit his knuckles for copying and his left eye had started twitching uncontrollably, or when his ear had started throbbing unbearably, a minute before his friend Babloo had slipped on cow dung and travelled down a manhole. His body had an inbuilt warning system and he knew something was amiss even now, since he was severely constipated ever since his conversation with Prachand two days ago.

Now as he sat in his shop, hardly paying attention to the customer before him, he felt a familiar sensation of doom.

'Mister, I need an adapter!' said an irate-looking man.

'Why are you screaming?' asked Yatish, frowning.

'I'm not! I've been asking nicely for the last five minutes and you're just standing like a statue.'

'Raju!' shouted Yatish to someone at the back of the shop. 'Where the hell are you? Go attend to the customer!'

He walked out of the shop and lit a cigarette. This was his guilty secret, something he resorted to under special circumstances. And he really needed to clear his head. Lying to his best friend was a burden on his soul, but it had to be done. Hadn't he promised Rachna Tripathi that he would look out for them? But if Prachand ever found out that Yatish was using a petty criminal, even for a good cause, he would be upset, not being fond of secrets or criminals.

It was clear from his last conversation that Prachand had suspected something. But did he really believe that Yatish was capable of betraying him? Tears pricked his eyes. Chachu Tripathi had called in the morning, desperate for some news but Yatish had nothing to share.

Bhima Shankar had come into his life about a year ago. Who cared if he was a petty criminal? He was an even better mole. Under the radar, connected, enterprising and greedy, an ideal choice for tricky jobs. But what seemed like a great plan was clogging his intestines now.

Ignoring the state of his insides, he ordered food from a stall he was passing by. While waiting for his spicy order, he fished out his phone and started calling Bhima Shankar. Five rings. No answer. Why hadn't the man been taking his calls? All he had been told was that they were headed to Mumbai. There has been no word ever since. He realized dolefully that his constipation wasn't going away any time soon.

Meanwhile at Ratan Lal Nagar Police Station, Navin Srivastava was trying to update Murli Dayal, the DG of Police, on the case.

'Sir, tea?'

'No, Srivastava.'

'Sir, samosa?'

'No, Srivastava.'

'Sir, any other snack?'

'Srivastava, I'm not here for a picnic.'

Navin Srivastava did not like Murli Dayal much. Every other senior of his had afforded enough opportunities for ego massages and appeasement, but this one was out of his league. This was their second meeting since his posting to the city and this lack of control was making his stomach rumble.

'So, Srivastava, what information do we have from the theatre group?' Murli Dayal asked with a raised eyebrow.

Navin Srivastava's chest fluffed up like a proud male turkey's.

'Sir, our detailed investigation has solved this case.'

'Can I have the information first, Srivastava, before you start patting yourself on the back?' The chest deflated. 'Sir, the car did belong to the group.'

'So who did it, and why?'

'After interrogating some of the staff, we found out that there were two actors, also part of the management team, who were kicked out a few months ago because of some fraudulent money transactions. They threatened to burn the place down while leaving. We caught up with them. All it took was a little bit of roughing up and they sang like birds.'

'But what is the connection with Shailaja Kapoor?'

'That's another angle we had to investigate to make sense of the whole picture. It turns out that these two actors were friends of Sujit Oberoi's driver. The driver was also Sujit's man Friday and the one responsible for the introduction. They agreed to abduct Shailaja Kapoor, hold her till a ransom was paid and were to be rewarded handsomely for this job, a big chunk going to the driver as well.'

'So that crook of a husband was behind all of this?' Murli Dayal looked skywards as if apologising to his ghost. 'May his soul rest in peace. Anyway, who would have thought that a man with his means would try such desperate things for money? But...' he seemed to be in some thought. 'Who would pay the ransom? The mother?'

'Yes, sir. Shailaja Kapoor had always been the sole beneficiary. The mother, a guardian.'

'Hmm. That's a bit odd,' Murli Dayal said. 'And where is Shailaja Kapoor if her abductors have been found?'

'This is where it gets confounding. They stole the car from their ex-office using some keys they had access to, kidnapped Shailaja Kapoor, brought her back to the office because they knew it was shut for a long Holi break. But they swear that she escaped on the very night of the abduction.'

'She escaped?'

'Yes, sir. You see, they're just actors and did not know much about holding abductees. According to them, they went to another room for a short nap and on waking up, found that she was gone. They said they were secretly happy because she was too talkative and kept lecturing and threatening them.'

'They could be lying but that's for us to find out. Has an alert been issued? Maybe she is hurt and is looking for help.'

'Yes, sir! Information, picture, all of it.'

'Well, I must say you and your team aren't as dumb as I'd expected,' confessed Murli Dayal.

It was unclear whether he had just been complimented or insulted so Navin Srivastava decided to maintain status quo.

'I'm hoping you've been in touch with Mumbai and have sent a team there to interview the mother?'

'Yes, sir. And I'll be joining them very soon,' said Navin Srivastava, smiling confidently while secretly sweating as no team of his was anywhere close to Mumbai. There had just been some calls with the Mumbai team and an initial conversation with Shailaja Kapoor's mother, even though jurisdiction was a problem while investigating in another city. Something else struck him then. He would have to seek his wife's permission to go to Mumbai.

'Okay. Please keep me posted. Remember, this is a priority as it's getting too much attention. The sooner we solve this, the better.'

'Yes, sir.' A salute later, Navin Srivastava relaxed visibly as his least favourite person walked away.

He had just about left the room when Murli Dayal turned around once again and Navin Srivastava inadvertently sucked in his stomach in anticipation.

'With the abduction story clear, that detective and his wife are in the clear now, at least with respect to the kidnapping. Is that correct?'

'Yes sir, but they keep popping up in all our investigations. And the detective was found standing next to the dead body. The wife was on the scene as well.'

'Hmm. Investigate. I'm just saying; don't start off a witch hunt while trying to get to the truth. Explore all angles.'

'Yes, sir!' Navin Srivastava clocked in another salute, very clear that he wanted to do exactly that. This case needed a quick closure and something in his bones told him the answers lay with the owner of Kanpur Khoofiya Pvt. Ltd.

CHAPTER 37

Louvar Lodge was a compact and clean hole in the wall on a side street of Andheri East. No one knew the place was named after the Louvre in Paris. Given the target audience the hotel catered to, even Shree Sai Residency or Goodluck Lodge would have been a good enough choice; but the owner, whose dream it had been to visit Paris and the Louvre, died chasing it and converted his hotel into an ode to his one wish. Every nook and cranny of this tiny lodge was covered with hideous paintings that looked like they had been produced by baby elephants in a fit of rage. But this was exactly the kind of hole in the wall that suited the needs of one Mr Abdul and his Missus Fatima Begum, the occupants of Room No. 8.

Prachand thought it best to hide their real identities and use some disguise in order to roam the city freely. He already had a beard and moustache on. Some quick surma and befitting headgear from his bag was all he needed to transform into Mr Abdul. As for Vidya, some more makeup and covering most of her head and face with a dupatta did the job.

The morning was spent in bed, recovering from the long, eventful and tiring journey. An afternoon stroll had then led them to a snack centre. That's where Vidya fell in love with a steaming bun filled with crispy fried potato and mesmerising condiments. The humble vada pav had claimed its latest victim and she didn't stop eating till an alarmed Prachand physically restrained her.

Exactly an hour after the meal, she started throwing up with such force that anyone would suspect she was secretly being charged with Duracell batteries. A few hours of this made her retire to bed, burping Eno bubbles.

Prachand stroked her head and watched her as she slept, feeling another pang of guilt. She was here because of his choices (barring her food ones). He desperately wished there was some way in which she could be sent back home. For now, he would have to be content with getting her some more antacids before she woke up.

The manager flashed him a smile as he walked out of the lodge. Prachand returned the greeting with an aadab by curling his palm slightly. He had been feeling melancholy all day and Vidya's state wasn't helping. The medical shop appeared to his left but he kept walking. Half an hour later, he found himself at a small garden, with a board that said 'Nana Nani Park'. Walking in, he sat down on one of the benches and was possessed by an immense sense of nostalgia and longing. Asking Yatish about his family wasn't an option anymore. All he wanted to do was connect with someone from home. So intense was the desire that he dialled his mother's number, knowing that he was taking a risk. The phone was picked up after two rings.

'Ma? It's me.'

'My son!' He could hear Rachna Tripathi crying.

'Ma, don't scream!' Prachand begged her. 'If the policemen are posted outside, they'll hear you.' Despite his requests, she wouldn't stop wailing.

'Ma, listen to me!' he finally had to raise his voice to cut through the din. 'We are okay. Vidya and I are not in Kanpur anymore.'

'What,' shrieked Rachna Tripathi.

'Don't repeat it! Don't say it out aloud. Please!'

'Where are you?'

'We are in another city to get answers. It might take us a few days. Don't worry.'

'Don't worry? I don't feel like doing anything, Ammaji is barely eating, Bhushan refuses to sing or study, your Chachu is distraught and your Pitaji's blood pressure is very high! We are all miserable. Please come home.'

'I'm sorry,' Prachand apologised meekly. 'Just know that we are okay. And that this will be over very soon. Please let Vidya's father know, very discreetly. They must be worried.'

'They are.'

'Have the police come around asking any more questions?'

'No. They just follow us around and ask if you have been in touch. Some reporters are keeping a constant vigil as well. Horrible people. They especially upset your father.'

'And has Yatish been in touch?'

'Yatish? Not since the last few days really.'

'Ma, please listen to me carefully. Do not tell him anything about this call.'

'What is wrong, Prachand?' Rachna Tripathi's stomach knotted up at the very possibility of being expected to keep a secret.

'Nothing. Just don't tell him anything for the time being.'

After promising to update them soon, Prachand hung up.

The short conversation brought him a modicum of peace. He picked up the few items that he needed on his way back, but his mind kept taking him back to all the questions that needed immediate answering. Where was Shailaja Kapoor? Was she alive? Was Yatish really involved in some way or was it a misunderstanding? Who was the man that attacked him? And the biggest question of them all: why would Pamela Kapoor help them when they finally met her?

CHAPTER 38

Hirwa mooed dolefully. Once a lover of the limelight, she was now fed up with all the attention. Reporters, photographers, the police, she wondered why none of her usual tactics were working to keep them away from Awadh Niwas. She watched the drama unfold and missed seeing her friend Prachand who chatted with her every day and fed her hay.

Meanwhile, inside Awadh Niwas, Rachna Tripathi knew exactly what was happening but was frustrated that she couldn't do anything to make it go away. Ever since Prachand and Vidya's departure, she barely managed to navigate daily chores and Ammaji's demands. Her remaining time was spent making pickles. With a vengeance. Nothing helped with the distraction. No house work, no errands, no conversations, no Gwaltoli Gilehris. But pickles were the psychologist she never hired. Through the chopping, washing, pickling and drying, she spoke to them continuously and no one dared disturb her. Unlike the usual jar every few months, the count over a few days was rivalling the number of bricks used in the construction of the house. As a result, anyone who visited, including milkmen or reporters, were handed a jar of pickle.

Chachu Tripathi, Bhushan and Ammaji were flocked like birds in a row on the charpoy, watching her make *karele ka achaar*. Through the constant muttering, she suddenly giggled.

'Chachu, should we talk to a doctor?'

'No, son. I understand what she is going through.'

'But we are all dealing with it without going mental.'

'She hasn't gone mad. She was speaking very normally to Prachand when he called, wasn't she? I think it's just that she finds making pickles therapeutic. I mean, look at how much she has to do at her age. Being made to run around all the time...'

Ammaji coughed and cleared her throat.

'What I mean is,' Chachu Tripathi continued, with one eye on his mother, 'she is exhausted on a good day. Add to that the possibility of seeing her children behind bars, public ridicule and throw in this media and police circus. Isn't it enough to drive someone off the edge?'

'But Chachu she even tried to sell my guitar. Said she can purchase fifty more pickle jars with my trash.' Bhushan pouted.

Chachu Tripathi put an arm around his despondent nephew. 'She is in shock. Don't worry, son. Hang in there. She'll be fine, we'll be fine. Just let your brother sort this mess out and get home.'

'That's the other thing. I am angry that I can't do anything to help them. We answer questions, hide our faces and sit at home.'

'I do know one way in which only you can help, Bhushan.' Chachu Tripathi looked Bhushan in the eyes as his nephew puffed his meagre chest out, ready for the responsibility.

'Yes, Chachu?'

'Please sing fewer songs at night when you practice. It'll help us sleep better.'

Instead of fetching a tart response from Bhushan, this seemed to have cracked the usually distracted Ammaji, who started cackling away. And looking at his grandmother cracking up, his straight-lined mouth curved into a sheepish smile as well.

'Okay, Chachu.' He laughed.

'There is always much to laugh about in stressful times!' A familiar voice made them look up. Ammaji let out a torrent of wind as a distress signal and scowled. It was Navin Srivastava with his sidekick.

'Is the door open?' Chachu Tripathi asked politely, trying to make a point.

Navin Srivastava looked over his shoulder and then at Chachu Tripathi. 'No, but it wasn't locked either. And I never need an invite, do I?' He winked playfully but silence ensued.

'Why the sullen faces?' he asked while stepping carefully around the sea of pickle jars. 'Even that cow, or cow-cum-watch-dog, of yours outside didn't try and stop me today.' Rachna Tripathi merely grunted and returned to chopping radish stems.

'Is there something you came to talk about, Inspector Sahib?' Chachu Tripathi wanted to dispatch the portly cop from Awadh Niwas as quickly as possible, especially before his brother returned.

'As a matter of fact, I did. Much as I love your company,' he drawled. 'I wanted to gauge your levels of excitement, now that your fugitive family members have reached the City of Dreams.'

'City of Dreams?' asked Bhushan, exposing his enviable general knowledge of the world beyond Justin Bieber.

'Are Prachand and Vidya in Mumbai?' Rachna Tripathi had finally woken up from her pickled trance. She walked up to Navin Srivastava and shook his arm, leaving an oily palm print on him. 'Tell me.'

'Hey hey,' Navin Srivastava sprung out of his chair as Inspector Ranganathan tried to clean the stain with his handkerchief.

'Tell me, are they in Mumbai?' To her, Mumbai stood for the big bad world full of crime, violence and Bollywood. Now her son was in its clutches.

'That's what our sources tell us. Two people who looked very much like them were spotted at a railway station there. But you already know that, don't you?'

'I don't know what you're talking about' the pickle maestro shrugged.

'Not a very convincing liar,' the inspector clicked his tongue. 'We know you received a call from an unknown number yesterday. Unfortunately we couldn't trace it, but I will bet my own hat that it was Prachand calling you.'

'Insector Sahib, you're badgering her now,' Chachu Tripathi intervened. She said she has no idea. Now if you could please shed some more light on this information for us. Are they really in Mumbai? But why?'

'That's what I came to ask you all. I find it impossible to believe that such a loving son would keep you in the dark and establish no contact.' Then he leaned in. 'We just want to talk to him. If there's nothing to hide, where's the need to run? If I talk to him, I might be able to make this go away,' he lied.

'Well, we really don't know where he is, Inspector,' Chachu Tripathi said.

Navin Srivastava got up. 'Okay, then. I tried. I'm going to Mumbai soon. And if I really do find them there, let's just say you won't have trouble locating his whereabouts for he will be in prison for a long time,' he declared ominously, turned on his heels and left with his lone entourage.

'Kambakhat,' muttered Ammaji. She wanted to set this man's hair on fire. Maybe that was the only way to get him off her poor grandson's back.

Just then Yatish walked in. While the others started chatting with him, Rachna Tripathi's hands had stopped moving. Her eyes were fixed on Yatish and the only words that echoed in her head were, 'Just don't tell him anything for the time being'. She had to prevent her family from talking about Prachand and Vidya being in Mumbai.

'Yatish, why don't you come to the kitchen?' she hollered abruptly. She washed her hands and walked into the kitchen. Despite feeling immense guilt, she knew she couldn't do anything to further jeopardise Prachand and Vidya's situation. Yatish Bhatnagar obediently walked in after her. He opened up a packet of hot samosas and placed them before her.

'Here, Mataji, eat hot snacks and cool your mind! Forget about that Inspector. So, what did you want to talk about?'

She stared at him, her stomach in knots. What should I do, she wondered.

'Are you alright?' Yatish enquired. 'You look like you've seen a ghost.'

'I ... I'm fine.' Her mind was racing, looking for any reason to distract him. 'I ... I need you to take five pickle jars to your mother.'

'Oh, that's great. I'll take them tomorrow.'

'No ... now!'

Looking at the wild look on her face, Yatish nodded and walked away with the jars. Rachna Tripathi sighed. She was now qualified to take on Kaikeye's role in the Ramlila play next year.

CHAPTER 39

'Sir, are you comfortable in your room?' the receptionist asked with a wide Colgate smile. An array of aromatic incense sticks had freshly been lined up before a picture of Shirdi Sai Baba and a large glass replica of the Louvre. The deification of the Louvre was possibly an important directive in the hotel's instruction manual and as all good, salaried employees; he was following through without any questions or objections.

'Yes, thanks Mr Gupta.' Prachand was skimming through newspapers while a small TV unit mounted on the wall was tuned to a news channel. His ears perked up when he heard the mention of Shailaja Kapoor. Apparently, she still had a respectable fan following and some of them got together and performed a havan praying for her safety.

'What a waste,' exclaimed the receptionist.

'Huh?' Prachand lowered the paper.

'All these film stars, small or big, are so pampered and adored, but they repay us by cheating on their taxes. So much money, so much fame but they don't even pay their taxes honestly.' Mr Gupta shook his head.

'But Mr Gupta, the report is not about tax evasion. The poor lady is missing.'

'Who knows what's happening with these people. What is true, what is false. Maybe she ran away to evade tax. They are a funny lot. I should know. I was also an artist, you know.' Mr Gupta announced proudly. 'My whole family has worked in Bollywood.'

'Really? That's amazing.'

'My father had a rental business. He was famous. Do you remember the ornate skirt that Hema Malini wore in Sholay? In the famous dance sequence towards the end?'

'Somewhat.' Prachand struggled trying to recall a skirt but could only conjure images of Gabbar, the dacoit. 'So, that ghagra was from his shop?'

'No, the shiny lace at the bottom! My father custom made it.'

'Aah.' Prachand smiled, trying to sound awed.

'And do you remember *Satte pe Satta*?'

'Of course! Classic movie.'

'My elder brother was in it. With Hema Malini.'

'Really? Wow!'

'You remember the scene where Amitach Bachchan and Hema Malini meet?'

'Sure. And he mistakes her for another girl and she gets upset with him.'

'Yes, and he leaves her a watermelon that an orderly hands over to her.'

'That man was your brother?'

'No, no, my brother was the man who gives the orderly the watermelon. Those idiots just edited out his part from the scene.'

Prachand couldn't articulate a response but Mr Gupta, in his own estimation, had clearly established his family as Bollywood veterans.

'I also started working in movies but then I decided to retire at my peak.'

'That's a dignified way to go.' Prachand said, wondering what the man's absurd association with Bollywood could have been.

'I used to dance. Should I show you?!' he enquired enthusiastically.

'Maybe a bit later,' Prachand suggested politely. 'So when did you retire?'

'When I was thirty-five, I became a spot boy on Subhash Ghai's film set. People used to line up after me to get closer to him. The fame was getting to me, affecting my family life, so I exited. My friend owned this place and I decided to join him and the rest, as they say, is history.' He shrugged humbly, with the shoulders of someone who had borne the terrible brunt of fame.

Prachand sensed an opportunity. 'So, Mr Gupta, you yourself are a celebrity, would you know a bit about where these stars live?'

'But of course. You need to know where your ex-colleagues live. Besides, my contacts in the industry keep me updated.'

'My wife is a huge fan of Amitabh Bachchan, Shah Rukh Khan and ... Shailaja Kapoor as well.'

'Really?' he enquired, surprised. 'I don't come across very many Shailaja Kapoor fans. She only acted in a few movies, you know. I think she is more famous because of her mother.'

'Pamela Kapoor, right?'

'Yes. She was a stunning beauty of her times. Didn't act in very many movies but her looks could kill. From what I can remember, she married a very wealthy and politically connected man who died a few years after Shailaja was born.'

'Wow, Mr Gupta! You seem to know everything about everyone. Say, will you be able to write down all these addresses for me on a piece of paper? That way we can plan out the sightseeing.'

'Sure. Let me write it down for you,' he said pulling out a writing pad with Rakhi Sawant on the cover.

'I've added a list of other places you can go to spot celebrities. If you are going to see Shah Rukh Khan, then you might as well try Salman Khan who is nearby. All you need to do is stand under the Galaxy Apartment building in Bandstand every evening after 7 p.m. You might catch him on his way back from the gym. My friend is a pantry manager at Gold's Gym so he knows his timings,' he announced officiously.

'Any idea what would be the best time to meet Pamela Kapoor?'

'I'm not very sure but I've heard she is largely homebound.' He then exchanged a few text messages with someone and handed Prachand the paper. 'I found out the number for Kapoor Villa. Here you go.'

Prachand had left the room directionless and dispirited, but now he had an address and number in hand, somewhere they could start. He found Vidya awake, propped up in bed. Prachand sat beside her and stroked her head.

'Would you like some more vada pav?' he joked.

Vidya made a face like she wanted to throw up.

Prachand updated her about the call he had made and the information he had managed to glean from the chatty receptionist.

'That's good news, Prachi,' Vidya said while emptying a quarter bottle of Digene syrup. 'But do you want to call first?'

'It might not be the safest thing for us to do but I'll have to. Apparently, you need appointments to see them.' Vidya nodded and then became silent. She leaned sideways to rest her head on Prachand's shoulder.

'You know, I really miss home, our small but normal life. If God ever delivers us from this mess, I'll never complain about our clients, or extra snacks being ordered, or Ma's complaints about my cooking, or...'

'Shhhhh,' Prachand whispered, hugging her. 'Very soon, Viddu, very soon. Oh, before I forget, do you know how to make authentic "Muslim" biryani?'

Vidya looked shocked. 'Absolutely not, Prachand. You know I can barely make an omelette.'

'Well, Fatima Begum, Mr Gupta downstairs is insistent he needs a recipe for his wife, so we best get to it.'

'Ya Allah!' exclaimed Vidya, holding her head.

CHAPTER 40

'Hello! This is Bertha. How can I help you?' a voice announced in a crisp accent.

'Madam, hello. I'm ... Pr ... Pritam Singh from Kanpur.'

'Yes. What can I do for you?'

'I want to meet Madam Kapoor.'

'Who is that? Pamela Kapoor, you mean?'

'Yes, yes.'

'What is the nature of work?'

'Good nature, madam. I laugh, I smile ... a lot.' Prachand was trying his best to piece together words from her heavily accented voice.

'Oh God!' muttered the voice. 'I meant, why do you want to meet her?'

'Umm. Personal work, madam. Very urgent.'

'Everyone says that. She has already finished her quota for donations this year.'

'But I don't want money, madam.'

'She will not be able to attend any event currently.'

'Event?'

'Well, unless there are free gifts or a free holiday provided by the sponsors.'

'I'm not doing any event, madam.'

'No fashion show appearances either. It's very difficult in her wheelchair. Everyone says there is ramp access but it's always a problem.'

Prachand could barely conceal the frustration in his voice towards this chattering monkey of a woman. 'It's my personal work, madam. I told you.'

She sounded miffed. 'If you can't tell me what work then I can't help you.'

The line went dead.

The question on the table was now what.

'I had a feeling this might not work,' Prachand said pacing the room. 'She stays in Pali Hill. Let's get there and figure out a way to her.'

'Give me five minutes,' Vidya said and disappeared into the bathroom.

'I'll put my beard and moustache back on till then,' he called out after her.

―

Kapoor Villa could easily be seen from a distance. It was part of the tribe of luxurious bungalows standing out amidst the fashionable high rises that dotted the Pali Hill skies. With a creamy marble – like exterior, large wooden gates allowed a partial view of the well-manicured gardens flanking the short driveway to the bungalow. In contrast, the outside walls were lined with a row of pan-beedi and grocery shops, that resembled inquisitive ants wanting to breach the boundaries and pour into the fantastical world beyond the walls.

Prachand and Vidya had stopped a few buildings away and were relishing some sugarcane juice to combat the humidity. It was 10.30 a.m. and the shops were just opening for business.

'There's a security cabin right behind the gate. I saw it when the gate opened. Trying to approach the bungalow from the front or the sides is pointless. Let's try the back.'

'If we are scaling walls illegally, that will officially be our first crime,' said Vidya, looking uncomfortable.

'Do you have a better idea?'

Vidya slurped her drink noisily and shrugged.

'Then let's at least give it a shot. We are running out of time and money.'

They started walking towards the house when Prachand's gaze fell on a man lighting a cigarette. Right by the gate of Kapoor Villa. He turned, saw Prachand and froze. It was the stalker from the station. White rage simmered inside Prachand thinking of the brutal way in which he had been attacked. Without a word to Vidya, his pace quickened to reach the man who was glowering at him now, with a set jaw. Vidya called after her husband but he was a man on a mission.

As the distance between them reduced, Prachand continued to stare, as did the man. Suddenly, the man darted towards Prachand. Instead of standing his ground and getting the answers he desperately needed, Prachand broke into a run. 'Vidya! Wait for me here!' he hollered as his voice faded.

Within ten minutes, Prachand had streaked through most of the neighbourhood and he now felt like a local. However, the hilly residences were sucking the life out of his lungs and legs. Every time he looked back, the strange stalker seemed to be getting closer. Out of shape and out of breath, Prachand soon turned a corner and found himself outside what looked like the back walls of the Kapoor Villa. The man was closing in and Prachand had no option but to scale a wall. No sooner had he started doing this than the stranger stopped and started backing away, looking puzzled. Then he disappeared around the corner.

'You keep walking, you crook!' screamed Prachand perched on top of the wall, infused with renewed bravado, now with the goon at a safe distance.

Imminent danger having being averted, he wanted to get back to Vidya first. As luck would have it, the wall seemed freshly painted and Prachand felt like a mouse caught in a sticky trap. While un-gluing himself, he lost his balance and fell inside the property, streaked with paint. That's when he heard the faint growl and turned around.

A big black beast of a dog was sitting erect, fangs exposed. Every time he growled, Prachand had a vision of his intestines being chewed by the reincarnation of Yamraj sitting before him. As the beast inched closer, Prachand started screaming the Hanuman Chalisa. The chanting continued as he ran to the nearest tree, but not before part of his trouser landed in the dog's mouth.

'I need to get off the ground!' he screamed to no one in particular. He ran as fast as his tired legs could carry him and started climbing the smallest tree he could find.

He recalled, most pointlessly, that this was the second time in the last few weeks when he had swung off a tree.

'Who is it?' he heard two voices coming his way. The dog's constant barking had attracted all the attention.

Now he apologetically peered into the faces of two angry security guards.

'Thief!' hollered one of them.

'No, no, sir. I am not a thief. I had made an appointment.'

'To hang from the tree and be chewed by Dabbu?' sneered the other.

'Dabbu?'

'Yes, Dabbu,' he said pointing at the barking beast.

'Please, just take me to Pamela Madam. I'll explain everything.'

After a thorough check, he was taken indoors, while pleading with them to let Vidya through the gates. She joined him at the beginning of a long corridor and they walked along to emerge in an enormous living room. Sitting there in a black wheelchair was a beautiful and elegant-looking lady. Curious brown eyes peered out of thin white frames.

'Who are you?' she asked Prachand.

'I am here to help you, madam. You must believe me!'

As an instant validation for his credibility, the fake beard decided to leave his chin and waft to the ground.

CHAPTER 41

Vidya couldn't take her eyes off Pamela Kapoor, with her alabaster complexion and soft brown eyes, her thick silver hair, arched neck and beautifully defined features told a story of past glory. She was wearing a long cotton dress with a silk scarf around her neck and small diamonds dotted her ears. Sitting in a wheelchair, she was a portrait of dignity and grace. Vidya had never seen anyone so lovely. Meanwhile, she also wondered how long the lovely lady would take before calling the police.

When she was asked to step into the house, she was relieved thinking that her reliable partner had somehow managed to gain entry to the house after giving the crazy guy a slip. Now as she looked at the paint-streaked man before her with a false beard at his feet, she started mentally preparing for their next adventure: behind bars.

'Madam, he wanted to steal,' announced one of the security guards.

'No madam, I told you, I don't need anything. I just wanted to speak with you,' said Prachand, while gracefully retrieving his beard from the floor.

'Breaking into someone's house is not the best approach,' Pamela Kapoor finally spoke, in a soft voice.

'Madam, I tried calling but I couldn't get an appointment.'

'Bertha?' called out Pamela Kapoor. A petite lady in a tight-fitting red business suit came tottering out in high heels.

'Yes, Ma'am?' She nodded her head towards Pamela Kapoor.

'Did this man try to make an appointment to meet with me?'

Bertha seemed like she was trying to remember.

'Ma'am, I think this might be Pritam Singh, the person who would not tell me why he wanted to meet you.'

'You could have tried to find out why.'

'I did!' Bertha said in a high-pitched voice. 'But if he still wouldn't tell me what business he had with you, how could I let him come here? What if he were a criminal or something?'

'How dare you call my husband a criminal!' spat out Vidya. 'Back home he is very well respected. He is a private investigator, the smartest one!'

'What does a private detective want with an old lady?' Pamela Kapoor asked with a quizzical look.

'Madam, for that I need to speak with you alone.'

Before Pamela Kapoor could respond, Bertha jumped into the fray. 'Then you will have to go and explain to the police. How can we leave madam with a stranger who broke into the house! I'm calling the police!'

Prachand's usual reservoir of patience had dried up and he snapped. He decided he had had enough of running around, hiding, pleading, being pushed around. The beard was the first casualty. He threw it on the ground, pulling out his moustache next. Then he folded his legs and sat down.

'Call the police then! Go ahead. Get that Dabbu, get him to bite me. I don't care. Just remember, this was your last chance at finding your daughter.'

Pamela Kapoor froze. Her eyes widened and filled with tears.

'You ... you know about Shailu?'

Prachand held his silence.

'Everyone, please leave us alone,' she announced and turned to Prachand again. 'Please, son, tell me where she is.'

Vidya walked over to Prachand and knelt beside him. 'I know how you're feeling, Prachi, but isn't this exactly what we wanted? She wants to listen to us. You want to help her. Come on. Let's talk to her.'

Prachand relented and stood up. They were both directed to a seating area nearby. Pamela Kapoor pressed a remote-like panel on the side of a chair that propelled her forward.

Once they were alone, she was full of questions. Prachand filled her in patiently.

'So, as I explained, we were keeping an eye on your daughter. Someone asked us to. If we knew she was in danger, we would have reported it to the police straight away.' Prachand couldn't help but feel a pang of guilt while narrating the facts. 'It was standard surveillance and she was under our watch for a few days till ... you know ... she was abducted.'

Pamela Kapoor shuddered and Prachand decided to give her some time to collect herself.

'Did she seem troubled to you? In any way?'

'Well, we did see her buying a gun, and she had a few arguments with her husband. By the way, was he also in some trouble? We ... happened to go through some of his belongings and it seemed as if he was on the run. Were you aware of what might have led him to leave town?'

'Aware?' she laughed. 'I know all of it. To the world he was a wealthy and established man, a sweetheart of the jet set and social circles. But he was struggling with loans. Money he had borrowed from dangerous people. He had to keep the charade going so he got sucked in deeper and deeper. He even came begging to me for money because some bad people were after him. And why do you think he was in Kanpur with all his baggage and his "estranged" wife? Because he was hiding from them!' She paused, wringing her hands. 'That rascal! I told Shailu he was not good for her. But she wouldn't listen. I ... I know he is dead but ... I can't forgive him. He destroyed her in a way. She had a delicate mental constitution ever since her father passed, but Sujit's jealousy and then his obsession with money made her more unstable. But I still can't imagine how he could stoop so low as to have his own wife abducted.'

Prachand and Vidya exchanged a look. He cleared his throat.

'You mean he was behind Shailaja's abduction? The police know this?'

Pamela Kapoor looked confused. 'Of course. Didn't you know that already? The police have been in touch with me. He had hired some ... some drama company, actors, I think to abduct her and keep her till he could get a ransom from me. Greedy pig.'

The shy Prachand Tripathi stood up right then and there, and started dancing. As passionately as he could. In pin-drop silence, his arms and legs moved to the silent happy tune of freedom that was playing inside his head. He stopped and shook Vidya by the shoulders.

'Viddu, we are no longer under suspicion for the abduction. Do you realize how amazing that is?'

Vidya smiled while trying to draw his attention to the shocked woman behind him, possibly assessing his mental stability.

He sat down with a flourish. 'I'm sorry.' He smiled. 'You cannot imagine what a relief it was to hear that. So then, Shailaja ji is with you?'

'With me?' Pamela Kapoor asked, with tears welling up again. 'She escaped her captors and no one knows where she is.'

Prachand's face fell again. 'So then, we are back to square one. We are not wanted for the abduction but she is still missing. And they still think we were somehow involved in Sujit Oberoi's murder.'

'Son, if you can help me find Shailaja, I am sure that with her testimony and the light she throws on the case, your innocence will be proven,' explained Pamela Kapoor.

'Madam Kapoor, this city is completely new to us. We can hardly find our own way back to the hotel. How could we possibly know where to look for her?'

'All I know is that you are a godsend. The police don't seem to have any answers and are going around in circles. There is so much pressure on them due to my husband's connections that they just want *any* answer instead of the *right* answers. The longer we wait the more trouble it will spell for Shailu. You are a detective. At least try. For this old woman, if nothing else.' Tears streamed down her face as she held Prachand's hand.

'I can't promise you anything, but I'll try my best,' he relented. Her eyes twinkled with gratitude. 'That's all I ask.'

'Also, it just occurred to me that you have a lot of help and servants who have seen us. Will they...'

'These are my people and their lips are sealed. Don't worry at all,' she assured them.

It was time to leave and figure out the least conspicuous exit strategy. Pamela Kapoor had a suggestion. 'There is a side entrance that opens onto a small by-lane adjacent to the house. You can slip out from there without drawing too much attention.' They moved towards an exit when Pamela Kapoor stopped them. 'Wait. It's getting dark. Alexa, switch on garden porch lights.' Prachand looked at the door, waiting for Alexa, the maid to appear.

'Switching on garden porch lights,' a voice boomed.

In response, the path lining the side garden lit up and Vidya leapt into the air. 'What sorcery is this?'

Pamela Kapoor laughed. 'Don't be scared. It's just Alexa. Let me call the driver. He will show you the way. Alexa, call driver.'

Just as Alexa called the driver, Vidya shot out of the door like a bullet, without waiting for Prachand.

CHAPTER 42

'Prachand, there is so much free food in the fridge!' Vidya was rummaging excitedly through the hotel minibar.

'Well I'm not sure it's free.' Prachand had his doubts. After only a few days in the city, he was sure of one thing. Whatever seemed to be free usually wasn't. Which is why he was also wary of Pamela Kapoor's offer. She had insisted they stay at a friend's private and uber luxury boutique hotel, of course, to be sponsored by her despite all their protests. The owners would be discreet and they could enjoy their luxury hideaway. When Prachand refused, she asked him to consider himself hired by her and that she would deduct this stay from his fee.

'I think we won't have much of a fee left after she has deducted the tariff for this hotel,' Vidya worriedly whispered to Prachand.

Prachand was also given a list of all of Shailaja's friends. They had no idea where she was but learning more about her from her small circle of trusted people couldn't hurt. It was imperative that all of this be done smartly without making anyone suspicious.

The luxury boutique hotel was nothing the Tripathis could ever have imagined. Everything seemed to be made of glass, gloss and metals. There were large art installations all over the hotel. Life-sized paintings adorned the walls and mobile human installations could be seen walking around and interacting with guests. Vidya had bumped into a man standing still in the reception area, with what looked like a commode and lid positioned on his top half. The rest of him, barring his eyes, was painted white. Vidya shrieked as he walked passed.

'Madam,' the face in the commode spoke softly. 'I am not a ghost. I represent the human condition. Everything we say or hear is worthy of being flushed down the toilet these days. Don't you feel life is too chaotic and the only place you can truly get some peace is in the bathroom?'

'Ammaji is also finding peace there,' Vidya added helpfully, latching on to 'toilet': the only familiar word in this monologue.

'Exactly, you get it then.' He smiled and pressed a button he was holding. From somewhere on his body, the sound of a flushing toilet was audible. He bowed and walked away.

Now safely tucked in their room, she was munching her way through all the snacks in the mini bar. Prachand meanwhile was making notes.

'Do you know, Vidya, that man who was chasing after me near Kapoor Villa was the same man who attacked me in the railway station toilet?'

'What? You were attacked in the toilet!' Vidya dropped the pack of cashews she had just opened. 'Why didn't you tell me this before?'

Kanpur Khoofiya Pvt. Ltd

'I didn't want you to worry,' Prachand shrugged. 'But I wish I could find out what he is after. I could tell that he was surprised when he saw me outside Shailaja Kapoor's house.'

'Because he didn't expect to see you there?'

'Maybe. Hard to get any answers sitting here, isn't it?'

While Vidya was checking out the many amenities in their room, Prachand continued to pour over the list he had been given. He had called some of the people on it. Though some had sounded suspicious, most others were satisfied with the explanation that the police was doing another round of questioning over the phone. So far, this exercise had yielded no results.

After another two hours of calling, Prachand had managed to gain one vital piece of information about a place Shailaja Kapoor used to frequent.

'It's an ashram. In a place called Ut ... Utan, I think. It's quite far from here,' he updated Vidya while checking his notes. 'A friend of hers called Ronnie told me she used to go there every week, at times accompanied by him. Most importantly, he said when he was there last week; he might have heard her name mentioned by one of the staff members. But he couldn't be sure. We should go there.'

'Rani? A boy's name? That's strange.' Vidya sounded confused.

'Not Raaani, Ro ... Ronnnie,' Prachand enunciated, to correct her.

Vidya nodded, secretly wondering what Ronnie meant.

'If she really is in Mumbai, wouldn't she just go home?'

'Maybe not. It's possible she thinks her life is still in danger, Viddu. We don't know who paid us to follow her.

Was it her husband? I can't be sure. I'm sure she isn't either. The ashram is the only place where she seems to have been spoken about since the abduction. Isn't it worth a visit then?'

'Okay,' Vidya said giving her consent.

'The ashram offers tours for visitors, I hear. That's all we need. But from my research it sounds like a fancy place, Viddu. A lot of celebrities and politicians patronise it. Which means there must be a lot of security. We need to be careful to look the part as well.'

Vidya bristled. 'What do you mean, Prachi? So I don't look fancy enough because I wear Indian clothes? You know what? I don't care. I don't want to blend in.'

'Calm down, Viddu,' Prachand tried appeasing his irate wife. 'You know you look beautiful in anything you wear. It's just that if we don't look the part, they might not even let us in.'

The logic eventually melted her guard but she still snorted in irritation. 'I don't have any modern clothes. No jeans-pant. Nothing.'

Prachand smiled. 'Then let's go shopping!'

Prachand's smile was replaced by palpitations when he saw the prices of the dresses at the shopping arcade. Vidya seemed to be reaching out for the most expensive ones. Oblivious of the price tags, she had seized the moment and was thoroughly enjoying herself.

'How about this one, Prachi?' she preened, twirling around. Prachand nodded appreciatively.

She picked up another yellow-and-white dress. It was conservative and long, but stylish. 'Maybe I'll try this one as well.'

Kanpur Khoofiya Pvt. Ltd

Prachand's throat went dry, trying to remember how much he had left in his wallet. Ammaji's stash had steadily depleted and he didn't know how long they would be able to survive with the paltry sum in hand. Now this makeover had turned into a complete shopping spree, which he could ill afford. But he didn't have the heart to stop Vidya. It was the first glimpse of happiness he had seen on her face since this wild goose chase had started.

'Are you from UP?' asked the friendly man behind the counter, as Vidya went into the changing room.

Prachand nodded, smiling. 'How did you know?'

'I can always tell,' he smiled back.

'Be careful!' he whispered conspiratorially.

'About what?' Prachand lowered his voice as well.

'All the men get their wives to the city. Then the simpleton women take in the city air and their heads get turned.'

'How?'

'They first start asking for things. Then they want to go to the cinema, eat out, and avoid house work.'

'So, yours is in control then?' Prachand humoured him.

This assumption seemed to touch a raw nerve. The exuberant shopkeeper suddenly looked defeated.

'I am living with my friend in the next shop for the last four days. My wife got angry and threw me out of the house.'

Prachand wanted to laugh out loud in light of the recent wisdom shared with him, but he said sympathetically, 'That's so sad. At least your friend is with you.'

The shopkeeper brightened up. 'Oh yes, sir. That's my great solace. There are many of us to keep each other company. Most of the liftmen, construction workers, taxi drivers, shopkeepers in my locality are from UP and Bihar, suffering the same fate,' he announced warmly.

Prachand smiled. 'Great. And don't worry. I'll try to keep my wife under control.'

The shopkeeper looked satisfied, as if his Good Samaritan deed for the day was done.

When Vidya came out of the changing room again, Prachand smiled with pride. She looked lovely! Her long hair had been set free and was cascading down her shoulders, middle parting had moved sidewards, making her look very different. She had even applied red lipstick; pouting and posing like the women he had seen in advertisements.

'Not bad?' she enquired, loving the effect she was having on her husband. 'Now all I need is a nice pair of shoes with this dress.'

Prachand's eyes opened further. 'Shoes?'

Vidya looked at him, surprised. 'Of course! And by the way, after that we need to get you a nice shirt and shoes as well. You're fooling no one with your current attire.'

The shopkeeper gave him a disappointed look.

CHAPTER 43

The ashram was a beautiful and spiritual escape for the high rollers and well heeled, sprawling across twenty acres of lush green landscaped gardens. While a sea of slums and hutments lined the extremities of the property, everything within the boundary wall was clean, pristine and heavenly. There were frequent protests from the MHADA colonies and hutment dwellers about the water supply that the ashram was usurping. But this part of the world brought them so much gossip, excitement and celebrity spotting that secretly they didn't really mind the forced coexistence with this strange world.

Alongside the east wall of the ashram, there was a small grassy patch of land where the local population collected to ease themselves early in the morning. They sometimes would be treated to a direct view of a terrace where celebrities and the glitterati were welcoming the rising sun as part of their daily yoga session. There was a mad rush every morning for the envious front-row seats. While the defecators were happy with this entertainment, the international subjects were happy to get a glimpse of 'real India' along with their rigorous yoga.

Oblivious to these matters or anything to do with the ashram, the passably sharp-looking Tripathis had finally made their way to its ivy-laden gates after an arduous, smelly, local train journey and a short bus ride. The local train ride had certainly been an experience. The sights, sounds and silent machinations of the seat mafia were bewildering and fascinating for the first-time visitors. Vidya had exchanged some sharp words with a group of ladies who pushed her out of her seat. Then the fisherwomen had arrived with their large baskets and her focus shifted to protecting her new dress, shoes and styled hair. Prachand hadn't had any great luck either. On stepping into the compartment, he had immediately been inducted into a singing group. He was promptly handed a set of manjeeras and he played them in auto-mode, momentarily transported back home to Awadh Niwas with his mother and the Gwaltoli Gilehris.

'Viddu, I can smell fish.' Prachand scrunched up his nose.

'That's me!' Vidya admitted, dismayed at the smell and her crumpled new dress. 'All that money spent and I smell like I just took a dip in the fish tank!'

'Don't worry. Just use some deodorant,' Prachand tried to reassure her while smoothing out his own formal attire.

Vidya looked at him fidgeting and winked. 'Don't worry; whether I smell like fish or garlic, they will not be able to refuse the most handsome private detective.'

The guard at the entry booth near the gate greeted them after giving them a quick onceover.

'Hello, sir. Your car can be sent to the parking lot to the left.'

'We don't have ... I mean, our driver dropped us and left,' Prachand replied, trying to sound as snooty as possible.

The guard gave them an odd look. 'You have an appointment, sir?'

'No, but we would like a tour,' Prachand said firmly.

'No one is allowed without an appointment, sir,' the guard shrugged.

'Well, in that case, you will lose your job once they come to know that you've turned away the richest man in Kanpur,' Vidya announced haughtily. 'Come, let's go.' She tugged at Prachand's arm.

The watchman bolted out of the booth and stood in front of them. 'Sorry, sir. Sorry, madam,' he pleaded. 'Please don't complain. And I would never say no to anyone from UP. I am from Baliya.' He beamed. 'Come this way.'

As the gates opened, Vidya gasped. 'This is what heaven must look like, Prachand.' Her husband was equally speechless.

There were gardens with row upon row of flowers in every colour imaginable; as far as the eyes could see. Artificial streams dotting the landscape bubbled under wood bridges. The result was a pleasant gurgle of running water permeating the air. There were squirrels, rabbits and exotic birds strewn around in large numbers. Several modern huts and some brick structures, of what could be administrative buildings, were clustered in the centre. Lush green ivy consumed the boundary walls, resolute in containing this paradise within the ashram.

A serene-looking lady in a green flowing gown walked up to them.

'Oooooooom!' She folded her hands in a namaste.

'Namaste ... I'm ...' Prachand started.

'Chant with me ... Ommm!' she insisted with a smile.

Slightly bewildered, Prachand collected himself and complied.

'Are you here searching for the meaning of life, brother and sister?' the lady asked them.

'Ummm. Well, we were actually looking for ...' Vidya promptly responded as Prachand elbowed her.

'Yes. I don't know the meaning of life at all. I've come to find it.'

'I can see that both your chakras need a bit of cleansing,' she said looking around Prachand and Vidya who looked around as well, trying to locate the said chakras. 'Your troubles are clear to me. They surround you,' the lady continued philosophically.

'Here, to my left?'

'Above my head then?'

The lady raised an eyebrow. 'No, no. Chakras stem from the energy inside of you and as a result they take shape around you.'

On receiving some more blank stares, she abandoned her carefully rehearsed lines and came straight to the point, albeit politely, 'How can I help you?'

Finally hearing something that made any sense to him, Prachand looked relieved.

'Well, we would like a tour of the ashram.'

'Do you have an appointment, brother?'

'No, sister. But we really want to take a look.'

'Sure. But please come back when you have an appointment.' She now sounded more like a call centre employee than the calm, wise woman who was chatting with them moments ago. She bowed slightly and started walking away.

'Ms Shailaja Kapoor, who recommended the place to us, will be very disappointed.'

The woman stopped in her tracks. For a few seconds she stood still. Then she slowly turned around with the same beatific look on her face.

'Welcome to the ashram,' she said politely.

CHAPTER 44

'Please change into these robes.'

Prachand and Vidya had been ushered into one of the brick buildings that turned out to be a sort of reception area. The lady who ushered them in handed them green robes similar to the one she was wearing. Another woman joined in and helped them fill some forms. Prachand duly complied with some fictional information.

'Why do we have to change our clothes?' Vidya asked churlishly, thinking of all the effort put into their 'look'.

Their usher did not lose her smile for a nanosecond and explained, 'Our bodies are diseased with the demands of the world. That's why we are unhappy. Clothes, makeup, gadgets, the list is never ending. When we enter the doors of the ashram, we cut off from the outer world. There are no TVs or laptops here. No internet, no mobile phones. Just one administrative phone line on the entire property. We must shed our outer layers along with our clothes and connect with nature, connect with our inner selves.'

They hoped nodding wisely would be sufficient. Before they entered the changing rooms, the second woman asked them if they would like a quick tour or the overnight tour. Since they were friends of Shailaja Kapoor, they were told that that either of the tours would be free of cost. Hoping that a night here would give him some more time to investigate, Prachand opted for the latter.

After all the formalities were completed, they were briefed about the tour.

'We will first cleanse the body,' explained their usher, who they were told was called Ek Satya.

'Then we will give you your ashram names. You will proceed to attend different sessions of the mind and body through the day and at night you will spend time separately, in isolation, to collect your thoughts.'

'But we have names already,' said Prachand, confused.

'In the ashram we shed our names, the experiences and entitlements that come with them,' Ek Satya explained calmly.

A few hours later, a spent-looking Jaivant and Jatasya, formerly known as Prachand and Vidya, were finding it difficult to maintain silence during their aqua meditation session. They were sitting in waist-deep water in a large swimming pool-like enclosure along with six other ashram inmates. A quick tour of the premises helped them understand very quickly that there was nothing close to luxurious offered as part of this experience.

Their 'cleansing' turned out to be a freezing dip in ice cold water. This had been followed by their rechristening. Their breakfast was *saatvik bhojan*, consisting of a variety of seeds and fruits while they both craved some real food. The morning was followed by a variety of sessions that included deep breathing, lying on the grass and connecting with the earth (which helped them connect with a lot of large ants), joining a meditative dance group, and now they were meditating some more, sitting in water. While navigating these activities, Prachand had tried his level best to glean any information about Shailaja but it was hard to speak with anyone given the ashram rules. Even on casually asking whether the Kapoors were regular patrons, Ek Satya had left it at 'they are great supporters of our community, especially Shailaja Kapoor.'

'I want to leave, Prachand!' hissed Vidya, trying to cover her legs as the green robe kept filling with water and rising to the surface. Prachand himself was unable to concentrate.

'Viddu, relax. Please. We have come so far. Bear with me.'

'We came here to look for Shailaja Kapoor. Not to be dunked in cold water, or get new names or laugh, cry and talk to trees. There are many outside our own house. I don't need to be called Jag ... Jug ... jig...'

'Jatasya.'

'Whatever! And be tortured while doing it.'

'Deep breath, Vidya, deep breath,' Prachand implored his wife as he saw the irate instructor making his way to the two most troublesome pupils in his class. 'I am sure we will find out something about her here. I can feel it in my bones. Everywhere else has thrown a dead end.'

'You feel everything in your bones! Stop saying that.' Vidya gritted her teeth as the instructor stood glowering at them.

Later that night, as they sat in front of food that resembled nothing they had ever ingested, Prachand was almost in tears.

'They went around the garden, plucked whatever they could get their hands on and placed it on our plates. This isn't food!'

Vidya played food hockey, pushing the food around her plate. Ek Satya, who was walking past just at that time, squatted in front of them.

'So how has the experience been so far for the both of you?'

'Nice, madam. Very nice,' they both answered insincerely, trying to look happy.

'Great!' she seemed satisfied with their response. 'Then after dinner, let's move you both to your 'isolation' rooms where you will be locked up for the night. There you shall contemplate the day gone by and decide what you feel about living here.'

The isolation rooms were in a silence zone. Their instructions were whispered to them as well.

'You are not supposed to speak. Just connect with your experiences of the day, assimilate all of your feelings, and in the morning I will check with you if you'd like to take the silver or bronze package going forward.' Ek Satya whispered and left them with a bunch of pamphlets.

The only saving grace was that their isolation rooms had a common wall. If they whispered loud enough at the windows, they were audible to each other.

'Have you seen the pamphlet, Prachand? People would pay lakhs to stay here and torture themselves??!' Vidya whispered incredulously.

'I'm not concerned about these pamphlets or this place,' grumbled Prachand. 'We came here for clues about Shailaja Kapoor's whereabouts and have zilch.'

Vidya sighed. 'I say we tried our best. Let's just go back to Mrs Kapoor tomorrow and tell her we can't help her.'

'Really, Vidya? You want to be the one to tell an invalid old woman that her only daughter can't be found? That we are washing our hands off this matter as well?'

'Stop getting emotional, Prachand!' Vidya raised her voice slightly. 'My mother also doesn't know where I am. Nor does yours. It's a horrible situation and I would like to help but we need to get our own lives back in order and put an end to this madness. Enough now!'

'Helping her is helping us. I can't believe that you won't understand me, Vidya.'

'You know what, Prachand? I don't care now! I want to go home! I'm sick of everything!'

'I want to go home as well! I'm sick of everything!'

'Who was that?'

'When?'

'Just now, after you spoke, I heard another voice.'

'I think I heard it as well!'

'Maybe we imagined it? I think that cold water damaged my hearing.'

'Maybe I imagined it as well.'

'You didn't imagine it,' piped up a third unknown voice.

After a moment's confused silence, Prachand spoke up. 'Who ... who are you?'

'Someone you're looking for. Shailaja Kapoor.'

CHAPTER 45

Prachand and Vidya watched Shailaja Kapoor keenly. She sat across the table eating watermelon. After the initial shock of the previous night's discovery, Prachand had quickly introduced himself. But his questions went unanswered as the attendant came to silence them repeatedly. They had expected a barrage of questions from Shailaja Kapoor in the morning but she sat silently.

'She isn't speaking. You could've at least let me have a bath. Oh wait, I'm sure we'll be dunked in cold water at some point today.'

'Shhhhhh.' Prachand elbowed Vidya and then trained his eyes on Shailaja Kapoor. She looked a bit otherworldly chasing watermelon seeds around her plate with a vacuous look in her eyes. Clearing his throat loudly, Prachand brought her back to the present.

'So you're saying Sujit was behind my abduction and was then murdered?' she asked.

'Yes,' Prachand nodded.

'I can't believe he would become desperate enough to turn on his own wife. I mean, getting me abducted? That's a bit much, even for him.'

'I'm sorry. I know it can't be easy to hear all this. And I'm sorry for your loss.'

She shrugged. 'He had managed to make enemies of most business associates. We received threatening calls all the time. That's why I found it essential to buy a gun when I was in Kanpur.'

'We know that.'

'You do?'

'You see, someone hired us to keep an eye on you. I was just doing my job. I ... I hope you can...'

She waved her hand absentmindedly.

'Who would want to keep an eye on me? I would say Sujit, but then Sujit knew where I was most of the time, and he even stayed with me sometimes.' She shrugged. The watermelon seed race was resumed. 'You said both of you are in hiding because you were found running away from the scene of murder?'

'Yes,' Prachand nodded. 'The murder itself was an accident. The man arguing with him pushed him and your husband hit his head against a table during his fall. I went to help him, but Govind saw both of us and told the police. Do you have any idea who could be behind this?'

She shook her head. 'No. Not a clue.'

Shailaja Kapoor shut her eyes momentarily, possibly playing out her husband's death in her head. 'We haven't really been like a husband-wife for a long time now, but I didn't want him to ... die.' A watermelon seed was declared victorious. 'How is my mother? When I came here, I had forbidden them from informing her. In case whoever kidnapped me went after her next.'

'She misses you a lot but is a strong woman.'

'Yes. She is strong. I'll give her that.' Shailaja shrugged.

'But what was your plan? To stay here indefinitely?' Vidya interjected, wanting some answers. 'And how did these ashram people not hear anything on the news and why did they give you shelter here?'

'We are cut off from all technology as they say it pollutes the mind. A very limited number of visitors are allowed here and I knew the ashram was a place that was isolated from the outside world. Besides, they will do me any favour I ask of them. Money can work like magic!' Shailaja Kapoor laughed. First softly, then very loudly.

Vidya and Prachand watched her with a blank expression. Given their lacklustre response to her theatrical laughter, Shailja stopped laughing, cleared her throat and continued with her explanation. 'Our family has been visiting the ashram for many years. I'm one of their biggest donors so they make exceptions for me,' she announced with an air of privilege. Then she abruptly turned, gazing at the garden behind her. This left Prachand and Vidya staring at her back. Slowly getting used to her odd ways, they knew she would eventually speak so they waited patiently.

'You know, my father used to bring me here. I was very young when he died but I remember him clearly. A little part of me died with him.' She turned around to face them. 'Hey, I'm not giving you a sob story. I've had a good life. Just that I've never really been happy, happy. You know what I mean? I think most of my memories are foggy and to do with clinics, institutions.' She seemed to be having a moment of normalcy and clarity.

Prachand nodded sympathetically while she spoke, surprised that she was volunteering so much information. 'My mother and Sujit kept me afloat I guess, but my life has been a bit of a blur, even while I was acting. You know, Sujit wasn't always the boor he became. He made me feel very special for a while. But over the years, he found a new love.'

Vidya clucked her commiserations on cue. 'Some younger bitch?'

'No. Money!' Shailaja Kapoor laughed. 'My mother warned me that he was no good. Typical of her, to make me feel like no choice of mine is good enough.'

Prachand, reluctant to intrude on mother-daughter turf, didn't respond but added: 'We came looking for you because she begged us to.'

'Thank you.' Shailaja Kapoor smiled, beaming at him. 'If you hadn't come along, God knows how long it would have taken for me to learn what's going on outside these walls.' She got up to leave.

Prachand hurriedly asked her. 'But how did you manage to get away from the kidnappers and reach Mumbai?'

'Oh, that was easy.' She waved her slim, manicured fingers about. 'Such amateurs! It didn't look like they knew what they were doing. One of them looked more scared than I did. I even managed to hit him with my shoes a few times when he was trying to feed me.' She cackled. 'All I had to do was wait till they dozed off. The fools had forgotten to lock the window and I escaped through it. I've learnt to trust no one, so I didn't go to Sujit or the police. I called the ashram and they arranged for me to be picked up and brought here.'

Prachand had to give it to the woman. She was odd but had grit.

'I think you should contact your mother. She is extremely worried.'

'I will. And then I'll go home.'

'One request. Please don't mention us to the police yet. They are still looking for us in connection to your husband's death.'

She pulled an imaginary zip across her mouth.

'By the way, I have spoken with the people here. When all of this is over, I want to gift both of you a weeklong stay here, all expenses paid,' she beamed magnanimously. To her surprise, however, she found that the husband-wife duo had disappeared from plain sight.

CHAPTER 46

A tearful Pamela Kapoor was informed by Prachand that her daughter was coming home. Overjoyed and grateful, she insisted they come home to be thanked in person.

'Thank you very much, Madam, but I don't know how to accept this invite.'

'Why?'

'I mean, I really don't know how. The police are looking for us. It's too much of a risk.'

'My house is a fortress. Besides, once Shailaja is home and they've spoken with her, there is one less reason for them to keep an eye on us. You came in undetected once, you can do it again.'

'Madam, if I climb one more tree, I will…'

'Wait, I have an idea. My secretary will bring you in her car. Just duck and hide till you reach the house. She will call you with the details.'

As per the plan, upon Shailaja's return the following day, a high-tea session was discreetly organised in a parlour room attached to hers. Salads, scones, tea cakes, healthy savouries, no effort was spared as part of Pamela Kapoor's celebratory effort.

'Eat, eat, you haven't touched your salad either.'

Vidya looked dolefully at the spread in front of them. Instead of hot steaming home food, they were staring at strange cold delicacies they had never laid eyes on. The one thing that sounded familiar was the 'salaad', but instead of the round rings of tomato, onion and cucumber, what arrived was a plate of leaves, topped with what looked like beetroot – something even Hirwa would reject. It took a lot of resolve to maintain a straight face and pretend to enjoy everything.

As if reading her mind, Pamela Kapoor called Vidya closer and spoke softly with a twinkle of humour in her eyes.

'I'm sorry darling. After all that hotel food, you both would have preferred some hot homemade food, I should have guessed,' she laughed. 'You know, Punjabi food doesn't even bother going through the stomach. Heads straight to the behind. I stopped eating that kind of food years ago. That's the price you pay for being an actress.'

'I don't know why you keep talking about being an actress. Three movies and eons ago! Some actress! Eat what you like now!'

There was an uncomfortable silence as the statement hung in the air like a cobweb. No one willing to disturb it. Prachand stole a quick glance at Pamela Kapoor who looked mortified. Shailaja, unrepentant, chewed on some cucumber.

Pamela Kapoor seemed to collect herself and replied, with an awkward laugh: 'Old habits die hard!'

The erratic Shailaja Kapoor seemed satisfied with this response and resumed eating. Prachand hastened to change the topic. 'So madam, did the police come checking this morning?'

'Yes,' Pamela Kapoor nodded. 'They took Shailaja's statement.'

Shailaja laughed while walking to a small trolley filled with drinks. 'There was this one large cop who looked dissatisfied with anything I said. About how I got away from the abductors or how I said I just decided to come home on my own.'

'Shailu, haven't you had enough to drink?'

Shailaja Kapoor waved her hand dismissively. 'He also got very riled up when I asked him if he had anything substantial on the both of you or whether he was just on a witch hunt for lack of any other leads. Anyway, I really think you're on his hit-list, so be careful.'

Vidya grunted. Prachand was silent.

'I've been giving this matter some thought. You're right. This is a witch-hunt and we can't win. I think we should go talk to the police.' Prachand shrugged with a faraway look in his eyes.

'How long can we keep running?'

'So you want to be arrested?' asked Vidya incredulously.

'She is right. How can you think of going to the police? They will lock you up before listening to you,' Pamela Kapoor chimed in.

'Why did that bastard Sujit have to go and die?' This sudden declaration by Shailaja took everyone by surprise.

Pamela Kapoor cleared her throat discreetly, looking embarrassed. 'Are you sure you want to finish that drink?'

'Ever the wise ones. Always armed with a lecture. Sujit and you. Am I that big a mess?' She stood up and looked at

Prachand and Vidya. 'Thank you very much, but I'm afraid I must leave.'

The closing ceremony for the evening had officially been announced.

Pamela Kapoor looked apologetically at her guests.

'Please do sit down,' she requested, wheeling herself closer to them. 'She is a good person, you know. She just needs her medicines and shrink to keep her in check.'

'Shrink?' enquired Vidya.

'Umm. Psychiatrist,' explained Pamela Kapoor.

'Aah. The doctor who treats mental people.'

'No, no, Shailaja is not mad. She just needs someone to talk to.'

Prachand nodded his head in sympathy. 'When I am extremely emotional, even I go and talk to Hirwa. She is an extremely good listener.'

'Oh, how progressive! So you have a shrink in Kanpur? That's very good.'

'No, no, Hirwa is our cow,' explained Vidya.

Pamela Kapoor opened her mouth and shut it, looking confused, but continued with her explanation.

'You see, Shailaja never truly recovered from losing her father. He was everything to her. She was doing well with time. Some movies came her way and lifted her spirits, gave her some purpose. But her drinking finally chased them away.'

'Such a waste.' Vidya shrugged. 'She is so talented and beautiful.'

'Not a day goes by when I don't think of that,' Pamela Kapoor teared up.

As Pamela Kapoor kept shedding more details on her daughter's plight, Prachand excused himself to use the washroom.

Walking down the long marble-laden corridor towards the guest bathroom he had been directed to, Prachand looked around in awe at the tastefully decorated walls and rooms he was passing. Around one such corner, he came to a sudden halt as his eyes detected a movement in a nearby window. Wanting to take a second look, he went closer but found no one.

He was about to enter the bathroom when a sickeningly sweet and familiar smell hit his nostrils.

CHAPTER 47

'Srivastava, you have not been sent there to perform lavani and eat vada pav. Shailaja Kapoor is back, but there's a dead husband as well, isn't there?'

'Yes, sir.'

'Well then, who murdered him?'

'Sir, we don't know but we have left no stone unturned. We are looking into Sujit Oberoi's business and talking to his associates, friends and acquaintances. No important information has emerged except that recently two very expensive construction projects of his were stalled due to illegalities and he suffered huge losses.'

'Any information from Shailaja Kapoor?'

'She is a strange one. Evasive and uninterested in answering any questions. Most unhelpful.'

'What about that detective?'

'Sir, he and his wife are still at large.'

'Well, that's one stone you haven't been able to turn. Even with the help of the Mumbai Police they are managing to stay hidden. Maybe I should hire him to solve this case no?'

'I'm sure I'll find them very soon. But you know what I feel sir? There is more to this case than meets the eye.'

'Do you know what I feel, Srivastava? That you are doing a lot of guesswork and have nothing concrete.'

'No sir ... I...'

'Srivastava, you have two days to show me some results. If you have nothing by then, please pack your bags and go home. But after that, don't ever expect me to take you and your career seriously. I need this wrapped up fast.'

Navin Srivastava wanted to strangle his boss with his bare hands but hung up with utter politeness and all due respect. That's when Ranganathan called out to him. He was looking at surveillance photographs of the Kapoor residence that the local team had captured over the last two days.

'Sir, I don't get it. Do you think these ladies see even twenty per cent of this property on a daily basis? What a waste. If I had such a house, I would utilise every room. One for my wife and me, one for each kid, one for my parents, one for her parents, one for my bua and her son. I would even keep a room for when my wife is angry with me. I would call it the "maika" room where she could go very often when upset with me, without wasting any money on a train ticket.' Ranganathan sniggered but ended up clearing his throat as his superior trained his eye on him.

'Can you just focus on the case and not indulge in frivolous chatter?' Navin Srivastava grunted. Somewhere inside, he was also realizing that for the first time in his life he was really invested in solving a case. Whether it was his acute need to get back home or the pressure on him, all he wanted was to get done with it.

'Sir, check this surveillance picture.' He handed his boss a slightly blurred image of a middle-aged man with a muscular build and very cold, sharp eyes. He had a square face and a thin mouth which looked like it was sealed shut. One's face is their fortune and this one was tailor-made for the top ten most-wanted criminals list.

'Who is this guy?'

'Sir,' Rangathan began, 'we found him in our records. Name is Bhima Shankar. From Kanpur. Been in and out of jail most of his life. Cheating, minor frauds, etc., mostly petty crimes but a long rap sheet.' Navin Srivastava was in deep thought.

'Is that him near the Kapoor house again?' he asked, jabbing his finger at the figure in another picture.

'Yes, Sir.' He picked up a few others. 'He seems to be around that house quite a bit. Never uses the front gate though.'

Navin Srivastava pointed at another picture. 'This timestamp shows Shailaja Kapoor exiting a few minutes after he left the house yesterday.'

Ranganathan looked at the picture closely.

'Yes, saar. You're right.' Then he continued with a frown. 'You know, that woman seems a bit ...' he made circles to the side of his head and whistled, '...off.'

Navin Srivastava nodded. 'I think I know what you mean. She does behave like a *paglait*, a complete basket case. When I questioned her, she started singing. In the middle of my interrogation! She even told me who the composer was.'

Ranganathan was excited at the prospect of his theory being indulged. 'Saar, she was so evasive when I questioned her as well. Not one single answer given clearly. We are supposed to believe that she escaped her kidnappers and made it all the way to Mumbai on her own, without any help? Her mother said she has been going to a mental doctor since she was a child. You think she could be...'

As Navin Srivastava walked into the men's washroom, he was overwhelmed with two mysteries. The first: how it was possible for police station bathrooms across the length and breadth of India to stink with the same intensity? The second was this damn case. Two suspects claiming to be innocent. A dead husband. A failed actress who needed psychiatric help and a criminal from Kanpur who was somehow connected to this mess. His mind was a jumbled knot as he returned and reached for the Eno sachet kept on his temporary table at the station.

Just then his phone started ringing and he knew it could only mean more bad news.

CHAPTER 48

'Chowpatty, Juhu Beach, Elephanta caves, Mahalaxmi Mandir, Siddhivinayak. Nothing. Imagine. Coming all the way to Mumbai and seeing nothing worthwhile.'

Vidya was irritated. They were still being chased by the police and there was nowhere to run. Not only was her life in shambles, she hadn't even managed to tick any tourist boxes in Mumbai.

'We only made it to Shah Rukh Khan's house and even there you couldn't wait till his balcony appearance.'

'Viddu, how can I be blamed for my bladder?'

'No, you can't. I'll just tell my friends we never saw Shah Rukh Khan because my husband wanted to do sussu.'

Shaking his head wearily, Prachand continued packing his meagre belongings. It was standard practice for them to pack up everything each time they left the room. They were stashed away in an unused utilities section on their hotel floor. If anyone even came checking after them, they would find nothing.

He also knew that when his wife was in this mood, it was best to leave her be. How could he blame her when what had started off as an adventure that she had embarked on with her husband had turned into a nightmare with no end in sight? As she packed and unpacked a handful of her things, she looked overwhelmed and he kept a respectable distance.

A call from Pamela Kapoor had been responsible for this sudden packing spree.

'Son, please come home today evening. I am very keen on helping you out of this mess. I think I know who killed Sujit,' was all she had divulged. There was now a small glimmer of hope and they hurried towards it.

'Viddu, that slipper is for the room guests. And why are you keeping that laundry bag?' Prachand enquired.

'So what if I keep the slippers. They are fluffy and soft. It's like walking on soft cotton and they make me happy. Is that a bad thing? And this bag, it's perfect for vegetable shopping. Big and sturdy. The one at home keeps tearing and has more stains now than the original design. Do you have a problem with everything, Prachi?' Then she burst into tears. At which point Prachand started throwing combs, shampoos, slippers and every possible hotel kit he could lay his hands on, into his wife's bag.

An hour later, Prachand and Vidya, with their disguises intact, went downstairs to grab a bite.

'Something doesn't seem right.' Prachand scratched his head. There was no traffic on the road. Some semi-naked kids were playing in the middle of the street and all the shops were shuttered. It looked more like a sleepy peaceful afternoon from the pages of *Malgudi Days* than a busy working day in Mumbai. A little boy in shorts, carrying a large consignment of tea cups, was walking towards them. Prachand called out and he walked up to them wiping the sweat off his brow. 'Tea, biscuits?'

Prachand took two cups of tea and paid him. 'Son, why is everything so quiet. Did something happen? Or is it a public holiday?'

'You don't watch TV?' the boy enquired.

'Not much these days,' Prachand shrugged.

'You don't read paper?'

Prachand shrugged again, unwilling to explain to the boy why current affairs of the nation weren't a top priority for him at the moment.

'Well, there is a bandh today.' The boy said, scratching his arm.

'But why?'

'Same old.' He shook his head like a wizened politician. 'Some dog shat in a BEST bus. The conductor wanted to throw the owner and guilty dog out of the bus. The owner slapped the bus conductor. The bus conductor complained to his union. The owner, part of some consumer group, went to the police with a case of assault. The union was supported by the opposition party and the consumer group by the ruling party. It became a political matter and there was a lot of *gondhal* (trouble). Now a bandh has been called by the opposition.'

'Same old? Strange city, stranger folk,' Prachand mumbled as he returned to his tea cup. For all the inane reasons for bandhs in Kanpur, he couldn't remember the last time dog poop had caused one. 'Now, tell me, how I can reach Pali Hill from here. I really need to get there.'

The boy, who looked like he had wasted too much time talking, started walking away. 'Try walking!' he yelled.

Vidya, who had composed herself by now, was looking around as well. There was a taxi standing nearby. She walked up to the driver and folded her hands. 'Namaste! Will you take us to Pali Hill, please?' The taxi driver with a big tikka across his forehead smiled. 'From UP?'

She nodded. He folded the newspaper and alighted from the cab. 'I knew it! I can always tell. Besides, you didn't say "Oye Boss! or Ey bhai!"' He chuckled. 'I would love to help you, madam, but they will burn my taxi if I even try to start it.'

Prachand stole a glance inside the taxi. It looked like Kedarnath and Badrinath had condensed into a cab-compliant format and poured in from every window. There were pictures of Lord Shiva in every size, covering every inch of the car and the smoke from the incense sticks wrapped the whole look in a dream-like spiritual haze. Prachand was about to cajole him on account of being a fellow Shiv bhakt when he remembered his attire. A Muslim gent's interest in Bholenaath would definitely spark curiosity and conversations, something he could ill afford.

'We can't possibly walk there. Is there no other way?' The taxi driver thought for a few seconds and then his face broke into a smile.

'There might be one.' He winked.

In keeping with the theme of the day which was 'strangeness', Prachand and Vidya had soon found themselves in a political rally. Everywhere the eye could see, there were posters and banners of sombre-looking politicians pasted next to large images of a dog pooping, crossed with a red and angry line.

The kind taxi driver who had brought them to the rally advised, 'Stick with these people. They will move in trucks and buses from place to place attending speeches all day long. Keep an eye out. Get off when they're passing your stop.'

Prachand was confused. 'They have been hired to attend these gatherings?'

'Of course,' nodded the driver. Even I am going to park my taxi and join them. Might as well make some money elsewhere if I can't drive my taxi.'

A man walked up to them and enquired whether they would like pav bhaji or 'Chinese'. And whether they would like a shirt-pant set or a steel plates-and-glasses set.

'More like a party with return gifts than a protest,' Vidya whispered to Prachand. He tapped a person squatting next to him. 'What is going on here?' The man deftly spat a long squirt of paan, without hitting the sea of humanity around him. 'How would I know!' he shrugged.

All they were required to do was shout some slogans and look upset whenever any news camera came by. Of course, short of hiding under people, Prachand was doing everything possible to keep a distance from any news crew.

After a few stops, it seemed that their destination was nearby. However, a few minutes later, the buses stopped abruptly and people started pouring out of the vehicles. Prachand stood up and asked someone. 'Excuse me, mister, why is everyone leaving when we haven't reached the venue?'

The man looked at him with a strange expression. 'We're going home, of course. There is some blockage ahead and by the time it clears, we might get caught in evening traffic.'

'But the protest?'

'What about it? Look, this is Mumbai. Convenience is key. Bandh, protest, rally, all only till 6 p.m. Then *khallaas*. Finished. Who wants to get stuck in rush-hour office traffic?' He shuddered as if the mere thought made him queasy.

After a few hours of chanting slogans that made no sense, eating Chinese, drinking tea, discussing the ill effects of dog poop and why steel plates made better gifts than clothes, Prachand and Vidya stood at the small side entrance of Kapoor Villa that they had been instructed to use. It was already dark by then and their shadows were dancing with the flickering street light.

Prachand looked around. 'Wasn't it more brightly lit the last time we left the bungalow? It's very dimly lit today, isn't it? Almost reminds me of...'

'Oh no, you don't!' interrupted Vidya. 'Don't remind me of that *manhoos* night at the Lily Bungalow. Nothing bad is going to happen tonight. Let's just go in.'

CHAPTER 49

A loud clap of thunder accompanied their arrival into the Kapoor mansion.

Dabbu was the first one on the reception committee. He sat snarling with his teeth exposed. If they didn't know any better, this could have been misconstrued as a welcoming smile.

'Brother Dabbu, why do you still hate us? Aren't we friends now?'

Another deep throated growl amply conveyed Dabbu's sentiments to Prachand.

'If you're done talking to the dog, please come this way.' The stern-faced Bertha quipped with a raised eyebrow. 'You're a bit early so you shall have to wait in the visitor's hall till madam is ready to see you.'

'Sure. Is Shailaja Madam also home?'

'Pamela Madam will update you when she is here.'

'Okay, but how long do you think we will have to wait?'

'It all depends on Pamela Madam.'

'Not much of a talker, is she?' muttered Vidya.

They were ushered into a large hall just before the main living room. It almost looked like the Golden Temple in reverse. The only difference was that instead of gurus or Gods, the deification was of human beings, namely the Kapoor ancestors. Large paintings and photographs of men and women, framed in gold, lined the walls. The remaining space was filled with ornate gold leaf designs, gold curtains, and gold-coloured furniture. The interior designer for this room had clearly graduated from the 'Bappi Lahiri School of Aesthetics'.

'I remember reading somewhere that the Kapoors have roots of Peshawari Khatris. Apparently, Mr Kapoor's ancestors were wealthy traders and landlords. These must be some of them,' Prachand said pointing at the smartly dressed men and women with Colgate smiles.

'Why are portraits of rich people so typical?' Vidya said thinking out loud. 'The men are always standing next to tigers, deer heads or holding a gun. The women look like no one bothered styling them. And look at all the expressions, like someone just made them lick a spoonful of vile-tasting Chyavanprash. I remember seeing one faded and torn picture of my great grandfather, standing next to his prized cows, but he had a big smile on his face.'

Prachand smiled in response but his mind was elsewhere.

'Are you okay? I can tell that something's bothering you.'

He shrugged. 'Don't worry about it Viddu. Just connecting some dots. But you know what the best part is?' He asked, changing the topic. We might be on our way home if the Kapoor ladies help us tonight.'

'Do you think Pamela Kapoor has also realized that her unstable and nut-job daughter is capable of murder?'

'Viddu, we mustn't speculate till we know the facts...'

'Yes of course, and I should wait till I'm fifty years old, by which time this jalebi of a case will have been solved,' she retorted caustically.

'Just be positive!' Prachand hugged her.

'How, Prachand?' Vidya asked. 'So they've come up with a plan and it is something that hasn't occurred to you already? I find that hard to believe.'

'Oh, believe it, my darling.' Prachand laughed. 'This case has many firsts.'

The heavy door opened noisily and Bertha walked back in.

'Madam will see you soon. Refreshments are on their way. Will you need anything else? I'm on my way out.'

'You're going home?' Vidya enquired.

'Is that a problem?'

Vidya looked like she was getting up to punch the petite woman and Prachand had to restrain her. 'No. Thank you. Goodnight.'

Bertha nodded and walked out.

'I'll kill that woman!' Vidya hissed. 'I was asking because I thought she could drop us back in her car when we are done, like last time.'

'Forget about her and getting back. Let's focus on tonight,' Prachand advised.

After an hour of staring at ancestral faces, Pamela Kapoor appeared at the door.

'I'm sorry to have kept you waiting,' she apologised. 'I had ... certain matters to arrange.'

'Please don't worry about it. We were keeping ourselves busy looking around at your ancestors.'

'My husband's, actually,' she said with a flicker of a frown on her face that disappeared quickly. 'Anyway, please follow me.'

She pressed a button on her wheelchair and it turned towards the living room. They followed her.

In keeping with the mood on the outside, the living room looked bleak with the few yellow lights that were twinkling in the centre of the living room. Pamela Kapoor shot out an instruction to remedy this.

'Alexa, switch on living room lights.'

Vidya looked at the little black box. It reminded her of some tantrik's paraphernalia she had once seen.

'Switching on lights.' The lights came on, flooding the room as Prachand and Vidya took a seat on a large, mahogany leather couch.

Lightning ripped through the night sky as unseasonal rain poured down in sheets.

'Very strange weather for this time of the year.'

Prachand looked around the house. 'It seems rather quiet around here today, well, barring the rain.' He wondered where the battalion of help had disappeared.

'You're right. It is. Everyone seems to have fallen ill or gone home due to the storm warning,' Pamela Kapoor explained.

'Oh. So it's just us tonight?' said Prachand.

'Yes.' She nodded.

'And Shailaja Madam?'

'She is in her room.'

Prachand decided to get to the point. He cleared his throat. 'So, you had said you might know who killed your son-in-law?'

'Oh, I'm so sorry. I keep forgetting. Yes, that's correct,' she nodded excitedly. Let me call Shailu as well.'

She yelled for Shailaja. A few minutes later, Shailaja Kapoor came sauntering out with a drink in her hand. 'What?' she asked her mother with a sour expression. That's when she saw Prachand and Vidya and smiled. 'Hi. What brings you both here?'

Prachand looked confused. 'Well ... your mother said she knows who ... killed your husband. Hasn't she told you already?'

'What?' Now it was Shailaja Kapoor who looked utterly confused.

CHAPTER 50

All eyes were now trained on Pamela Kapoor. Her face, inscrutable.

'Wow, mother!' mocked Shailaja Kapoor, clapping her hands slowly as she spoke. 'More secrets. Just when I thought I could give you a benefit of doubt. You supposedly know who killed my husband and I'm the last to find out?'

'I was waiting for the right time, Shailu. Why are you always...'

Shailu was in no mood for explanations and bit back. 'Oh, come on! You always have an explanation ready. Why can't you just be normal? Like everyone else's mother?'

'If I ever spoke with my mother like that, she would break my legs,' Vidya blurted aloud and then clamped her mouth shut, realizing what she had said.

Shailaja Kapoor sighed. 'I would happily switch mothers with you, Vidya.'

'Here we go again, the boring "poor me" speech!' A voice announced languidly. Shailaja Kapoor turned around to look at her mother who was staring at her with a steely look in her eyes. It was as if the docile and pliable Nirupama Roy had suddenly transformed into Lalita Pawar.

Shailaja Kapoor was seething. 'Don't you dare mock me!' She walked up to her mother and shook her by the shoulders.

Prachand stood up and warned Shailaja. 'You might hurt her.'

Pamela Kapoor laughed. 'I can take care of myself, mister. I'm not an old helpless hag like your mother!'

Prachand was incensed as he thought of his sanskaari, spunky and very loving mother with her crop of silver hair.

'What has happened to you all of a sudden? And please don't bring my mother into this,' he said in a clipped tone.

'I will bring whomever I please, you nosey two-bit detective!'

Vidya's jaw dropped. 'She has killed and eaten Pamela Kapoor. This can't be the same lady.' She tugged at Prachand's sleeve.

Prachand focused his attention on the woman in the wheelchair as he needed some answers.

'Why are you so upset with me? I found your daughter, didn't I?'

'I wish you hadn't!' Shailaja said. 'Can't you see how psychotic this woman is? And she tried to convince everyone that I'm the one with the problem.'

Instead of answering him, Pamela Kapoor stood up and walked towards Shailaja. Not like someone who had walked out of a wheelchair after struggling for years, but with a 'tottered down rampwalk in stilettos' kind of confidence. The scene was unfolding at normal speed but it seemed like it was unfolding in slow motion. All three spectators stared at her in silence as she catwalked her way to her daughter.

She traced her daughter's face with her fingers as Shailaja stood with her mouth open trying to pull away. 'Always so uptight with me. The little princess. The perfect little princess. With the perfect father. In their perfect world, that never had any place for me.' She sounded so venomous that it seemed as if she was hissing.

'You ... you can walk? So you were fooling everyone, and me, all these years?' Shailaja shook her head in disbelief. 'How selfish can a person be?'

'Selfish?' Pamela Kapoor bit out. 'I gave up my career for you ingrates! But your stupid father was too busy making money. Stingy bastard had none for me though. The purse strings were loosened only for the darling daughter. So what was a beautiful woman like me expected to do? Wait around for scraps? I did what I had to. And by the way, I didn't invite him for a show in our bedroom when I was with Harish. I mean, who comes back all the way from work to change a tie. Seriously!'

'He had a heart attack soon after he saw you with that lawyer Harish, didn't he?' yelled Shailaja Kapoor.

'I guess.' Her mother shrugged. 'And simmer down. I'm sure you don't remember, but even at that age you were always spewing venom at me. Treating me like it was my fault your superhero was dead.'

'But, why were you pretending to sit in a wheelchair?' Prachand couldn't help intervening.

'I was driven to it! This stupid child was blaming me, behaving like a fool, screeching and shouting at me all the time. It made everyone suspicious, especially under those circumstances. People started talking. I had to do something so I pretended to injure my legs permanently in an accident.

She didn't stop hating me but, I think somewhere it made her feel bad for me and behave herself. That's all I wanted. Otherwise, the lawyers wouldn't release any money that my conniving worm of a husband left in Shailaja's name.' She jabbed her finger at Shailaja.

'How I have suffered just to keep up this act. So much planning and drama, acting helpless, looking old and worried. I'm just fifty-something, damn it. And I'm hot! I had to keep colouring my hair to make myself look older, keep the sympathy card going. Beat that! I think I deserve a lifetime achievement award for this performance! And don't even get me started on this wheelchair.' She kicked it savagely. It rolled away, possibly happy at having created a distance between itself and the raving lunatic. 'My leg goes off to sleep all the time. And do you know what happens to the behind if you sit on it all day long with the kind of skin I have? It itches! Constantly! I've tried every cream but nothing will stop it.' She subconsciously reached for her bottom and gave it a good scratch.

'So typical! You cheat, you liar, you manipulator! You wanted us to feel sorry for you. Knowing what you're capable of, I was naive enough to think that my mother would eventually come around for me. Stupid, stupid stupid.' Shailaja Kapoor whacked her forehead repeatedly.

While absorbing all the information being bandied around, pieces of this jigsaw puzzle finally started falling into place in Prachand's head. But he still needed to get the vital piece of information that could save them. The problem was getting the mad woman to tell them.

'We were also fooled, Shailaja Madam.' He shook his head in disappointment.

'Your mother has no idea who killed Sujit Oberoi and she just lied to lure us here.' He was deliberately trying to goad Pamela Kapoor and he succeeded.

'You fool! It is beyond your intellect to even fathom my genius. You couldn't imagine in a million years who the murderer is.'

Prachand tapped his fingers thoughtfully and said, 'As a matter of fact, I can tell you where the murderer is from.'

'Oh really?' She smirked. 'Did he send you a postcard?'

'Not exactly. But it didn't take much to figure out that he wasn't just sent there as a one-off, but that he is in fact from Kanpur.'

Pamela Kapoor's eyes widened.

'That perfume ... well, the smell he carries with him, I remembered where I've smelt it before. There is an *ittar* shop in the old part of Navin Market. Very popular but mostly amongst old timers. They make very unique scents. I'm positive it's from there. Besides, he spoke briefly but his Awadhi accent was very clear. He also had a monkey cap in his hand, possibly to mask his face, that I saw while he was running away. Unless you stay in the city, it's odd to have a winter accessory handy at this time of the year. So you see, he is most definitely from Kanpur, according to me.'

Pamela Kapoor's jaw dropped ever so slightly and Vidya's chest puffed up with the pride of redemption. But Pamela Kapoor recovered quickly and resumed her monologue.

'Baah. Humbug. Guess work won't get you beyond a location. While you can just pin down a city, I happen to know exactly who killed Sujit Oberoi.' Looking in the direction of her room, she called out to someone. 'Bhima!'

In a few seconds, a grim-faced man of medium build appeared in front of their eyes. Prachand drew a sharp breath as he recognised who was walking towards them. It was the man that had been following them, the one who had attacked him. And as he drew closer, a pungent and familiar smell hit Prachand's nostrils. 'You ... you have been following us since Kanpur and ... and you ... Shailaja Madam, your mother is right. This man murdered your husband.'

CHAPTER 51

'Surprise!' Pamela Kapoor shouted, as if she was announcing the winning number in a game of Bingo instead of revealing a murderer. 'Don't you recognise him, Shailu?'

'You filthy animal!' Shailaja screamed and lunged at Bhima Shankar, the notorious criminal who Shailaja had considered her mother's man Friday over the last few years. Instead of defending himself, he darted out of the way as he saw Shailaja Kapoor mid-flight, descending on him like a ninja warrior. Vidya joined her. 'You scoundrel, you attacked my husband and made our lives hell!'

Pamela Kapoor seemed to be enjoying herself and made no attempt to intervene. Prachand caught hold of Shailaja and Vidya, pulling them away.

'We need answers from him. You both can attack him later.' He then turned to Bhima Shankar. 'So why did you do it?'

Bhima Shankar shrugged without compunction. 'I do what boss lady asks me to do.'

Kanpur Khoofiya Pvt. Ltd

Prachand shook his head and looked at Pamela Kapoor with disbelief. 'Why would you have your own son-in-law murdered?'

'Oh, he had it coming.' She waved her hand about. 'The imbecile thought he could outsmart me. He came crying to me one night, drunk, asking for money to bail him out of his troubles. Said he was in over his head and that Shailaja would never give him money for illegal paybacks. As if I had money to give.' She scoffed. 'I told the fool that I had massive gambling debts as well.'

Vidya stared at her with censure in her eyes. Pamela Kapoor shrugged. 'How else is a poor woman leading a double life supposed to keep herself busy? He was the one who hatched the kidnapping plan, don't look at me. Said that it would be easily done in Kanpur and that the ransom money would be enough to help us both out. But he bungled it by trying to outsmart me. Thank God for Bhima here who told me about Sujit hiring you.' She patted Bhima on head and he almost purred like a cat. 'The nerve. He thought he could create alibis for himself, implicate me and keep the money.'

'But he died accidentally. We saw the whole thing.'

'That was Bholenaath making things easier for me. Before I could strangle him, he slipped and fell,' said Bhima.

'You both will rot in hell for this. I'm sure Sujit is roasting there as we speak,' Shailaja Kapoor said icily, but tears were rolling down her eyes. 'How could I have been so blind? You know, I think my father knew what his wife was capable of, so he left most of the money and estate in my name. But she made such an effort with me, especially after the accident, I ... I really thought she had changed and that she was trying very hard to show me that she loved me.' She wiped her eyes and held her head in her hands. 'Now it's all clear. Why she insisted that I start seeing the psychologist at such an early age and had me overmedicated. Why she kept sending me to rejuvenation retreats. Why she had me and the world convinced that there was something wrong with me. Because she wanted the money, and had to keep me distracted.' She blew her nose. 'We all were puppets in her hands.'

Pamela Kapoor yawned. 'Now if you're done walking down memory lane, let's get down to business. You could have made it easier for yourself, you know, and lived. But the last couple of days have convinced me that as long as you're alive, you'll always make me beg for money.'

'As long as I'm alive?' asked Shailaja Kapoor in a tremulous voice.

Prachand interjected. 'Are you really planning on killing your own blood now?'

'Oh, not just my own blood, I'd be delighted to spill a lot of Tripathi blood as well. You and your wife are a big pain in my behind. Ever since you walked into our lives. Instruction: Follow Shailaja. "No. I will enter her house and find out more." Keep away from the husband. "No, I will go meet him instead." Remain hidden. "Oh never! I will run all the way to Mumbai for answers and find Shailaja Kapoor." Didn't they teach you in some dumb detective school that you should stick to the brief?'

'That's what makes him great!' said Vidya, with tears in her eyes, remembering her parents, now that it seemed like they would be minced meat soon.

'Middle-class people and their emotions. That's why you guys won't get anywhere in life.' Pamela Kapoor said

Kanpur Khoofiya Pvt. Ltd 265

dismissively and tottered in her heels to a small side table. She pulled at a drawer and out came a gun.

Everyone around her gasped and ducked, including Bhima Shankar. She saw the reaction and laughed.

'Aah. Everyone shuts up when this big boy comes out. Hmmmm, so back to business.' She waved her arms theatrically. 'I mean, let's end this business once and for all.' She looked like she was making some mental calculations while using Bhima Shankar as a sounding board. 'Okay, then. So, for the police, the story goes back to when the abduction plan was made by Sujit. He hired Kanpur Khoofiya Pvt. Ltd to tail Shailaja and then to abduct her. The actors fronted it but it was these two tiresome people all along,' she prattled away in a singsong voice. 'Abduction botched. Duo gets greedy and has a scuffle with Sujit over their payment. Sujit pops it. They're seen. They run but their greed brings them to Mumbai. They pretend to be concerned about finding Shailu so they have a cover for being in the city. The gorgeous, gullible and helpless mother ... ahem ...' – she fluffed her hair – '...falls for their act as well.'

'You liar!' hissed Vidya.

'O shush! So their greed leads them to the house today. We are fast asleep. Snore snoooore. They come to demand money from mother-daughter. Scuffle breaks out. Shailaja is accidentally shot by Prachand's gun, pop pop. Prachand and his nuisance-of-a-wife are shot by Shailaja ... pop pop.'

She turned to look at Prachand. 'Oh, don't look so shocked. I got your desi gun pulled out of your bags at the hotel. I have friends everywhere.' She winked. 'Now where was I ... hmm. So the police comes, I wail, I beat my chest – wait, that'll hurt – I just cry bucket loads, tell them about what happened, go into complete shock, am taken ill for a few weeks and then the smell of lots of crisp notes will bring me back to life when all the money is mine. La dee da ... yup. That sounds about right!'

After this long speech, Prachand was now certain that mental illness ran in the family.

Prachand turned to Bhima Shankar.

'Listen, I'm ready to forget everything. You know your boss is crazy, right? Why don't you just help me call the police?' Prachand tried to reason with him.

'Of course.' He laughed out loud. 'Listen, she pays me handsomely. The murkier her deeds, the more money I get to help her and keep my mouth shut. It's a fair deal.'

'You fool!' Shailaja snapped. 'That's my money. And I'll give you a lot more if you help us now.'

He still didn't seem impressed. 'Fat good your money will do me if she chops me into little pieces for betraying her. Haven't you figured out how ruthless she is, even now?'

'You're really going to kill me?' Shailaja Kapoor asked her mother by way of confirmation. 'You're my mother, you psycho.'

'Yes. Say these things,' Pamela Kapoor retorted. 'They will augur well for you, darling. I would have been happy with a large ransom but you are becoming more unstable by the day. One fine day I'll wake up and find out that you've donated all our money to the milkman.'

'He will be more deserving than you!'

'Be that as it may, this ends tonight.'

'You're right about one thing.' A voice boomed from the direction of the main entrance. 'It does end tonight.'

CHAPTER 52

Everyone turned around to see who the latest addition to this odd party was. As the amorphous entity walked into the light, Prachand remembered the wild chicken that sometimes ran around Awadh Niwas. The man before him looked like something that had been thrown up after an undigested meal of Chicken 65. He wore a bright yellow suit with red buttons. A feather-infested cravat rose from his collar area and stood around the circumference of his head like proud plumage. His hair was puffy and slicked back while a thick long moustache moved around animatedly as he spoke. But you had to give the man points for confidence. To exhibit such a confident disposition when one, in reality, is looking like roadkill is a rare trait. He was trailed by a larger man-mountain who presumably was his body guard, characterised by the absence of any expression on his face.

'P ... Patty Bhai,' Pamela Kapoor stuttered but collected herself quickly. 'How nice of you to come.'

He laughed. 'Madam ji, you are behaving like you invited me to your birthday party.' His expression hardened. 'Where is my money?'

'Patty Bhai ... why don't you first get comfortable.' Her voice tinkled as she coyly took hold of his big arm and tried to make him sit. But he sprung back up like coir. 'I am not falling for your drama or excuses tonight.'

'Patwardhan Bhai will not entertain one more excuse,' the bodyguard suddenly spoke, making his presence felt.

'I want all my money tonight,' Patty Bhai announced.

'You must give all the money tonight,' the bodyguard reiterated.

Patty Bhai looked annoyed. 'Oh, shut up!' he shouted at the man-mountain behind him. Man-mountain obliged.

Patty Bhai sat down heavily. 'Aye shapath, this woman is too much.' He complained, looking around the room as if gathering support. 'I lent her so much money in good faith, for years. She's hardly paid anything back. Always a new excuse for more money. She took advantage of my kind heart.'

'Couldn't you just force her to give it to you? I mean, that's what bhais do from what I've heard?' Prachand goaded him.

'Oh, I tried. Warnings, threats, stalking, my friend had suggested I even send her a ... what was that ... yes, a horse's head. It seemed to work for some bhau in one English movie. Aye Ganpat, what was the name?' he turned around to enquire.

'Ghodphadar,' Ganpat, the man-mountain, responded proudly.

'Aah, yes. But these days you touch a goat and people start chanting slogans, plus it is so costly and so messy to find a horse, and then cut its head. So I sent her the cut head of a stuffed horse with a threatening letter. Clearly, even that didn't scare her. She has a rhino hide.'

'Patty bhai,' Pamela Kapoor pleaded, all sass and venom having deserted her in the presence of the new guest. 'How can I possibly give you all the money now? Give me a few days please...'

Prachand jumped into the fray. 'Fatty bhai ... I mean Patty Bhai ... trust me, she has no money. She was planning to steal it from her daughter here. She got Shailaja Madam kidnapped and due to her insatiable greed, she has hatched a plan to kill her! If a mother can kill her own daughter, she will definitely double cross you!'

'Shut up!' yelled Pamela Kapoor.

'Don't yell at him. He's only speaking the truth. You shut up!' yelled Shailaja Kapoor with equal might.'

The big burly Patty Bhai looked appalled and stared at Pamela Kapoor. '*Tujhi pori*?' (Your daughter?) *Kashala*?'(How?) Even we have principles,' he said, looking disgusted.

'You don't worry about that, Patty Bhai. I have money for you,' said Pamela Kapoor desperately trying to steer the conversation in her favour. 'Bhima! Get the black bag from my room.'

Prachand sensed an opportunity. He pointed an accusatory finger at Bhima Shankar.

'Patty Bhai, on her instructions, this man even killed Shailaja Madam's husband Sujit Oberoi. She has blood on her hands!'

Patty Bhai seemed even more agitated. 'You are a terrible woman. I always had a bad feeling about you. You act like Langda Tyagi when you can bounce around like a horse. I never asked you why because it was your business and I am just bothered about my money. But now you want to kill your own daughter. And this man says you got another man killed. Next you will want to kill me because you can't pay me.' He stuck his hand in his bodyguard's trouser pocket and a pouch full of chana fell out. He reached up and whacked the man-mountain on the back of his head. 'Did you come here to watch a movie?' The bodyguard looked sheepish. 'Ghoda ... nikaal!' He was promptly handed a large revolver that he aimed at Pamela Kapoor. She instinctively moved back. 'I want all my money today. Every penny. Or you won't leave this house alive.'

Seeing the gun in Patty Bhai's hand, Bhima Shankar pulled out a gun as well.

There were now more guns in the room than flowers blooming in the gardens outside. Everyone sat still, wondering what would happen next. Prachand's mind was racing. He had managed to turn Patty Bhai against Pamela Kapoor but all that had ended up doing was adding another gun to the blossoming bouquet. Never in his life had he been in such a situation. All the guns he had seen were in the movies, the most sinister killer he had caught was Bholu the Alsatian, who used to like chewing on the neighbour's chicken and the craftiest criminal he had dealt with was Arpan Kumar, the ex-husband who had filled his ex-wife's beauty parlour with a sack of firecrackers. However, this level of deceit, violence and danger was out of syllabus for him. But as his eyes scanned the deadlock of affairs in front of him, he suddenly had an idea.

Without a warning, he said loudly. 'Alexa, switch off hall lights.'

'Switching off hall lights,' Alexa announced.

In a second, the living room was plunged into darkness.

'Where's my phone?'
'I'm going to shoot!'
'Whose hand is on my behind?'
'Prachi, where are you?'
'Give me that gun, you rascal!'

In this commotion of people and voices, it took Pamela Kapoor some time to persuade Alexa to switch the lights back on. When they did come back on, the scenario had changed.

Prachand had knocked the gun from Bhima Shankar's hand and had fallen to the floor. Pushing Prachand with one hand, Bhima Shankar was trying to tackle Patty Bhai to get the gun from him. Shailaja Kapoor had mounted the bodyguard's back and was hitting his head with a small vase. Vidya had leapt at Pamela Kapoor like she was attempting an Olympic high jump.

'*Nautanki budhiya!*' she screamed while pulling at Pamela Kapoor's voluminous hair.

'Leave me, you bitch!' screamed Pamela Kapoor, trying to relieve Vidya's grip on her hair.

A deafening gunshot ripped through the chaos and made everyone freeze in their tracks.

CHAPTER 53

Pamela Kapoor looked like a woman possessed. Post her combat session with Vidya, her clothes were crumpled, her eye make-up was runny and her hair looked dishevelled. The cool, collected Pamela Kapoor was looking like she had been thrown into a washing machine. Holding the gun that she had just fired into the air, eyes smouldering, she looked positively deranged.

The gun was pointed at Vidya, who had just dismounted her.

'Now now, what is the need for guns here?' Vidya stole a desperate glance at her husband and then smiled, trying to placate the angry lady staring at her.

'Shut up!' screamed Pamela Kapoor. 'Everyone put their guns on the table. Now!' She waved the gun around and the remaining ones were placed on the centre table.

Patty Bhai looked around puzzled. He muttered to his bodyguard, 'This is the first time I am on the wrong side of a gun.'

'Didn't everyone hear me?! I said shut up! I should work with the Planning Commission of India. Who else is cursed with ever-changing plans more than me!! All of you, line up on this couch.' She pointed at the largest couch in the hall. 'Sit down.' Then she looked at Bhima Shankar. 'Go get a long rope.' He walked away obediently and came back with a very long rope. 'Tie them all up.' They squeezed on top of each other as he walked around them.

'You're stepping on my foot.'

'Move a little, will you! How much space can one person take up?'

'Why don't you just sit on my lap.'

'Shh! I have a headache already. Because of all of you. Each one of you has played a part in ruining my life.' She hissed and then turned to Patty Bhai. 'You couldn't wait could you, fatso.' Patty Bhai bristled but held his peace as the gun was an inch away from his nose. 'Now along with the original plan, I'll have to think of what to do with you and this lump that you brought along. But, for me...'

Pamela Kapoor was interrupted with the sound of gunshots as the main door was pushed open.

'We'll take care of them, don't you worry.'

Navin Srivastava walked in with Inspector Ranganathan and several cops from the Mumbai Police.

CHAPTER 54

Pamela Kapoor was not ready to go down without a fight.

'Listen, you constable. You have no idea who you're dealing with! Do you know who my husband was?'

Navin Srivastava retorted, 'Why, don't you know who your husband was, Mrs Kapoor?'

'Act smart all you want. He was a very connected man and there are many ministers and policemen who are still loyal to our family. You just watch where I get you transferred.'

'You can? Amazing. Please just ensure I don't get posted to Bastar. I mean, I don't have a problem. Just that my wife wouldn't feel comfortable with naxals around. And if she leaves me, eating out will give me a lot of gas, which I'd like to avoid.'

'Un-cuff me and I'll give you something to laugh about,' she growled. Navin Srivastava looked at the lady constable who had handcuffed her. 'Madam, please un-cuff her.' The constable looked surprised but started to comply. 'Oh, and please give her phone to her. She needs to make a call.'

Pamela Kapoor looked smug as Navin Srivastava continued speaking. 'Ranganathan, go inside and get everyone out here.' Then he turned to Pamela Kapoor. 'As for you, please make that call. Just be sure to let them know how you have admitted to the fraud of handicap, using disability benefits for so many years, one deep dive into your financial records and they'll see all the tax evasions, money laundering, banned financial instruments, illegal betting, umm, what else, oh yes – plotting the murder of your son-in-law, planning the abduction and then murder of your own daughter and two other people. Umm. Am I missing something? In case I have, I'm sure Mr Prachand, who was incidentally recording everything, will fill in the blanks.'

The colour drained from her face.

Meanwhile, the rest of the party came trundling out the main door. Bhima Shankar looked like he had swallowed a pigeon. The threads of loyalty unravelled as fast as the threads of a cheap suit in the face of self-preservation.

'It was her all along, sir. She was giving me money to kill her son-in-law and then the detective and his wife.'

'Why?' Navin Srivastava shook him by his collar. That's all the coaxing Bhima Shankar needed. 'She was livid when she found out that Sujit Oberoi was planning to double cross her and the detectives needed to go because he and his wife had seen me in the house when Sujit Oberoi died.'

A red pair of heels came flying through the air. Aimed at Bhima Shankar's head, they were launched by Pamela Kapoor, 'Shut up, you fool! They have no evidence. Just seal that mouth of yours!' she growled.

'Don't listen to her. Your fingerprints were all over the crime scene. You might as well give us information and buy some leniency for yourself. So, Prachand saw you when you had the scuffle with Sujit Oberoi.'

'Yes, sir. I had gone with the intention of killing him, but it was an accidental death. He slipped and fell. I swear on my mother!'

'Save your performances for impressing your prison mates.'

Before he was led away, Prachand ran up to him. 'I can't understand something. How on earth did you know that we were heading to Mumbai by train?'

Bhima Shankar shook his head. 'That friend of yours, Yatish, begged me to watch your back. Gave me your whereabouts in Banda. Said you were his brother. Fool didn't realize he was helping make my job easier,' he smirked as the police officer pulled him away. Prachand felt an acute sense of contrition at having doubted his friend and vowed to make things right once he got back to Kanpur. He walked over to Vidya and held her hand tight, both absorbing the enormity of what they had been through, adrenaline rushing through their veins.

Sensing an opportunity, Patty Bhai tried to escape with Ganpat but an Inspector from the local team managed to identify him. '*Kya bhau. Kutha jato tumi*? (Where do you think you're going, brother?) We've been looking for you. Come, come. Your friends are waiting for you in prison.'

Shailaja Kapoor was the only one sitting quietly on a bench near the main door. Prachand, Vidya and Navin Srivastava walked up to her. Vidya sat next to her and hugged her. There were tears streaming down her cheeks. 'I mean, I always knew the woman wasn't Mother Teresa but ... but ...

she was still my mother ...' She gulped. 'Someone should make a movie on my life and I'll star in it for free. A mad mother, a bastard of a husband and the worst luck on the planet, it has all the right ingredients.'

Prachand put a hand on her shoulder. 'It's not your fault. There was no way you could have known. She really is a very good actress. Now you're safe.'

Navin Srivastava thumped Prachand on the back. 'Thanks to you, Mr Prachand. If you hadn't called me earlier in the evening and also had the presence of mind to record everything, we might not have been able to close this case so quickly.'

Vidya's eyes widened in disbelief. 'Prachi? You knew? And you didn't tell me?' Shailaja Kapoor's eyes were trained on him as well.

'Viddu, I just had a hunch. But it made me reach out to Inspector Saheb anyway. I didn't want to alarm you.'

The door of the police van shut with a loud thud. Pamela Kapoor's light and unrepentant eyes were boring into all of them as they watched her disappear down the driveway.

Shailaja Kapoor sighed, rubbed her head and stood up. 'Inspector, may I be excused for a few minutes before I give my statement? I need some medicine for my headache.'

'Of course.' Navin Srivastava nodded.

She started walking away and then turned around to face Prachand and Vidya. 'I don't know how to thank you guys. Thanks for not giving up on me when everyone else did.'

They smiled back shyly.

'And don't think I've forgotten my promise. Along with a handsome fee for this case, I will be sending both of you for a fully paid, weeklong stay at the ashram,' she announced, beaming.

Before Shailaja Kapoor could say another word about her gracious offer, Prachand and Vidya disappeared from her sight like two rabbits in a magician's hat.

CHAPTER 55

'Please tell us. How in the world did Prachand Bhaiyya figure out that that Pamela was the real culprit?' A cross-eyed little boy looked quizzically at the best friend of his newest idol, Prachand Tripathi. Yatish was used to answering all kinds of questions related to the now famous 'Nautanki Budhia' case.

Being a close friend of the most famous detective of Kanpur, had its perks. Like people hanging on to his every word. In Mumbai, after the police formalities were completed, the press had taken over. The scandal, the celebrities involved and the drama was too delicious a combination to resist. Overnight, Prachand and Vidya became famous, splashed across newspapers and TV channels all over the country. When they came back to Kanpur, it was as if Lord Ram had returned after a *vanvaas*. Fireworks paved a deafening welcome, diyas were lit, programmes organised, and even a play was enacted based on the case. Prachand was of course played by Yatish.

Reporters thronged the city and many neighbours were seen standing against their houses giving soundbites about Prachand.

'He found Billo, my beloved cat. When the whole world had given up on her. Prachand slaved for two whole days till he found her locked in an abandoned flat.' The camera zoomed into the teary eyes of Ramkatori Chachi.

'My wife and I became ... estranged ... I had contacted him for collecting evidence against her but he helped us get back together. Nunu would not be here, if not for him.' Camera zooms into little Nunu, perched between his grateful father and his excited-looking mother who had caked her face with talcum powder to make it look camera-ready.

Prachand was still not used to all the attention and struggled to keep up but Vidya, Yatish and the rest of the family were basking in it.

'You see, very few people are blessed with the gift that my friend has. He is the smartest man I know. And of course,' he smiled, brushing his collar. 'He has always had my invaluable support. He values my advice greatly...'

'Bhaiyya, you were telling us how he figured out it was the budhiya?' interjected the impatient cross-eyed boy.

Yatish cleared his throat. 'Oh yes, of course. So as I was saying, you remember that crook Bhima Shankar?' A lot of people squatting around him raised their hands. Every person in the case was etched in public memory due to the extensive media coverage.

'So you see, when Prachand da saw him outside the Kapoor house as well, the same person who had been following them doggedly, attacked them, it was too much of a coincidence and made him suspicious. Shailaja Kapoor was out of the picture so it had to be someone on the inside.' Everyone nodded vigorously. 'But what about her shoes?' Yatish turned around to see a beaming Chachu Tripati standing behind him. He smiled and asked the proud uncle to be part of the conversation.

'Why don't you tell them?'

'Arey, Prachand had also noticed that Pamela Kapoor was always wearing fancy new shoes. And they were mostly heels.' This information was met with blank expressions. 'What I mean is, those tall shoes heroines wear. So much interest and careful selection of footwear for someone in a wheelchair piqued his curiosity.'

'I buy one pair of shoes every two years,' offered someone in the crowd, providing validation for the theory.'

'And,' Chachu Tripathi continued, 'on his way to the bathroom at Kapoor Villa, he passed by her room and saw a lot of dirt around the shoe rack. His gut told him she was hiding something. So he continued being normal on the outside while keeping an eye on her. Once her phone call came, he was convinced that she had hatched some plan, requested me to get Navin Srivastava's cell phone number, which I did, and then called him.' Chachu Tripathi finished the explanation with a flourish.

'Hello, check, check. Hello, check, check. Testing, testing. The show is about to start, please take your seats.' Once the mike tester was convinced that people from the next locality had also registered his announcement, he asked the sound in-charge to raise the volume further.

'You idiots!' thundered Dinanath Tripathi. 'Are you deaf?' He chastised the people doing the sound check. 'And why is my son's name slanting on that banner? Straighten it right now.' He couldn't let one thing be out of place. After all it was a function for his son and his daughter-in-law. The local MLA would be the chief guest to give them an award for Bravery and Service to the community. Prachand, who was watching from a distance, couldn't help but smile. He felt a hand on his shoulder. 'I'm so glad you're going to try and help Pitaji at his shop as well.' Vidya smiled. 'The father-son duels were becoming a bit boring.' She laughed. Prachand turned to face Vidya. 'You know how amazing you are?'

'Do you know how amazing *you* are?' she responded and laughed.

A decked-up Rachna Tripathi, who was walking past with her gang of Gwaltoli Gilehris, shouted out to them. 'Why don't you tell us what khichdi you're cooking now? If you're done looking for cats and being famous, how about working on a new case?' Prachand shrugged. 'The case of making baby detectives.' And the entire gang burst out laughing in support as they made their way to the front row seats being part of the 'It' crowd now.

Suddenly, an unearthly sound ripped through the gathering. It sounded as if someone was wailing.

'*Kauno maatam manavat hai.*' (Someones in mourning.) explained an elderly gentleman with a worldly-wise look on his face. Yatish, who was standing nearby, looked incensed. 'He is my nephew. He will be auditioning for Indian Idol Junior next year. Then you will see.' He defended the opening act of the show with gusto: 'The child tried his best to stitch together a few notes but the tune got away from him in terror.'

Thankfully, the MLA arrived just then with pomp and show and a cavalcade. His angry-looking bodyguards, acting like they were on presidential detail, eclipsed him and the only pictures the press managed to take were of the bodyguards' arms and buttocks.

The venue was packed, the crowd was sweating, and the excitement was palpable as Prachand's eye caught a big banner of Kanpur Khoofiya Pvt. Ltd. He squeezed Vidya's hand and smiled the biggest smile ever. Life was good and his dream, after playing kabaddi with him all his life, had finally landed in his palm.

'Ladies and gentleman, presenting, the biggest singing sensation of Kanpur, from the famous Tripathi family, put your hands together for ... Mr Bhushan Tripathi of KPB Rocks!'

As the wannabe Belieber started belting out one song after the other, which not one person in the gathering understood, a few blocks away, the doyen of Awadh Niwas lay back, far from the madding crowd in her favourite charpoy, sucking on her churan. She looked down and smiled at the fancy new gadget that had found a home in her legendary trunk – a gift from her loving grandson. Reaching for her hookah, she announced in a shaky voice. 'Alexa, play *"Where's the party tonight"*.'

ACKNOWLEDGEMENTS

This part is where humour and brevity desert me! When you feel so blessed and grateful, then all you want to do is, look a whole bunch of wonderful people in the eye and tell them how thankful you are. This is me staring you in the eye!

Ravinder Singh, I know you've heard this enough, but you'll have to live with a bit more, I'm afraid. Thank you for being a kind friend, the voice of reason, the gentle mentor and the reality check. I'm making you sound like a wise old man with a white beard but that's what you are in spirit. This journey started with you and I hope to have you along for the ride, for good. Besides, your awesome workout videos make me feel guilty when I'm feeling lazy, so I'll add fitness prodder to that list as well. Big hug!

To all the wonderful people at HarperCollins who have made a publishing house truly feel like a home. Prerna Gill, your stellar editing almost made me harbour the illusion that I had made fewer mistakes. Thank you for making sense of and enjoying this odd stew of confused detectives, cows, actresses and life in the heartlands. Diya, Akriti, Swati, Ananth (who I respect immensely and aim to meet now outside Twitter land), the sales team and so many others I cannot name, every interaction has been encouraging and warm. I thank you and wish you the best. Thank you to Prateek Agarwal for helping craft the best path to the readers and Wasim Helal for such a wonderful cover.

How can you thank bits and pieces of yourself? It's possible. Thank you, my sister-moms Mudita, Namita, Deepika, for being the best parts of me and for letting me bask in your love and warmth. Deepika (a.k.a. Vinkey di). From thrashing the hell out of me as a kid to being my sounding board and co-editor for this book, it would have never seen the light of day if you hadn't given me a thumbs-up. Thank you! Banu (a.k.a. Anirban Mukherjee). You're pretty much as important as the ink that flows out of my pen when I write. There's no sounding board, no 2 a.m. editor, no imagination, no love, no wonder, well, no me without you. Thank you for every single time you grinned at me and said: You can do it! Papa, like you said, you are the root and I'm the twig. This little twig hopes to make you very proud and become an ounce of what you are. Anika baby, you're my brightest star and my happiest place, but since I've already dedicated my first book to you, I'll keep this short.

Mumma, I know it was you who helped me finish this book. When I had nothing left in me. I would give absolutely anything to see you hold it, but I know you will stand with me through many more. You never gave up and I never will. Ma Baba, I try and feel a little more whole everyday and your kindness, warmth and love help me along. Thank you.

Kanpur will always make me smile. Its winding lanes, quaint buildings, curious customs, aroma of frying food, chatty people, songs, folktales and immense warmth have knitted many childhood memories. I hope this book does justice to this wonderful city.

Lastly, a big warm hug for all my other cheerleaders. This includes so many wonderful readers and the Bookstagrammers whose reviews lit up my heart, fellow authors and writers who prodded me on and the various communities that supported me. Thank you very much!

ABOUT THE AUTHOR

After finishing her MBA, chasing around a few criminals and their lawyers as a journalist and spending years in advertising selling shampoos and juices to unsuspecting housewives, Richa finally decided to write a book of soul-searing poetry. She is a celebrated blogger and writes for several online platforms. Her first novel, *I Didn't Expect to Be Expecting*, was a humorous take on the roller-coaster ride of pregnancy. She now lives in Mumbai juggling work, writing, and often, her five-year-old daughter as well. This is her second novel.

She would love to hear from you:
@richashrivas (Twitter) / @mukherjeericha (Instagram) / richasmukherjee@yahoo.com (Email)